PUMMELED TO DEATH BY
HAMBURGER

Second edition

David A Dawson

Printed in the United States of America

Library of Congress Control Number: 2020907950
ISBN: Softcover   978-1-64908-163-6
        eBook   978-1-64908-162-9

Republished by: PageTurner Press and Media LLC
Publication Date: 06/01/2020

To order copies of this book, contact:

PageTurner Press and Media
Phone: 1-888-447-9651
order@pageturner.us
www.pageturner.us

DEDICATION

This book is dedicated to all the people of the world who suffer from Bureaucratic Stress Disorder.

ACKNOWLEDGMENTS

An acknowledgment should be made to the pharmaceutical industry, the insurance industry, organized religion, the criminal justice system, bureaucracies in general, and the paradigm of medicine that punishes physicians economically if they think for themselves. I feel I must also thank the County of Peoria in the State of Illinois for their kindness in allowing me to purchase the court transcripts that make up a significant section of this book. While this book is a work of fiction, many of the events are real. I feel I must acknowledge the contributions of these entities because, without their greed, arrogance, and avarice, I never would have been able to describe or even imagine the events presented in this story.

David A Dawson

CHAPTER 1

Michael cringed as the blue and red lights flashed in his rearview mirror. He had just made a right turn off a four-lane bridge. Michael was lost in Peoria, and now he had to deal with the police.

Carefully positioning the shoulder harness of his seatbelt to cover the logo on the breast of the green polo he was wearing which spelled out *Medical Cannabis Consultants*, he watched as the officer approached. Michael's company trained physicians and patients in everything there was to know about medical cannabis. This was a bad time for a cop to find out he was "in the industry."

Illinois had not yet begun their long-awaited medical cannabis program, and the police were always on the lookout for medical cannabis patients to harass. The Illinois state attorney general had informed local police departments that she no longer wanted to prosecute medical cannabis patients, but the police were always on Michael's mind. He figured he could get away with a warning as soon as the officer saw his wheelchair in the cabin area of his van, and Michael knew he had a chance if he could keep the officer from viewing the logo.

"License, registration, and proof of insurance, please, sir." the cop said.

"What'd I do?" Michael asked.

"That was a construction zone back there, and you were speeding through it," replied the officer. "License, registration, and proof of insurance, please, sir."

"My license is in my chair; it'll take me a minute to get it."

"In your chair?" the cop asked.

"Yeah, it's in the pocket in the very back."

"Well, I can't do anything without a license."

Realizing he was defeated, Michael released the seat belt, and the officer's eyes opened so wide when he viewed the logo, Michael thought they were going to explode. He placed his right hand on the passenger seat, and gracefully transferred his body across. His next step was to press the switch on the left side of the passenger seat, which would electronically maneuver it back so that he could transfer to his power wheelchair and retrieve the wallet. Suddenly realizing he could save the officer some time by retrieving the requested registration and insurance information from the glove compartment before he transferred to his wheelchair.

"The insurance and registration are in here," he said, reaching for the glove compartment. That's when the cop's gun came out.

"You make another furtive movement, and I'll blow your fucking head off!" The cop screamed. "Just give me your God damn name and where you're from. I'll look it up myself. I don't have all day to watch you dick around."

"Michael Dunston, Willow Springs, Illinois," Michael responded, exasperated. The cop turned on his heel and strolled back to his patrol car, and Michael transferred back to the driver's seat and reattached his seat belt making sure the shoulder harness covered the logo, but he knew the damage had been done. After about 15 minutes, the cop came back.

"I'm citing you for speeding through a construction zone. Sign this; it is not an admission of guilt, but this is a class A misdemeanor, and you damn well better appear in court, or I'll throw your pothead ass in jail for as long as I legally can. You remember the rough ride that nigger got in Baltimore? A severed spine is nothing compared to what will happen to you when you and your wheelchair go bouncing around all the way to the station."

"There were no signs indicating that it was a construction zone."

"Those orange cones on the sidewalk should have been a pretty good indicator. If your head hadn't been so fucked up by the drugs, you would have known not to go barreling through it."

Realizing he had messed up in a big way, Michael thanked the officer for his courtesy and watched him goosestep back to his patrol car. Michael pulled off the road, retrieved his cell phone, and called the wheelchair company.

"Mobility Specialists, this is Kim," the receptionist answered.

"Hi Kim, this is Michael Dunston, is Dave still around?"

"Just one moment." The Hold music of Blue Suede Shoes was interrupted after about 45 seconds.

"You're late!" Dave snapped.

"Yeah, I'm lost and got pulled over."

Dave chuckled, "What'd you get pulled over for?"

"Speeding in a construction zone."

"Oh yeah, I should have warned you, the whole city of Peoria is considered a construction zone. Was he rude?"

"Nothing out of the ordinary."

"Where're you at?" Michael gave him the address. "Oh yeah, you're close. You shouldn't have crossed that bridge. You need to come back. When you cross the bridge again, turn right, and there's a black building about a block and a half up on the right-hand side. That's us."

Michael pulled his van into the Mobility Specialists parking lot and spied a handicapped-accessible parking spot right in front of the building. *"That's pretty convenient,"* he thought as he pulled into the space. As he was transferring across to the passenger seat and then to his power wheelchair, a red Miata pulled alongside.

Realizing he could not lower his wheelchair ramp without damaging the Miata, Michael went through the series of transfers again to the driver's seat and pulled the van to another spot so that nobody could park beside him. He then transferred back, lowered the ramp, and entered the building.

Dave was waiting for him. "You realize there's not much we can do until Medicare approves your need for a new chair." Medicare had been verbally denying Michael a new wheelchair for the past seven months. "There's nothing much we can do until we get an actual written denial. But these are the chairs."

"I contacted Senator Kirk about a written denial, and hopefully, he can get something done." Replied Michael, "But I need to be prepared when he does. I understand I've been in this loaner chair for seven months, and you want it back, but let's look at some chairs to replace the one that broke down last year."

"The best chair for your condition is this one, but Medicare will never approve it." Dave said, "See how the seat kind of cradles you. It'll take care of the damage the loaner has been causing your body over the past year. Try it out."

Michael went through the perfunctory test drives of wheelchairs he knew he had no chance of getting so that he met his insurance company's requirements. He agreed the chair Dave recommended was the one he needed.

"Why won't Medicare approve this?" He asked.

"The base is okay., but Medicare doesn't have a code for the seat. You need this seat because the loaner has broken down your spine over all this time."

"If Medicare approves the base, can I pay for the seat myself?"

"Of course, as long as we get our money, we don't care where it comes from."

"Cool."

CHAPTER 2

M ichael had a two-hour drive to get back home, and this gave
him time to reflect on his life on the fringes of the medical
cannabis industry.

Technically, that life began in high school when he met the first
girl with whom he fell in love. He was entering an English class where
a group of students was discussing the newly released show *Star Trek:
The Next Generation.* Every student there had an opinion about the
characters Paramount had introduced.

"I hate the captain."

"The storyline is terrible."

"Yeah, the original was better."

As Michael approached this group, he noticed Carol, a junior, the
most beautiful girl he had ever seen. She was unlike any girl Michael
had ever been attracted to before. Her hair was brown, straight, and
cut short. He was usually attracted to long hair blonds, but her short
brown hair accentuated the beauty of this girl's face. It particularly
complimented her big brown eyes. *"These are eyes you could lose yourself
in."* Michael thought.

That's when Carol made her comment. "I liked the one where
Spock had a beard."

"Mirror, Mirror," Michael said, identifying the episode's title, his nerd knowledge of Star Trek finally paying off.

"Yeah," Carol responded, her amazement and respect apparent. From that point on, they were inseparable. Early on, they spoke mainly of Star Trek, and through other conversations, Michael discovered that besides being extremely sexually appealing, she was also incredibly brilliant.

One day they met in the school's library. The year was 1976, and women's rights were in the nation's political eyesight. The first thing Carol said to him was, "Do you agree with the equal rights amendment? Hold on. Before you answer, this is what it is." She then put down a typewritten sheet of paper with the 24 words of the amendment.

The Equal Rights Amendment:

Equality of rights under the law shall not be denied or abridged by the United States or by any State on account of sex.

"I believe in that," Michael said, sliding the paper back to her.

"No!" Carol exclaimed, "I wanted to get into a big argument with you today, and you took that away from me." From that point on, Michael was in love. Here was a girl with a brain and someone who would stand up for what she believed.

It wasn't until a few days after that he learned she was a pothead. She let him know in hushed tones, again in the library. They had been spending study halls together there pretty much constantly, both hungering for the knowledge the stacks contained.

Until he met Carol, he believed the school propaganda: "Marijuana kills brain cells," "Marijuana makes you lazy," and "Marijuana makes you stupid."

This was a marijuana user who was anything but brain dead, lazy, or stupid."

By Michael's senior year, they had both scheduled study halls before and after lunch so they could leave the school together, and they returned completely baked so that Michael could attend his Geometry class.

Fortunately, the final period of school was often canceled for the drug awareness assembly. Michael and Carol got to sit together and watch the people from Drug Abuse Resistance Education (D.A.R.E.) teach them about how the world is full of dangerous drug peddlers waiting to ambush you at every corner so they could shove wads of pills, needles, and reefer down your throat and get you hooked for life. By the time they reached their concluding remarks, Michael and Carol were in hysterics.

When the program concluded with the claim that "for every one joint of marijuana; four teenagers become burdened with pregnancy," Michael and Carol were so horny, they couldn't see straight. They both had their first sexual experiences that afternoon.

There was no question Michael would wear a condom. He didn't want to get four girls pregnant the first time he had sex.

When they were finished, Michael remarked that cannabis helped alleviate the pain from his muscular dystrophy. That was when Carol gave him a rudimentary lesson on the history of cannabis as medicine.

As they lay in bed, the blanket covering her breasts, she lectured the way a college professor would. "When we look at medicinal cannabis from a historical perspective, we have to start with the ice age. The last ice age ended about 12,500 years ago. This history is circumstantial and is merely an attempt to reverse-engineer the missing prehistory of cannabis, which hasn't been told. To do this properly, we have to go back 75,000 years to when humans survived as hunter-gatherers for 55,000 years. 12,000 years ago, the ice-age ended, and humans migrated into Northern Asia.

"The first contact between humans and the hemp plant is lost to history, but that contact was to change the course of human evolution by providing survival resources to small nomad bands allowing them to produce more offspring. The hemp plant ended up accelerating human evolution by contributing to a radical shift in human behavior called the Neolithic Revolution.

"The Neolithic Revolution was a period of significant transition where humans went from a hunter-gatherer subsistence existence to primitive agricultural settlements. The first agrarian settlements likely originated as hemp/cannabis-based farms.

"Humans now started to settle down in one place with one goal; find a niche with an optimal environment to grow plants for food. Surplus food meant greater chances for infant survival because, in times of famine, females stop ovulating since pregnancy is calorie expensive.

"There is a Chinese Neolithic legend that says the gods gave humans cannabis to fulfill all their needs. Early humans quickly discovered hemp's usefulness in making food, rope, cloth, medicine, and most likely religious sacrament, and this encouraged further growing of the plant.

"This hemp farming kind of put a "kick start" into the Neolithic revolution and, in time, the first pieces of civilization. Civilization implies cooperation over hostile tribal conflicts, and it's likely a shaman from this culture used cannabis as a sacred plant of peace and as something to worship.

"The Neolithic Revolution occurred in six different early cultures around the world in 5000 years, but the first area in the world it took place was in northern China, very close to where wild hemp originated. Human's first cultivation of hemp also started there. China is the oldest culture in the world and has a rich historical connection to this plant. Their export of hemp seeds and products progressed west and started the development of new Neolithic Revolutions in India and then into the Middle East and Europe.

As soon as cannabis arrived in each region and culture, we see the development of cannabis-based religions in those areas.

"Chinese archaeologists agree that hemp was one of the first known plant species to be purposefully grown. When you're one meal away from starvation, you don't waste energy on tasks that don't fit your needs. Also, this plant was the only one cultivated dioeciously, meaning they have separate male and female plants. This is interesting because it gives us insight into what they were thinking about cannabis and how they were using it. There is only one use for the female plant, medication.

"Hemp is a 'first foundation' crop that gave humans an evolutionary advantage by producing food, fiber, fuel, and raw building material. Over time this plant yielded something new; a 'medication for the soul'—a plant which could satisfy a unique higher purpose, the ability to positively change human consciousness. This is the fourth drive in Maslow's hierarchy of human needs after food, shelter, and reproduction.

"The leading theory of what drove the origins of human agriculture is known as the Evolutionary/Intentionality Theory. The theory states that certain plants formed a symbiotic, co-evolutionary relationship with early humans. It started with the mere protection of wild plants and progressed until their domestication was improved to help humans increase in numbers. If humans and plants both manipulate the other's environment to produce genetic changes in their DNA that favor reproduction using the least amount of energy, it offers a substantial evolutionary advantage to both species.

"Plants want to make seeds and spread them. Humans are similarly programmed by their DNA to reproduce and increase in numbers. If both species benefit from this arrangement, and they can accomplish their primary task, a symbiotic relationship is formed between both species. How special is this bond? Cannabis has never taken a human life due to overdose. The big smile on your face is just a freebie.

"Once the seeds are produced, a genetic algorithm will always find the most efficient method of dispersal, be it animal fur/feces, water, wind, or by influencing human behavior. In exchange for providing its medicine (the plant's gift to humans), humans were only too happy to help the whole process along by sheltering the plant, providing it with nutrients, water, and protection from predators and the elements. A win-win.

"Additionally, the plant provided humans with many necessary survival products, high-quality complete food containing essential fatty acids. It offered oil for cooking, lamps, lubrication for skin and hair care products in addition to rope, which is naturally salt-resistant and extremely durable. It also provided clothing and, best of all, a spiritual change of consciousness.

"Don't underestimate how important joy is to a robust human immune system and survival. To early humans, discovering hemp was like hitting the evolutionary lotto!

"The earliest known farming culture to use hemp/cannabis was the Yang Shao culture whose origins go back to 5000 B.C. This culture existed until 3000 B.C., and for 2000 years, the economy of this culture was cannabis driven. It's easy to imagine excess cannabis being traded with other tribes. Hemp probably played a massive role in the founding of human commerce.

"The Yang Shao culture was established precisely where cannabis originated, just south of Siberia. Chinese archaeologists have firmly concluded that cannabis use in China extends deep into our prehistorical human past. In fact, recorded history started because of hemp. Approximately 10,000 years ago, humans began to write information on hemp paper. Hemp replaced bulky clay tablets and expensive silk. Hemp paper became available to all people. It was very durable and easy to make in large amounts. In fact, the first King James Bibles were printed on hemp paper. Hemp paper literally shaped humans' first 'information age.' Hemp made the first books possible. Hemp, the plant started civilization by recording what happened in the past from which others could learn. The first books were made from hemp paper. They were printed in China and were medical journals, and the first information written in them was the suggested uses of medical cannabis.

"Cannabis was human civilization's first effective widespread medicine, a medicine that has been used for over 12,500 years, a medicine which never caused a fatality and was legal in the United States until 1937."

Michael was transfixed, first at Carol's knowledge and secondly at her ability to make the history of a plant seem interesting. He interrupted her lecture, "Okay, now we're up to 1937. That was when they began finding evidence that cannabis has no medicinal value and has a high potential for abuse. What's the story on that?" Carol continued her diatribe.

"If you look for the roots of America's decision that cannabis has no medicinal value, you'll find nearly all roads lead to a man named Harry Anslinger. It was he who established the precedent that in the United States, it is the politicians and law enforcement officers that make the medical decisions. Anslinger was the first commissioner of the Federal Bureau of Narcotics, which laid the groundwork for the modern-day DEA, and was the first architect of the war on drugs. He coined the word 'marijuana' because it sounded foreign and scary.

"Anslinger was appointed to the bureau in 1930, just as the prohibition of alcohol was beginning to crumble and remained in power for 32 years. From the moment he took charge, Harry was aware of the weakness of his new position. Anslinger needed to be able to justify his new bureau's existence financially. He knew he couldn't keep an entire department alive on narcotics alone. Cocaine and heroin were simply not used enough to sustain a whole bureau. Very few people were using heroin and Coke. He needed more.

"To fund his newly established bureau, Anslinger made it his mission to rid the US of all drugs except alcohol and tobacco. This included cannabis, which he chose to pursue with a vengeance. His influence played a major role in the introduction and passage of the Marijuana Tax Act of 1937, outlawing possessing or selling of cannabis without a tax stamp, which he ensured would be virtually impossible to obtain.

"Anslinger claimed that cannabis could cause psychosis and, eventually, insanity and death. In a radio address, he stated young people are "slaves to this narcotic, continuing addiction until they deteriorate mentally, become insane, turn to violent crime and eventually murder." The problem was, he had no scientific evidence to support this. He contacted 30 scientists, and 29 told him cannabis was not a dangerous drug. He hired the 30th, Dr. James Munch as the US government's 'official expert' on marijuana. In this position, Dr. Munch was responsible for presenting the scientific evidence indicating that ingesting cannabis caused psychosis and, eventually, insanity.

"This is probably a good time to introduce the concept of anecdotal evidence. It is the government's position that any success stories of individuals attaining successful medical results as individual stories that that should be ignored as unscientific. Anecdotal evidence does not qualify as scientific evidence, because its very nature prevents it from being investigated by the scientific method. The evidence the United States uses to support the claim that cannabis has no medicinal value is based on the research of experts. One of the most notable experts was the aforementioned Dr. James Munch, a professor of physiology and pharmacology at Temple University in Philadelphia, PA.

"Dr. Munch was employed as the US government's 'official expert' on cannabis from 1938 to 1962. In 1937 Dr. Munch testified for the Federal Bureau of Narcotics during the Marihuana Tax Act Hearings of 1937. His court testimony demonstrates the importance of medical decisions being based on evidence, and America's decision that cannabis has no medicinal value is primarily based on the findings of the esteemed Dr. Munch. During the hearing, Munch incorrectly testified that cannabis was introduced into human medicine by William Brooke O'Shaughnessy in 1838. This was 37 years before Louis Pasteur came onto the scene, and Munch testified that before Pasteur, cannabis was used to treat rabies and corns. He correctly stated that synthetic medicines were better options for these conditions and went on to testify that cannabis has no medicinal value because there is no established method for standardization of dose that compares to the exacting standards of synthetic narcotics. Dr. Munch further testified, without producing studies that cannabis use causes degeneration of the brain, extreme laziness, violent irritability, and disintegration of personality.

"He then stated in open court that he had conducted a series of experiments with cannabis on dogs and had, for scientific purposes, tried the supplement himself. When asked how cannabis affected him, Dr. Munch testified, under oath that, after two inhalations of a marijuana cigarette, he was turned into a bat, flew around the room and down a 200-foot-deep inkwell."

Michael chuckled, nuzzled her ear, and whispered, " We should find the stuff that'll turn us into bats." Carol ignored his attempt at distraction.

"Interestingly enough, this was not the evidence President Ronald Reagan was referring to when, in 1984, he declared, "I now have absolute proof that smoking even one marijuana cigarette is equal in brain damage to being on Bikini Island during an H-bomb blast." The study Regan used was the Heath Tulane 1974 study, and this study has been repressed and is only available by filing a request through the Freedom of information Act. We'll get to that study in a moment, but by the time Dr. Munch and Harry Anslinger retired from the Federal Bureau of Narcotics in 1962, the government's paradigm had been established. And this paradigm was to flourish within the government for the next five decades. In a nutshell, the paradigm is this: Ingesting cannabis kills brain cells, causes psychosis, criminal behavior, and insanity.

"The next step in the advancement of this paradigm was 1971, when President Richard M. Nixon declared war on drugs, explicitly targeting the cannabis plant and mandating that the cannabinoid molecules it produces not be studied. On July 1, 1973, President Richard Nixon created the Drug Enforcement Administration, a paramilitary division tasked with the responsibility of ensuring no US citizen would ever be allowed to possess or research the cannabis plant. However, an exception was made for Robert G. Heath.

"The history of psychology is filled with tales of researchers pushing the boundaries of science and ethics. Dr. Heath had the background and credentials the government wanted because he was one of the first physicians to implant electrodes deep inside the brain as a psychosurgical intervention. He is best known for using electrical stimulation in an attempt to cure patients of schizophrenia and as a method of conversion therapy for homosexual males. In addition to these studies, Heath conducted and published the results of a study in which he claimed to have administered to rhesus monkeys the equivalent of 30 joints per day for a period of one year, which conclusively demonstrated the harmful effects of ingesting cannabis. This is known as the Heath/Tulane study, and it is probably one of the most important studies in cannabis history. In reporting, Heath claimed after the year was up, he killed the monkeys, counted the dead brain cells, and compared that number to the number of dead brain cells in monkeys that hadn't ingested cannabis. The result of this study demonstrated conclusively that the cannabis ingesting monkeys had significantly more dead brain cells than the monkeys that hadn't ingested cannabis. This study is cited quite frequently as proof that cannabis use kills brain cells and is still used as evidence by the DEA to advance their paradigm that cannabis is one of the most dangerous substances a human can ingest. The Heath/Tulane study is the evidence the DEA cites when pressed for scientific justification for cannabis remaining a Schedule I substance as destructive as heroin.

"The actual methodology used in the study and the way the results were disseminated provides an interesting lesson about the nature of science. To avoid having to pay an assistant's wages every day for a full year, Heath strapped gas masks to the monkeys, made certain they were sealed, and pumped marijuana smoke into them for five minutes not providing the monkeys any oxygen. According to the *Red Cross Lifesaving and Water Safety Manual,* "Three to five minutes of oxygen deprivation causes brain damage." It turns out The Heath Monkey study was actually a study in animal asphyxiation. The monkeys suffered brain damage due to being completely deprived of oxygen and exposed to smoke with carbon monoxide and carbon dioxide instead. The brain damage was the result of a lack of oxygen. This was the study cited by Ronald Reagan and is still the study cited by the DEA when pressed for the scientific evidence justifying its decision that cannabis has no medicinal value."

By the time she finished, Michael was passionately in love, and so turned on, he probably would have taken her forcefully if he had had to. They had sex virtually every afternoon until he went to college. Since Carol was still in high school, he chose a college near their hometown of Wapello, Iowa. He tried to always come home on the weekends so that he could be with her.

Michael quickly discovered that choosing a college by location rather than the quality of education was a bad mistake. This became apparent when he was presented with the reading list for the Freshman English class. The instructor was an overweight woman of about 55 years of age.

"Class." she began, "You can address me as Miss Fatima. This semester you will be required to read ten books. I have personally selected these books because they cover a wide array of subjects, and

I, therefore, believe that many will be enjoyed by a diverse group such as this. I will expect a written review of each book at the end of the semester. Here is your reading list, and you will be required to summarize the plot and the lesson of the story.

"You will spend your class time reading these books. I will leave you here in the classroom together so that you can read and discuss the subtleties of each book among yourselves. I will be in my office having a cigarette, and if there is a word you don't understand, you can come and find me. Get started."

She then walked out, and Michael didn't see her again until finals week when they met in her office, and he presented his reviews while she smoked one cigarette after another.

By the time he left her cloud-filled office, Michael understood he was not getting a quality education, and he transferred to Princeton University. Carol had already been accepted at Princeton, and they vowed to continue their relationship there.

CHAPTER 3

Two weeks before Carol and Michael were due to leave for Princeton, Michael's father sat him down and spelled out the plans for Michael's future.

"Son," he said (he never actually used Michael's name) "I am the nations' top anesthesiologist, and I know of which I speak. Your future is in molecular biology. Studying this subject will get you everything you want and provide you untold riches. Molecular biology is the future of medicine, and it is your future as well."

Deep down, Michael knew his father was right. He always was. Michael had grown up with the privilege great wealth provides. He and Carol used to spend their free time canoeing and getting high on the fifteen-acre lake his father privately owned and walking through the thousand acres of woods surrounding it and screwing like dogs. It was during these walks Michael developed an appreciation for nature. Carol was going to pursue a degree in entomology, and she spent hours teaching him the scientific names of various species of plants, insects, and animals.

Carol's favorite scientific name was *Rana clamitans,* and they used to find northern tree frogs all over his father's property. He often took his mother on walks around the property and impressed her with his knowledge of ecology, which he had learned mostly from Carol. Carol had spent her senior year of high school studying entomology and preparing for her entry into Princeton.

They decided to take separate cars to the New Jersey College. Michael would take the direct route and arrive a few days earlier than Carol. Carol wanted to see Canada, and though they left the same day, she would arrive at Princeton some days later. This way, he could move most of their stuff into the house they had rented near campus together.

He had been in the house for two days when he received a message in a French-Canadian accent on their answering machine.

"Greetings from Canada. My name is Sergeant Pelletier of the Royal Canadian Mounted Police. I am calling you because I found your name and number in a wallet owned by Ms. Carol O'Donnell. I'm sorry to inform you Ms. O'Donnell was T-boned and killed by a drunk driver in Thunder Bay, Ontario, on Thursday. I am sorry for your loss."

Michael was never able to find the officer who left the message, who had hit her, or what happened to her body. After months of searching, he gave up trying and began focusing his mind on becoming a molecular biologist. By the end of his junior year, Michael figured out he despised molecular biology. At the beginning of his senior year, his academic advisor suggested he add a second major to his degree.

"Pick a discipline as different from molecular biology as you can think of to add to your diversity as an individual." She suggested.

He quickly chose the field of Psychology with a focus on animal behavior. It took him an extra year to receive his degrees, but it was his parent's money, and they were only too happy to provide it for his education. They would have preferred to put the money toward a doctorate program than another bachelor's degree but decided they couldn't always get what they wanted in life and were willing to compromise.

Michael began to focus his attention on what he enjoyed and only did enough with the hated molecular biology to receive a degree. After five long years, Michael finally graduated. All he had for the tens of thousands of dollars his parents had spent was a piece of paper certifying him as an animal behaviorist and molecular biologist and no job or prospects. One thing was certain in Michael's mind. He had no interest in pursuing a career in molecular biology. His real interest was animal behavior. He decided to attempt to create a business centered on that discipline. After attempting to enlist his services at various zoos, he focused his attention on birds of prey. The raptors interested him immensely and seemed to interest everyone else. He put together a collection of hawks, owls, falcons, and vultures and joined the lecture circuit.

He commandeered a huge building his father had constructed to house the creatures and presented assemblies in much the same way the people of D.A.R.E. did.

The content and the financing were, of course, different. Rather than receiving a 13.7-million-dollar grant to rehearse "just say no" skits and teaching corny rap songs about how "drug-free is the way to be!" environmental education programs receive no money from the federal government and Michael's father had to fund the program himself. The students loved seeing the birds fly around, and when he added a skunk as an example of a prey species for great horned owls, he became a smash on the lecture circuit. Beautiful young female teachers were all over him. He was a perfect one-night stand for horny instructors.

His favorite closing line was after the teacher would say, "Michael, you are so impressive!" Michael's response was invariable, "You think you're impressed now? Just wait till I get you into bed."

That line never failed. Michael was never really sure how impressed they were, but by the time he was done, it didn't matter, and it was time for him to move on to the next town and a new crop of teachers. He spent an entire school year lecturing and flying birds and screwing his way throughout the Central United States.

Ironically, it ended in 1984 when the federal government initiated a program known as Operation Falcon created to stop a falcon smuggling operation that existed only within the mind of the Federal Government.

When machine-gun bearing agents of the U.S Fish & Wildlife Service dressed in riot gear broke down his parent's front door, handcuffing and accusing them of flying into the tundra, trapping peregrine falcons and gyrfalcons, bringing them back to Wapello, Iowa and selling them to Arabs, Michael knew this aspect of his life was over. He decided to go back to school and pursue his Master's degree. Because of the positive experiences he had in his interactions with teachers, he decided to pursue education as his next adventure.

He chose Columbia University in New York as his next college because it had the best science education program he could find. Michael enrolled and stole a school year's supply of codeine from his father to treat the pain resulting from the progression of his muscular dystrophy. His parents sent Columbia a butt-load of money, and he was on his way.

The Master's program at Columbia took two years, and after graduating in 1986, he was immediately offered a teaching position at a small college in Northern Wisconsin. That is where he met Patrick, a cannabis cultivator who had been growing since New Mexico initiated their Medical cannabis program in 1978.

From that point on, Michael had access to the finest pain medicine ever produced in America. That access ended in the summer of 1988 because during summer hiatus, as a lark, he took a job with the first casino to operate in the State of Illinois. Michael was hired to train their employees how to be effective managers and quickly tripled what he made teaching at the college level. He never went back to teaching college.

Because he worked in the casino industry, Michael was now subject to random drug screenings to assure the State of Illinois he wasn't using marijuana, and he was developing a tolerance to the codeine he was periodically stealing from his father. Michael decided it was time to see a doctor to control the pain in a manner that would be acceptable to the overseeing administrations.

"Well, marijuana is useless for pain." Dr. Schneider told him. "And the reason you are no longer getting relief from the Codeine is that you're not taking a high enough dose. These pills are only 100 milligrams. I'm going to increase you to five hundred, and if that doesn't work, we'll switch you over to Hydromorphone, fentanyl, Oxycodone, or Opana. We have a ton of good opiates to choose from, and the marijuana that you're so fond of is a schedule I drug and, therefore, one of the most dangerous substances on earth. Didn't you see a few years ago when President Regan said smoking even one marijuana cigarette is equivalent in brain damage to being on Bikini Island during a nuclear blast? It's also likely to get you thrown in prison, and prisoners get really crummy health care. Relax, my specialty is pain management, and I can promise you that I will control your pain using the best medications Western science has to offer. So, don't worry, I am here for you."

Michael felt positive about the potential success of this pain management doctor but was transferred to Las Vegas shortly after the visit. Dr. Schneider recommended another pain management specialist in Las Vegas, so he knew he was going to get the best pain management medicine legally available in the nation. Michael began with Dr. Sanjay in Las Vegas shortly before he started working at the Golden Fleece Casino Hotel & Resorts Inc. He switched Michael to fentanyl and changed the dosage to fifty micrograms.

Michael knew from his molecular biology classes that fifty micrograms is very little medicine, about a thousand times less than codeine. He figured the fentanyl must be a pretty powerful medication to require such a miniscule amount. Obviously, this medicine was more potent than grass, and he didn't have to worry about getting thrown in prison for using it. He knew the casino would have no issue with him coming up positive on a drug test for opiates in his system but popping positive for cannabis would have him wandering the streets of Las Vegas homeless.

CHAPTER 4

Michael worked for The Golden Fleece Casino for thirteen years. During this time, he witnessed slot players putting counterfeit five-dollar bills into machines and table games players create elaborate scams to cheat their table games. He observed entire craps crews cheat everybody, and all the while, his pain level increased exponentially.

During this time, Michael developed a tolerance to virtually every opiate imaginable. Finally, Dr. Sanjay referred him to a surgeon in the hopes that cutting him open would relieve his pain.

The procedure was called a tendon release and entailed cutting his tendons and breaking the bones in his foot so that it could be placed into the proper alignment, thus relieving the discomfort.

The procedure might have worked too, except for the fact that the hospital was crawling with MRSA, a bacterial infection that kills about thirty-six thousand people a year. Michael spent three months in the hospital and lost his job.

The attending physician was appalled to learn Michael had been prescribed fifty micrograms of fentanyl and changed his medication back to five hundred milligrams of morphine. He said morphine was a better drug than fentanyl because it wasn't as strong, and the morphine had been in existence longer, and therefore its effects were better understood.

Michael went along with it because it kept him out of prison, and he figured traditional medicine simply had to be better than something that wasn't even allowed to be researched in the United States. The government was here to protect us, and why would they make the plant illegal if it wasn't one of the most dangerous substances a human could ingest?

He still had comped passes to play golf on one of The Golden Fleece's luxurious courses, and before he teed off one gorgeous Friday morning, he dropped the 500 milligrams of morphine to control his pain.

By the 16th hole, he had such a headache he couldn't see straight. He went home and went right to bed. The next day was Saturday, and when Michael woke up that morning, his headache was unbelievably severe.

He called the emergency number the surgeon had provided. The doctor was obviously annoyed at being disturbed on a Saturday, and Michael was sorry to have bothered him. He promised the doctor that no matter how severe the headache became, he would not call and ask for help. The physician seemed relieved that his weekend would no longer be disturbed, and Michael went back to bed.

He woke up twenty-four hours later in agony. He hadn't taken his morphine since the golf course two days ago and figured the drug would alleviate his headache. He took five hundred milligrams and lay in bed until the evening. His headache never subsided, and he slept for twelve more hours and went to the doctor's office at eight that Monday morning to beg for help.

The receptionist informed Michael that the doctor was booked all morning and that he *might* be able to get in to see him that afternoon, but there were no guarantees. Michael realized he hadn't eaten for two days, and he went to a Denny's Restaurant for breakfast. He hoped he might be able to see a doctor that afternoon.

He walked into a Denny's in Las Vegas, Nevada, at 9:45 a.m., and that was the last time Michael would ever walk again. The massive stroke took place in the middle of the restaurant shortly after he ordered a mushroom and cheese omelet.

CHAPTER 5

Michael woke up when the paramedic picked him up and shook him. "Sir!" the paramedic yelled at him which was no help to Michael's headache,

"We're going to take you to the hospital now!"

"Oh, the hospital," Michael thought. *"Someone passes out, and suddenly they belong in the hospital."*

Since he was unable to do anything else, he vomited on the paramedic and passed out again.

He woke up in a hospital bed two days later with a nurse standing over him.

"Sir," she whispered, "You've suffered a stroke. I'm going to ask you some questions to determine if you have brain damage. These questions come from the Nevada Mini-Mental State Determination Examination (NMMSDE). The questions will start out easy and become increasingly more difficult. Question number one. What is the day?"

Michael knew the answer to that. "Today is Monday, July 8th, 2010."

"No, sir. It's Wednesday, July 10th. You've been sleeping for two days."

She marked on the record Michael's first wrong answer. "Question 2. What is the name of the Governor of the State of Nevada?"

"I've been working pretty much constantly since I arrived in this State, and I haven't had time to become politically aware." Another wrong answer was checked off.

"Question three. Starting with 100, I want you to count backward by 17."

"100, 83..." As soon as Michael tried to subtract 17 from 83, his headache became so intense he nearly fainted again. He laid his head back on his pillow and wept. The nurse stood up, exited the room, and went back to the nurse's station where the doctor was waiting.

"How is he?" the physician asked her.

"He's pretty bad." The nurse replied.

"I'll make the diagnosis, nurse!" the Doctor snapped. "Just give me the NMMSDE form."

He snatched the form from her hand and, after reading it, apologized. "He only lasted three questions, huh?"

"Yeah, the brain damage is pretty apparent. He'd never make it through all ten."

"I suppose I'd better stick my head in. Otherwise, I can't charge him." Michael was sitting at the edge of the bed, looking for his clothes when the doctor came in.

"How are we feeling today, Mr. Dunston?" The physician asked.

"I still have a headache, and I hurt, but I'm ready to get out of here," Michael replied.

"What do you mean, you hurt?"

"I have a form of muscular dystrophy, and I always hurt."

"What are you taking for pain?"

"Either Fentanyl or Morphine."

"What dose?"

"50 micrograms of Fentanyl or 500 milligrams of Morphine."

"Well, what you need is a real drug. You have chronic pain. I'm going to write you a prescription for one thousand milligrams of Mondine. It's a new medication the FDA just approved. One thousand milligrams should be enough to take care of your pain and eliminate the headache as well. I'm going to send you home with a bottle of these. No more than one per day. I'm going to have you sign a pain contract. To get this drug, you must agree not to take any other drug, including marijuana. Alcohol is okay, of course, but only in moderation. I'm going to run some Mondine into your IV now. Tell me if this relieves your pain and your headache."

Warmth flooded through Michael's body. "Oh yeah," Michael responded dreamily, "that feels great."

"I thought it would." The doctor smiled.

Chapter 6

When Michael was picked up by his wife, he was in such a Mondine induced haze; he had forgotten he even had a wife. She informed him she had been back in Illinois taking care of the sale of the house. She and the doctor had conferred in the physician's office, and he explained to her what had happened.

"Michael suffered a stroke." He said. "He's lost the use of his left arm, and it's unlikely he'll ever walk again. There also may be some cognitive impairment. It might be so bad that he doesn't even remember who you are. The only real suggestion I have is to enter him into hospice care and for you to take him home and try to let him live out as normal life as possible. If you find you can no longer live with him, I would be available to console you privately."

"Oh, that's subtle." Michael's wife replied, "I think I'll just take my husband home now."

"Here's his medication." The Doctor said, handing her the bottle of thirty Mondine tablets. "Only give him one per day. No alcohol except in moderate amounts."

"Oh, Michael doesn't drink," She replied and turned on her heel and left the office.

When she stood by Michael's side, he realized why he must have married her. This was obviously an angel.

When she got him home, she sat him down at the foot of the bed and said, "Look, we're together through this like we've been together through everything else. I'm along for the ride. Like you always say, 'This will be an adventure.'"

Michael didn't remember ever saying that, but he replied: "That's not a bad philosophy."

"You know what's been screwing you up all this time? Synthetic drugs." She said, answering her own question. "Let's get you on some medicine that works. Just because a doctor tells you to do something or to take something doesn't mean you shouldn't think. We're going to wean you off that shit and start medicating you with cannabis. You remember how it worked for you when we were in high school?"

He suddenly realized who she was - Carol! This was his first, and his only true love. He couldn't believe he had been allowed to marry this Goddess. She sat at the foot of his bed and explained to him everything she had learned about cannabis as medicine over the last 33 years. He wished he could remember marrying her.

"The opiates have been messing with your mind for the past twenty-four years, and the only remedy your doctors have provided is to make them stronger. This shit is garbage." She declared, throwing the Mondine bottle into a nearby wastebasket.

Michael watched dejectedly, realizing he would never again have that warm, delirious feeling.

"We can't stay here. Nevada has no sense of humor when it comes to medical cannabis. I think we need to move back to Illinois. They're beginning a medical cannabis program there through the Illinois Department of Public Health."

"We really don't have much choice, do we?" Michael replied. He didn't relish the thought of returning to the snow and the cold winters.

Preparing for the move took six months. In those months, Carol reintroduced Michael to cannabis. But this wasn't the cannabis he remembered from high school. This was medicinal grade cannabis, and a quality of medicine he had never known before.

"You don't smoke joints of this," Carol told him. "Smoking joints is wasteful, and you shouldn't set your medicine on fire. Any time you set something on fire and breathe the smoke into your lungs, it is unlikely to be good for you."

She then introduced him to the wonders of vaporization and went into her teaching mode. "Vaporization is the logical choice for most health-conscious cannabis consumers. For the most part, the cannabinoids evaporate at around 356 degrees. Because the medicinal compounds in cannabis known as phytocannabinoids and terpenes are volatile, they can be vaporized at a temperature level significantly lower than that needed to reach combustion or smoke. As a result, hot air can simply be drawn through the cannabis, which in turn evaporates the cannabinoids and terpenes and frees them for inhalation. Vaporizers steadily heat the flower to a temperature that is high enough to extract the THC, CBD as well as the other medicinal cannabinoid and terpene molecules but too low to release the potentially harmful toxins associated with combustion."

Michael quickly discovered that by vaporizing, he only had to use a tiny bit of the medicine to control his pain. Carol always hung around and medicated with him while teaching him everything she knew about the medicine. It was an extraordinary amount. At first, Michael couldn't understand how she could know so much when he did not remember her working on it during their marriage or anything else about their marriage, for that matter.

She assured him the reason he didn't remember was a result of the stroke and all the narcotics he had been taking. She further assured him she would stay with him forever, and he felt elation at having a wife that was so devoted to him. It wasn't until later he discovered she was lying to him and had spent the last twenty-four years watching his deterioration from Canada until she could stand it no longer. She decided to rejoin him and attempt to make him believe she had been his wife the entire time.

In the morning, they used an activating strain, which helped Carol to do her research online and packed for the move to Illinois. In the evening, they medicated with a sedating strain that relaxed them while they spent hours talking and watching movies on Netflix until they went to bed.

A few months passed, and by this time, Michael had weaned himself off the opiates entirely and was only medicating with cannabis. Before they moved, Michael had to apply for disability through the Social Security Administration. They were more than happy to grant him disabled status when he went into the office in his newly purchased, slightly used electronic wheelchair.

"If you could have waited four months for the forms to be processed," The Social Security agent told Michael, "The government would have bought the chair for you."

"Yeah, I know." Michael replied, "But I understand how much the government spends on fighting the war on drugs, so I figured I could do my part by buying my own wheelchair." He didn't think it was appropriate at this point to inform the Federal Government he was medicating with the demon weed.

"You understand, "the agent said, "because you are now enrolled in Medicare's disability program, you're only allowed to travel between your bedroom, bathroom, and kitchen. When you go back to your dwelling, do not come out again unless we permit you to see your doctor and then only travel between your dwelling and the doctor's office. This is according to our regulations in the Medicare code. This code was established to protect you."

"I certainly understand and respect your regulations," Michael replied, knowing full well this was the first one he was going to defy.

While Michael was at the Social Security office, Carol secured an apartment at a Federal housing facility in Willow Springs, Illinois. They understood that neither Michael nor Carol had any money other than Michael's newly awarded disability insurance and were willing to give them a break on their rent. It also helped that when the facility conducted a credit check on Michael, they discovered he had half a million dollars in unpaid medical expenses.

They moved on June 2, 2010. On this day, Michael met Stacy, a woman who would have a profound effect on his life for the next five years. Stacy was the Director of the Willow Springs Federal Housing Project (WISFHP). She was also one of the most gorgeous women Michael had ever laid eyes on. Her hair was blond, long, and luxurious. She also seemed to be an incredibly nice person. She was opposite to anyone Michael had previously met who worked for the Federal Government. This was no officious bureaucrat, only interested in filling out forms and not making waves. She promised to make Carol and Michael's life at WISFHP as "enjoyable as she possibly could."

Michael did what he could not to read sexual innuendo into that phrase, but Stacy's throaty voice tugged at Michael's nether region. Michael and Stacy dealt with rent issues, and Stacy fingerprinted Michael for his federal background check. When the beautiful blond held his hand during the fingerprinting process, Michael was too aroused to even speak to her.

When he returned to the apartment, Carol was in bed. "My leg is messed up." She said.

He looked at her left leg and was horrified to see swelling throughout the entire thigh clear down to just below the knee area. There was a dark red (almost black) spot three inches above her knee.

"You have a blood clot." He stated. "We need to go to the hospital. Sit on my lap, and I'll take you to the van and drive us there". When Stacy observed the two of them cruising the hall on the video monitor she regularly watched, she became apoplectic. *How could this newly arrived couple disrupt the serenity of her precious housing complex by messing around this way?*

She decided to confront Michael when she could catch him alone. Stacy understood she was more intimidating when there were no other females present.

When Michael and Carol arrived at the hospital, the nurse looked at the swelling in Carol's leg, started an I.V., and immediately summoned the doctor. After confirming Michael's initial diagnosis of a blood clot, the doctor injected her with heparin and warfarin. He then took Michael aside to explain the possible ramifications.

"The disorder of venous thromboembolism" the doctor began pedantically, "is a relatively common and potentially life-threatening condition that refers in its simplest form to a blood clot forming in the lower extremities as deep vein thrombosis or causing a blood clot to the lungs known as pulmonary embolism.

"Annually," the doctor continued, "one in every one hundred adult Americans will develop deep vein thrombosis or pulmonary embolus. Most patients do extremely well; however, in some cases, the patients do not fare as well because of the risk factors for thromboembolic diseases. In the minority but a substantial number of patients, VTE may be the first sign of a hidden malignancy."

"What does that mean?" Michael inquired.

"Cancer," The doctor replied. "We're going to take her in for tests now. We'll do a CAT scan as well as a PET scan. Understand," he continued, "The likelihood of finding cancer increases with the extent of testing carried out. While it remains to be seen if extensive studies help provide early diagnosis, early cure and prolong life, consideration for a CAT scan and PET scan of the abdomen and pelvis and cancer-related tumor markers require careful consideration."

"What does that mean?" Michael inquired again. This doctor was using terminology with which he wasn't familiar.

"The more tests we do, the higher the likelihood that we will find cancer. The medical community is split regarding the advisability of launching a cancer search involving uncomfortable, expensive, and mostly nonproductive tests. It's going to be up to you to decide whether or not you want to pay for these tests."

"Aren't the tests covered by insurance?" Michael asked.

"That depends." The doctor responded. "What insurance do you have?"

"Medicare," Michael answered apprehensively.

"Oh, that shouldn't be a problem. Medicare is always willing to pay for tests for cancer. They even pay for cancer surgery. You only have to pay for twenty percent of the cost."

Michael was glad they wouldn't have to pay full price for the tests and was happy to learn he and Carol had quality insurance. He instructed the doctor to perform whatever tests were necessary for his beloved Carol.

"You're doing the right thing." The doctor said, "You don't want to mess around with cancer. We'll begin the tests immediately. I'll inform you of the results. You might think about getting something to eat while they are performed."

Michael had dinner in the hospital cafeteria and worried. The doctor found him when he was almost through with the Hungarian goulash, which was the hospital's '*Special of the Day.*'

"We found it." The doctor announced proudly. "Modern medicine triumphs again. Carol has ovarian cancer, but we should be able to take care of it with surgery. What I intend to do is take all the tumor I possibly can and send a sample of the tissue to UCLA and have it analyzed to determine the best chemotherapy regimen to destroy any remnants surgery might miss."

Michael was elated they had stumbled upon a doctor that could take care of Carol properly. He waited in the hospital chapel and prayed while the surgery was performed. While the surgeon would have completed his duties properly, it was the hospital that messed up.

It is well known that if a patient is deprived of oxygen for 4-6 minutes, they will experience brain death. More extended periods will lead to cardiac arrest. When a general anesthetic is administered, the airway is protected by an endotracheal tube inserted into the windpipe. If that tube is placed into the esophagus instead, oxygen is not delivered to the lungs, and the patient will turn blue and suffer cardiac arrest. The hospital had chosen not to invest in the device designed to determine whether the endotracheal tube was appropriately placed, and Carol died after 6 minutes without oxygen.

"Why didn't she breathe by herself if the tube wasn't in the right place?" an observant surgical nurse asked.

"We had to paralyze her to place the tube." The anesthesiologist explained. "We'll have to come up with a plausible explanation to explain her death to the husband and protect the hospital. I'm going to tell him the cause of death was an unknown allergy to medication."

Michael was happy that this time when Carol died, he had a body to grieve over.

Chapter 7

The funeral was, of course, small, mainly because Michael couldn't remember who their friends were, and he figured no-one would be able to travel for a 30-minute event. The casino he used to work for was kind enough to have a small vase of flowers delivered, but the mortuary supplied the remaining guests.

During the eulogy, while the Christian preacher described how great a person the deceased (whom he had never met) was, a stabbing pain shot from the bottom of Michael's foot right up through his ankle. Michael realized his muscular dystrophy was progressing, and he needed to find a pain management specialist in Illinois before he did anything else. He went directly from the funeral home to the hospital.

At the hospital, the nurse was extremely helpful and referred him to Dr. Hahn, a pain management specialist affiliated with the Triumvirate Healthcare organization, which was part of Michael's Medicare insurance network. Michael couldn't get an appointment with Dr. Hahn for another week, so he dropped a tablet of Mondine, which he had covertly rescued from the trash. From experience, Michael had found that when blood tested, it was always best to have some opiates in your system. He again enjoyed the warm sensation the Mondine provided.

Once he had control of his pain level, he began to search through Carol's computer. When he opened the files, he found logos, a business plan, documents, and tens of thousands of research studies from all over the world. All the files had to do with detailing the medicinal properties of cannabis. He also located deep within the documents, a journal chronicling Carol's life from 1976 almost to the present day. By the time Michael found this journal, it was time for his appointment with Dr. Hahn, and he planned on coming back to it after the meeting with the physician.

He rolled his wheelchair out of his apartment at WISFHP, fully aware his actions from this point until he left the building were being closely monitored and went out to his van. He pushed the external button on the van, which lowered the ramp and rolled into the cabin area, turned around, raised the ramp, then maneuvered the chair into position so he could transfer to the passenger seat. He then pushed the switch, which electronically moved the passenger seat back and relocated there so he could move across to the driver's seat and drove to the doctor's office.

When he arrived, there were no handicap spots available, so he had to park on the street about a block away. By the time he entered the doctor's luxurious office complex, he was six minutes late for his appointment, and the receptionist glared at him.

"You have to try to arrive at your appointments promptly at the appointed time, or the doctor won't be able to see you in the future. Dr. Hahn is a busy man, and he must stay on schedule."

A blond big-bosomed woman dressed in white approached, and the receptionist introduced her. "This is Gretel. She's the Nurse. She will escort you back to the waiting room and take your vitals and any medical history you might have."

After taking his vitals, Gretel asked him if he had anything documenting his medical history. Strapped to the back of Michael's chair was 28 years' worth of documentation from the Muscular Dystrophy Association totaling 1,346 pages.

Michael struggled to lift it, and Gretel helped. "Oh, my," She commented, "are you sure you have it all?"

"I never know what a doctor will find useful," Michael replied. "There are also notes from my doctor in Las Vegas who has me on Mondine, and I need a refill of that." He figured it was best not to let anyone know he had experience with the devil's lettuce.

"Mondine? That's a relatively new medicine. Okay, I'll let the doctor know." Michael sat facing the wall for the next hour and 15 minutes and thought about getting back to Carols' journal.

When the doctor came in, he was obviously in a hurry. He was German and, in a thick accent, said, "Mr. Dunston, I've reviewed your medical history, and I believe I might be able to help you. Your problem seems to be chronic pain, am I right?"

"Well, no, Dr. Hahn. Chronic pain is defined as a continuous constant pain level. What I have is intractable pain, which is pain that isn't controlled by pharmaceutical medications."

"Okay, explain the difference to me as you see it." Dr. Hahn asked, trying not to appear condescending.

"Well, the way I understand it, chronic pain is one constant pain level all the time. Like on this 'Rate your Pain Level' on a scale of 1 through 10 poster which you have bolted to the wall here. Many of your patients probably come through and are at consistent pain levels every time you see them, say 4. With my form of muscular dystrophy, I am at 4 for a period of time and then bam! It's at 7 or 8."

"Well, as you know, I am the pain management specialist Triumvirate Healthcare sends all their patients to because I am the best. I'm going to take you off the Mondine. It's simply too powerful. I'll provide it to you in the hospital intravenously, but what I'm going to do is switch you back to the fentanyl."

"The fentanyl doesn't work," Michael protested.

"Ja, I know. Here's how we're going to handle that. I'm going to surgically place a tube in your spine so that we can inject the narcotic directly into your spinal cord. I can promise you; you will feel nothing after that."

Michael thought about it quickly and realized that this was his ticket to intravenous Mondine and the warm feeling he craved. "When can we do it?" he asked.

"You're in luck." The doctor replied. "I had a patient cancel on me, and I can get you in this afternoon. Just show up at the hospital at two, and we'll schedule the surgery at three. Don't eat anything."

CHAPTER 8

When he arrived at the hospital, no handicapped spots were available, so he had to park at the physical & occupational rehabilitation facility on the other side of the hospital complex. It took him about 5 minutes to cross the compound in his wheelchair, and he arrived three minutes late.

The receptionist glared at him. "Try to arrive at your appointments on time, Mr. Dunston. The nurse that scheduled your surgery said that you came to your doctor's appointment late and showing up for surgery late is just bad form." Michael apologized for being such a bother and was escorted to his room. The attending nurse took his clothes as well as his vital signs and gave him a hospital gown.

"The attending physician asked me to give you a Mondine IV for your pain and to prepare you for surgery. What would you say your pain level is right now?" She stabbed the needle into Michael's right arm, and Michael cried out, "Ow! Seven."

"Well, this IV will help with that." Warmth flooded throughout Michael's body, and he couldn't help but smile. Through the Mondine induced haze, he could make out the nurse asking him about the scars on his feet and ankles.

"I had a tendon release years ago that became infected with MRSA," Michael said dreamily.

"You've had MRSA?" the nurse asked.

"Yeah, it was a trip." The nurse quickly left the room, but Michael was warm and happy and didn't really care.

After a timeframe, Michael was too wasted to determine, the doctor came in, removed the IV, and said, "I'm sorry, but I am unwilling to perform the surgery because you have a history of MRSA. The administration of the hospital has requested that you vacate the premises before you infect the whole floor. It would be in your best interest to leave. You should have told me you were infested."

"It was in my records," Michael replied, wishing he still had the IV. Anyway, I no longer have MRSA because medicinal cannabis killed it."

"Ja, I heard something about cannabis killing MRSA." The doctor said.

"Just Google cannabis and MRSA, and you can get all the information you need about it, but the pharmaceutical companies won't tell you anything about it because a natural product can't be patented." He glanced around the room. "Where are my clothes?"

"The nurse put them in the autoclave so that they're sterile. They might be a little damp when you get them back."

They were not only damp but cold. The temperature only decreased on the way to his van.

When he arrived at his parking spot, the van was missing. He asked the man shoveling the snow from the sidewalk what had happened.

"Oh, the rehab center closes at three on Fridays, and they have all the vehicles towed that are using their spaces. You can pick up your car at the county impound lot. It's about a mile and a half in that direction."

Michael had no transportation to the lot and couldn't ride in a cab with his wheelchair, so he set off in the direction the man had pointed. By the time Michael arrived at the impound lot, it was nearly dark. He paid the attendant the $400.00 to retrieve his car and set off for WISFHP. He was glad it was after office hours, and he didn't have to worry about being harassed by Stacy.

The minute he got into the apartment, he went straight to Carol's computer. What he found within would change the course of Michael's life until the moment he died. Along with tens of thousands of research studies about medical cannabis from throughout the world spanning 30 years, he found a letter written to him from Carol. This letter was created on the day she died the first time and answered every question Michael had wondered about over the last 28 years.

Michael my love,

I know you aren't going to understand this, but I'm leaving you. I can no longer live in a country that does not allow its citizens to have the medicine they need to survive. I met a girl up here in thunder bay, Ontario. Her name is Christie, and she has Dravet's Syndrome.

Dravet is a crippling form of epilepsy. She medicates with 200 mg of CBD spray to control her life-threatening seizures. Her husband had to perform CPR on her many times when she had seizures. The United States will not let her have this non-psychoactive medicine because your nation is engaged in Richard Nixon's drug war. You know he seems to be kind of a warmonger, and he also appears to have a penchant for extending your country further into unwinnable wars.

I say "your country" because it is no longer mine. I am renouncing my citizenship and doing something that you will hear about in the future. It is called "going off the grid," and it's now considered a crime in your country.

Going "off the grid" simply means going into hiding and living off the land. Living off the grid, off the land, and without government assistance is now a crime that can land you in jail in the United States. Government officials across your country are forming so-called "nuisance abatement teams" to intimidate people into giving up their land and forcing off-grid homeowners to conform to the governments' demands and hook back into the grid.

Counties across your country are jailing people for choosing to live the off-grid lifestyle.

I am now living with Christie, and we are in love. A drunk driver killed her husband about a year ago, and she is teaching me about how medical cannabis works. I am using the knowledge I got from you and your father about molecular biology to refine her ideas into a more scientifically acceptable approach.

If you and I ever see each other again, I will give you a Ph.D. quality dissertation so that you can fulfill your fathers' plans for you in molecular biology. That way, he can finally be proud of you.

I love you, Michael, and I always will, but I simply cannot live in your country. Please don't try to find me.

----Carol--

Michael dug through her files and found the dissertation she mentioned.

Utilizing Microdialysis Sampling Techniques to
Numerically Measure Balance of the Endocannabinoid System

Carol O'Donnell
Manitoba University

Abstract:

The endocannabinoid system (comprising of cannabinoid receptors and their endogenous ligands, as well as the enzymes involved in their metabolic processes) has been implicated as having multiple regulatory functions in many central and peripheral conditions, including diabetes, Rheumatoid arthritis, fibromyalgia, addiction disorders, chronic pain, PTSD, ADD/ADHD, Alzheimer's disease, anorexia nervosa, anxiety, autism, bipolar disorder, bulimia, Chronic Traumatic Encephalopathy

(CTE), depression, Down's syndrome, epilepsy, obesity, obsessive-compulsive disorders, and sexual dysfunction.

This research proposal is divided into three stages.

1) Find the basal levels of six endocannabinoids of healthy animal subjects. These endocannabinoids are Anandamide, 2-arachidonoylglycerol (2-AG), Oleamide, Virodhamine (O-arachidonoyl ethanolamine), Lysophosphatidylinositol, and N-arachidonoyl dopamine (NADA). 2) These levels should be available in the literature. If they are not, they will need to be determined experimentally.

2) Determine the differences in basal endocannabinoid levels in the animals with specified qualifying conditions. These can be determined later, but the ones of most interest are those that result from or result in an imbalance in the endocannabinoid system. These include diabetes, fibromyalgia, post-traumatic stress disorder (PTSD) Side effects of chemotherapy, rheumatoid arthritis, causalgia, Crohn's disease, lupus, neurofibromatosis, Sjogren's syndrome, fibrous dysplasia, severe chronic anxiety, asthma, epilepsy, syringomyelia, traumatic brain injury (TBI) and myasthenia gravis. Many of these are autoimmune disorders and, therefore, obviously the result of an imbalance of the endocannabinoid system. Considering the conditions which aren't, the imbalance of the endocannabinoid system is often the result of trauma. For example, PTSD, Traumatic Brain Injury, and the side effects of chemotherapy. Severe chronic anxiety may fit in here, but research needs to be done to determine this. Again, these base-level differences should be in the literature, but the researcher believes that this is as far as anyone has gotten.

It will be necessary to whittle this list of qualifying conditions to a list of qualifying conditions that are appropriate for this study.

Of the original list, these three would have to be considered as the "appropriate qualifying conditions for this research because they either cause or are the result of an imbalance of the endocannabinoid system and control animals are available experimentation.

• Diabetes • Crohn's Disease • Side effects of chemotherapy

3) By incorporating mimetic phytocannabinoid molecules as supplements to the deficient endocannabinoid molecules identified in stage 2, clinicians should be able to successfully treat these three qualifying conditions as well as the others previously mentioned.

By the time he had read through the abstract, Michael realized he was tired. He knew the vocabulary in the remainder of the proposal was going to get pretty complicated, and he suddenly remembered why he hated Molecular Biology.

CHAPTER 9

Michael was rattled when he finished reading Carol's letter. He thought about all the things they hadn't been through together. He knew she had lived her life the way she wanted and felt unable and disinterested in summoning up any anger towards her for blowing off Princeton and living her life in Canada.

She had always been interested in medicinal cannabis, but he never thought she could make it into a career. There was no way she could have pulled it off in the United States, and he really couldn't blame her for staying in Canada. He would have been able to have a good life without her except for his dependence on the drugs the US Government had forced him to use for 28 years.

In her memory, he vowed to change that. Michael maneuvered his Wheelchair from the desk and towards his bedroom. He got halfway across the room when his left wheel locked, and he was suddenly only able to travel in a circle. He tried going backward, and that direction worked fine. However, when he tried to move forward again, he could only make a small circle to the left. He tried everything he could imagine trying to fix it himself but quickly realized the problem was too complicated for him to repair, and he needed a professional to fix it.

Michael backed into his bedroom, transferred into bed, and thought about what company might be able to help him. He quickly fell asleep.

He woke up the next morning refreshed, grabbed his phone and Googled wheelchair repair, replacement, and supply companies. He called the closest one listed.

"Global Medical Supply Company," the receptionist answered.

"Hi, my name is Michael Dunston, and I have a wheelchair that needs to be repaired."

"What insurance company do you have, Mr. Dunston?" the receptionist snorted.

He read the information off the back of his insurance card, "National Care United, A Division of Medicare solutions."

"I'm sorry." The receptionist responded (not sounding sorry at all), "We no longer accept Medicare customers because Medicare doesn't pay their claims. I suggest you call Medicare and find out what companies are in your network."

Michael could sense that this was going to be a long, frustrating day. He called the number on the back of his Medicare card.

"Hello," the computer voice said, "and thank you for calling National Care United. We're happy to get you the information you need today. I've matched your phone number to the information we have on file. Please listen carefully as our menu options have changed. Briefly tell me what you are calling about today. For example, I need to make a payment".

Michael sensed where this was going. "I need to get a medical device repaired."

"Sure. Now to get you to the right department, just tell me what you are calling about. Your account balance, how to make a payment, or you can say give me some choices."

"Give me some choices."

"Sure, Now, to get you to the right place, just tell me which area you are calling about, your bill, your account balance, how to make a payment, or adding new benefits to your plan. Or you can also say, help me with something else."

"Help me with something else."

"OK, "Which service is this about? For your bill press one, for your account balance press two, for the benefits of your plan press three, for a change to your benefit plan press four. Or you can say help me with something else."

Michael had figured out the drill at that point and didn't say anything.

"All right, let me get someone on the line to help you. I just need to get one piece of information before we proceed. Please key in the last four digits of your social security number."

Michael Keyed in 6817.

"All right then, which service is this about? Your bill, a change to your benefit plan, setting up a payment plan or, to speak with an agent, say 'agent.'"

"Agent!" Michael screamed into the phone.

"All right, let me get someone on the line to help you. We also offer customer support services on our website: NCU dot support slash-dot accounts dot gov. We also offer free live agent chat support on our website: support dot National Care United dot heath dot backward slash-dot gov. We also offer our customers apps for smart-phones and I-pads. Simply search for Medicare on the apple I-store or on Google Play."

Once more, Michael said nothing.

"I've matched your phone number to the information we have on file. So, to get started, tell me your date of birth."

"Four, twenty, nineteen-fifty-nine."

"Thank you. In a few words, tell me why you are calling today." Michael sat back, stunned. "Here are some examples of things you can say. 'I have a question about my bill, I have a prescription drug question, or I have a question about my benefits.' So, tell me, what can I help you with today?"

"Medical device repair."

"All right, I just need a little more information to get you to the right department. You can say, I have a question about a payment, or I have a question about a claim. Or to speak to a customer service representative, simply say representative."

"Representative!" Michael was screaming into the phone by now, and he told himself to calm down. If he did get to talk to an agent, he knew he couldn't take his frustration out on them. If he did, he would never get the information he needed.

"All right, I'm transferring you now." The welcome phone ringing signal caused Michael to believe his luck was about to change.

"Thank you for calling National Care United; My name is Kala. How may I help you?"

"Hi Kala, my name is Michael Dunston. I have a situation you might be able to help me with."

"Well, I'll certainly try my best. Could you verify your date of birth, the last four digits of your social security number, and your mailing address?"

Michael and the agent went through the mandatory session, where he proved he was who he claimed to be.

The agent then asked, "What can I help you with Mr. Dunston?"

"My wheelchair is breaking down."

"Oh, I'm sorry to hear that. What kind of wheelchair is it?"

"Well, it says Victory on the side, so it must be a Victory Wheelchair."

"I see. Well, Victory changed its name to Spirit 4 years ago, so I'm going to put Spirit under wheelchair type. I have some information for you. There is a company that sells and repairs this brand of wheelchairs in your network near you. They are based in Peoria. Would you like their phone number?"

Michael certainly wanted the phone number. He had just gone through mechanized hell to get it, and he took down the information Kala provided. He then called the number the agent had given him for the company in Peoria.

"Mobility Specialists, this is Kim." the receptionist answered.

"Hi Kim, my name is Michael Dunston, and I have a wheelchair that is in the process of breaking down."

"I'm sorry to hear that, Mr. Dunston. What insurance carrier do you have?"

"I have Medicare," Michael responded, fearing the answer was going to turn into a problem.

"Okay, Mr. Dunston. My name is Kim. Let me take down some information, and I'll transfer you to a specialist who should be able to help you." Michael gave Kim the required information, grateful he had found a company that seemed to be willing to help him.

"All right, Mr. Dunston, thank you for being so patient, the insurance process is quite convoluted, but I will do everything I can to get you through it."

"Thank you, Kim. I appreciate that. And you may as well call me Michael. We are obviously going to be working together for a while, so we might as well be friends."

"Well, thank you, Michael, I can always use another friend, and I look forward to working with you. The name of our specialist is Dave, and he will take care of your chair. I will submit the proper forms to your insurance carrier, and it is my role to get them the forms they require. I want to warn you, though; things are going to get weird for you for a while with your insurance carrier."

"That's Okay, Kim; I'm beginning to get used to weird."

"All right, Michael," Kim replied, chuckling, "I'll transfer you now."

The Hold music of Walking on Sunshine was interrupted after about 45 seconds.

"Mobility Specialists, this is Dave speaking."

"Hi Dave, Kim transferred me to you. My wheelchair is beginning to break down."

"What do you mean 'beginning to'?" Dave asked snidely.

"Well, it goes backward fine, but when I try to go forward, it will only turn in a tiny circle to the left."

"Hmm. It sounds like you might have a bad bearing. Where are you located?"

"Willow Springs."

"Okay, I'm going to be in your area on Friday. Do you think you can get by until then?"

Friday was only two days away, and Michael was surprised that the company was going to come to him.

"Sure, Dave, I appreciate your help with this."

"No worries, Michael. Plan on me being there early in the afternoon."

Michael hung up the phone and realized he had dedicated the entire day to figuring out how to get his wheelchair repaired, and that he now had nothing to do. He decided he would spend the next few hours looking through Carol's computer and learning about the subject that seemed to have taken over her life. He then allowed it to take over his.

He spent the next couple days analyzing the dissertation paper she had presented so proudly and started to examine the tens of thousands of research studies she had compiled from all around the world. Her dissertation was pretty good, but she didn't get deep enough into the use of microdialysis as a method of obtaining the desired molecules. Fortunately, he had been trained in the technique at Princeton and realized he could expand on the research she had already begun.

Looking over the hundreds of research studies she cited in her dissertation Michael was flabbergasted that so many nation's scientists had spent so much time studying this plant while at the same time the United States spent billions of dollars trying to destroy it.

He only really took a break from his studies to eat, drink, and go to the bathroom. After a couple of days of this, Dave called.

"Hi Michael, this is Dave from Mobility Specialists, is your chair still having issues?"

Michael thought to himself, *"Well yeah, the thing isn't going to fix itself."* He realized he was becoming irritated because he had been studying molecular biology for two days.

"Yeah, Dave, it still only goes backward efficiently, but when I try to go forward, it will only travel in a small circle to the left."

Okay, I'm going to be there in about 15 minutes. Which apartment are you in?"

Michael realized he hadn't showered since he had started studying and that he and his apartment probably stank. He needed to air out.

"How about I meet you outside, in front of the building?"

"That would be great. It's a beautiful day outside. Can you travel that far?"

"Oh yeah, that's no problem. I'll just ride in reverse all the way and meet you in the visitor's parking lot."

It was a beautiful day outside, and Michael reveled in the warmth of the June breeze blowing through his hair. The sun beamed down on him like a warm blanket. He backed to the visitor's parking lot and laid his head back to enjoy the rays. He was almost asleep when Dave's van pulled up with the words *Mobility Specialists* emblazoned across the sides.

PUMMELED TO DEATH BY HAMBURGER

"You look pretty comfortable out here," Dave observed.

"Yeah," Michael replied dreamily. "I love days like this."

"Well, let me get my tools and see if I can't fix your chair. Can you transfer to that park bench over there?"

"Sure. No problem. Do you mind if I stretch out on it and sleep while you work?"

"Do what you gotta do, Michael."

Within 5 minutes, Dave had the wheels off and was covered in grease and hair that had wound its way around the axle.

"Well," Dave announced, wiping his hands on a white handkerchief, "this thing is shot. I'll have to take it back to Peoria to fix it. You'll need to contact Medicare and get their permission to either fix this one or get a new one. Either way, they should cover 80%."

"If you're taking this one, how will I get back into the building?"

"I figured it was going to be this way, so I brought a loaner with me that you can use until Medicare makes a decision. It's not designed for your condition but should get you by until Medicare decides to either fix this one or approves a new one."

Dave replaced the wheels and backed the chair into his van and the loaner out. He maneuvered the chair over to the park bench, and Michael transferred into the loaner.

"Kim can help you deal with Medicare, but trust me, it's going to get weird for a while."

"That's okay, Dave. I'm beginning to get used to weird."

Michael assessed the loaner chair. It was an old model and slightly uncomfortable but tolerable for a short time.

"Okay, now take care of that chair and try to stay out of the rain. Rain will kill it." Michael promised to try to stay out of the rain and headed back into WISFHP, where Stacy was waiting for him outside her office.

"Could I see you a moment, Mr. Dunston?"

He followed her through the swinging door to her office, her tight dress accentuating every curve of her body. Michael looked at her from her high heels to her legs and then to her ass and hoped he was about to be disciplined.

"Mr. Dunston, this afternoon, I observed you in our hallway driving backward. Now I've warned you about messing around in these halls, and you persist in doing it. I am going to present a written policy concerning the appropriate use of wheelchairs and scooters, and I will be calling a mandatory meeting of all the tenants, so everyone is familiar with it."

"Yeah, well, I doubt I'll be traveling backward again," Michael responded and turned and left the room. He went back to his apartment and called Medicare. After 15 minutes of negotiating with the computerized menu, Michael was transferred to an agent.

"Thank you for calling Medicare. My name is Crystal, can I have the last four digits of your social security number so that I can verify you into my system."

Michael recited the numbers, and Crystal said, "Thank you, Mr. Dunston. How can I help you?"

"I called a couple of days ago about my wheelchair breaking down, and the repair company came about half an hour ago and took the chair. They said to get an order from you to either repair or replace it."

"Okay, that's no problem. All you need is a doctor's prescription that states that you must have a wheelchair."

"That should be easy to get but probably a waste of time. I could come into your office, and you could tell I need the wheelchair."

"Oh no sir, I can't authorize that. I can only authorize you to go to your physician."

"Okay, I'm willing to jump through whatever hoops I have to to get the chair."

"Well, there is a process we have to go through, and the first step is to get your doctor to certify that you truly have a medical need for a wheelchair." Do you have an in-network doctor? I can name you some doctors who are in your network."

"Yeah, that would be great." I just moved into town recently, and I haven't had time to find a doctor. Any doctor will certify that I have to have a chair."

"Yes sir, I have a list of doctors who are at a clinic in Willow Springs. Any of these should certify that you truly are disabled and actually in need of a wheelchair. Do you need more than three?"

"No, three should be plenty. Any one of them will attest that I need a chair."

"All right, Mr. Dunston. Here are three names, and they all are at the Inception Healthcare Clinic right there in Willow Springs."

Michael took down the names as Crystal read them off. "Robert Packton, Theresa Granger, and Julius Santana." Michael thanked Crystal for her help, and the call was at an end. He then looked over the list to choose who his next doctor would be.

His decision was immediate. Michael believed that women were generally smarter than men and had to work harder to be accepted in their field. Women also had the advantage of not thinking with their little head the way men sometimes do.

He called and set up an appointment with Theresa Granger for Friday of the following week. He then got online and searched a website for doctors in Illinois willing to recommend medical cannabis. He found one, located in Chicago, which was on the other side of the state. Her name was Kristina O'Neil, and Michael phoned her office.

Amazingly he was able to get an appointment on Monday – only three days away. Michael then took a shower, put on clean pajamas, ordered some cashew shrimp from a Chinese restaurant, and spent the weekend analyzing the 22 thousand studies contained in Carol's computer. Some of those studies, of course, were simply garbage, and Michael eliminated them quickly. He knew the research that would be accepted by the scientific community were randomized, double-blind placebo control studies. These were considered the "gold standard" in the epidemiological community. He found a number of them and selected three, which he thought he could use to make doctors understand that they were killing their patients with their opiates in a slow, systematic manner.

He only stopped studying to drive to Chicago to begin the process of becoming certified to legally medicate with cannabis within the boundaries of the State of Illinois. It took him 4 hours to get there, and he spent 15 minutes with the doctor. The doctor would send for the Medical records verifying that Michael indeed had a qualifying condition, and he was told to come back in on August 2nd. Michael spent the 4-hour drive back to Willow Springs, feeling positive he was finally going to have legal access to the medicine that controlled his pain.

When he got home, he went right back to his research. He was able to process what he learned from Carol's dissertation and apply it to what he had learned about molecular biology as an undergrad and ideas were beginning to connect in his mind. Friday seemed to come quite quickly, and Michael road his loaner chair to the clinic and met Theresa Granger.

"Well, Michael, I don't see any reason why Medicare would deny you a new wheelchair or repair the old one, and I'll attest that your medical condition requires you to have a chair. I'll send them the paperwork they need this afternoon."

He left the clinic feeling positive he was going to get either his wheelchair repaired or a new one. He went back to his studies and, on the following Friday, received a call.

"Mr. Dunston, my name is Michele, and I'm from the Medicare Department of Compliance. I'm calling to let you know that Theresa Granger is listed in our records as a nurse practitioner and so can't certify you as truly in need of a wheelchair. You'll need to go to a different doctor. Do you need a list of doctors that meet our criteria and are in our network?"

"No, I've got two others. Does either Robert Packton or Julius Santana meet your criteria?"

"Yes, Mr. Dunston, either of those physicians, are qualified."

"I'll set an appointment up with one of those."

He then called the Clinic and set an appointment with Dr. Packton for the following Friday and went back to his research. After a few hours, his brain began to hurt, and he knew he was close to having all of these studies coalesce with the molecular biology he learned in his undergraduate studies. He knew there was a concept that tied it all together, and he went to bed, trying to define that concept. He lay back and considered the unifying principle. It was all about measuring balance in the endocannabinoid system. His memory went back to the notes from Carol's computer.

"So, the question becomes, how do we measure the balance of the endocannabinoid system? Researchers are currently trying to determine ways of analytically determining whether the endocannabinoid system is in a state of balance. Scientists like to put numbers on things, so why would the endocannabinoid system be any different? It is usually apparent when the endocannabinoid system is out of balance."

Carol included in her notes a message from a laboratory technician who wrote: *"Just about anyone with clinical signs/symptoms of obese-central metabolic syndrome, pain, anxiety, depression, sleep disturbance or inflammatory - immune dysfunction will likely have some sort of ECS imbalance that can be part of a multifaceted therapeutic strategy to manage these conditions....in healthy (or not-so-healthy) individuals."*

So, are there any techniques to numerically measure balance in the endocannabinoid system? In Carol's research, she had found two methods. The first was brain scans, but very few doctors have access to this technology, and insurance companies would be unlikely to pay for it if they did. The second was called liquid chromatography, and many laboratories in the United States were doing some amazing things using this technique, especially with PTSD patients. There had to be another way to go. Balance of the endocannabinoid system needed to be numerically established, but nobody seemed capable of doing it methodically. Michael knew he had to let his subconscious marinate on the problem, and he fell asleep.

CHAPTER 10

When Michael woke up Saturday morning, the last thing he wanted to think about was molecular biology. He got out of bed, and made a four-egg cheese omelet with onions, mushrooms, and green peppers.

While he was eating, he considered what to do next. It was time to create a business. The cannabis industry was literally about to explode, and Michael needed to figure out a way to make the most of this opportunity. His medical bills at this point had reached half a million dollars, and it was important he figure out a way to pay them. There were several angles he could play within the medical cannabis industry, and Michael understood that because of the politics involved, he had to avoid any association with either the growing or the sale of the plant. He had to come up with a way of being a part of the industry while remaining neutral with regard to whether or not the medicine was produced.

He needed to be considered an ancillary business, a business that enhances the primary services or product line of the industry. Traditionally these ancillary businesses helped with either the growing or the ingestion of cannabis.

Ancillary businesses that related to growing the plant were businesses that produced grow lights, soil, and hydroponic companies. Ingestion companies were companies that produced rolling papers, pipes, bongs, and vaporizers.

All the traditional ancillary businesses were already out there, and it was virtually impossible for him to start a new one. It was doubtful any of the established ones would even consider hiring a one-armed person in a wheelchair. He needed a plan. He had 14 hundred dollars a month coming in from his Social Security disability payments. Five hundred went to rent, 150 went to food 50 went to making sure the lights stayed on, another 50 covered the heat and water. At 3 dollars a gallon, gas for the van ran him around 200 dollars, and that amount was sure to increase. That was a total of 950 dollars.

He wanted to buy ounces of medicine when they became available, but it was likely they would run at least 300. That left him 150 a month on which to survive.

If he could make enough money to pay for his medical cannabis, he'd be set. It wouldn't take much. Michael considered. *"What industry does society look to for knowledge but not want to spend any money on?"*

And then it dawned on him. *"Education!"* All he had to do was pay for his medicine. It wasn't necessary for him to make a living. He had plenty to survive if he ate Romaine noodles for dinner every night. All he needed to do was pay for this new medication that his insurance wouldn't cover. It really wouldn't take much. He went through a little less than a gram of medicine every three days, about two grams a week or eight grams a month. Eight grams cost him about 75 dollars. He decided right then and there that his would be a company of medical cannabis educators. He had the knowledge needed on the computer right there in front of him. Carol had even left him nine PowerPoint presentations that he could use to train both doctors as well as his future patients.

He figured if he couldn't generate 75 dollars with the knowledge he now possessed, he probably shouldn't be allowed to live. He had no idea what the business would end up costing him.

CHAPTER 11

The nation was almost ready. If he didn't align himself with the cultivation centers or the dispensaries and aligned his company with the physicians and patients, he was golden.

Michael understood he was going to run into resistance and hatred from the ignorant portion of the population but understood their perspective because the government had spent the last eight decades conditioning its citizens to be against what his company was going to represent; Education.

The question was going to be how to get the doctors on board. Illinois was having a hard time finding doctors willing to recommend medical cannabis to their patients, and the pharmaceutical industry had purchased the three largest healthcare organizations in the state and was actively punishing doctors who recommend medical cannabis to patients. They did not want their expensive narcotics to be replaced by a weed.

There was only one doctor in the entire state willing to recommend medical cannabis, and that was the one Michael had seen on Monday.

"Most of the doctors are afraid of the politics," she told Michael. Some think they will lose their license because they would be prescribing a schedule one drug, and that would be the same thing as prescribing LSD or heroin. What they don't understand is doctors don't prescribe cannabis. They recommend it based on the fact that it might benefit the patient who has at least one of a limited number of specific medical conditions. Most of the physicians practicing today are completely ignorant about how and why cannabis works the way it does. Many have never even heard of the endocannabinoid system. Most of the better medical schools are teaching it now, but practicing physicians are ignoring it."

Michael considered the opportunity he had of approaching a doctor when he met with Dr. Packton on Friday. He felt confident he could make a doctor understand that the opioids were messing people up and that it would make more sense to balance the endocannabinoid system rather than to try to target the endocrine system. Any doctor should understand this, and Michael felt certain he could convince any physician that the science behind this medicine was sound. Michael had tens of thousands of studies to back him up, and he looked forward to his meeting with Dr. Packton on Friday.

There wasn't much he could do at this point, and he looked out the window of his second-floor apartment. It was another beautiful day. The leaves on the tree outside fluttered in the warm summer breeze. He hesitated to go out because he didn't want to leave his apartment and appear on Stacy's tape for fear he might do something else wrong. After determining there was nothing good on TV, he decided to go outside.

As the elevator door opened on the first floor, a drooling canine was staring him in the face. This animal was four feet tall and massive. It also had the best smile Michael had ever seen on a dog. This was a happy animal, and Michael was immediately impressed. He could tell instantly the dog was satisfied and well taken care of.

Michael cruised out of the elevator, and he and the animal quickly became friends. After a short time, a second equally gigantic animal lumbered up, dragging a befuddled stranger behind. The second dog was also 4 feet tall and weighed at least 140 pounds. Its owner was dragged along behind and weighed about 103.

"Stanley!" she exclaimed, admonishing the first animal, "You can't be taking off like that; people around here already hate you." The dog looked at the floor, seemingly embarrassed.

"They seem to be pretty well behaved, considering the fact that they're under no real obligation to listen to you at all," Michael observed.

"Yeah, well, we really kind of take care of each other. These are therapy dogs; I usually don't make them wear their vests here at WISFHP."

"What sort of therapy do they provide?" Michael inquired.

"Essentially, they keep me sane, alleviate some depression, and mollify my desire to rip people's faces off."

Michael knew he should be frightened by this little spitfire but wasn't.

"How do they help?" he asked.

"You'd have to spend some time with them when life tries to destroy you to understand." She replied.

"I'd like to spend some time with them, especially Stanley. He seems to have a good attitude."

"Yeah, he's kind of a party animal, but he's the dumbest dog imaginable. If you look deep into his eyes, you can see the back of his skull."

"What's the story on the other one?"

"Oh, this one is Stella. She's the serious one. If I ever allow them to provide you a therapy session, you'll see how it works."

Michael chuckled at this statement and asked, "Why do you get depressed and the desire to rip people's faces off?"

"My doctor says it's because I have fibromyalgia. It causes pain, depression, and I think for me in particular, it causes anger."

Michael thought back to the list of qualifying conditions that you needed to have in Illinois to medicate with cannabis legally.

Qualifying Debilitating Conditions

Cancer, glaucoma, positive status for human immunodeficiency virus, acquired immune deficiency syndrome, hepatitis C, amyotrophic lateral sclerosis, Crohn's disease, agitation of Alzheimer's disease, cachexia/ wasting syndrome, muscular dystrophy, **fibromyalgia**, spinal cord disease, including but not limited to arachnoiditis, Tarlov cysts, hydromyelia, syringomyelia, Rheumatoid arthritis, fibrous dysplasia, spinal cord injury, traumatic brain injury, and post-concussion syndrome, Multiple Sclerosis, Arnold-Chiari malformation, and Syringomyelia, Spinocerebellar Ataxia (SCA), Parkinson's, Tourette's, Myoclonus, Dystonia, Reflex Sympathetic Dystrophy, RSD (Complex Regional Pain Syndromes Type I), Causalgia, CRPS (Complex Regional Pain Syndromes Type II), Neurofibromatosis, Chronic Inflammatory Demyelinating Polyneuropathy, Sjogren's syndrome, Lupus, Interstitial Cystitis, Myasthenia Gravis, Hydrocephalus, nail-patella syndrome, residual limb pain, seizures (including those characteristic of epilepsy).

"I think I might be able to help you. I'm forming a company that specializes in the research and development of cannabis as medicine. I'm going to help patients get certified and teach them how to medicate with the plant effectively."

"I would love to be involved in something like that. I already know it works because I use it to treat my fibromyalgia. I've also got a bunch of friends that are qualified but don't know how to get certified. They've been to doctors all over and can't even find one willing to discuss it."

"Tell you what; if you want to start getting them together, I'll make it my mission to find them a doctor willing to allow them to use a medicine that works legally. I'll guarantee I'll get them certified as long as they have a qualifying condition. If I can't get them certified, I'll give them their money back."

"How much are you charging for this miracle? I smoke joints to treat my fibromyalgia, so I already know it works. What can you teach me?"

"Well, first of all, you shouldn't be smoking it. It's wasteful and has the potential to lead to some health consequences. As a company, we are against smoking anything. Any time you set something on fire and breathe the smoke into your lungs, it's unlikely to be good for you.

Come by my room, and I'll begin to get you started on the certification process. I'll also provide you with training on how to dose correctly, nine methods of ingestion other than smoking, medical cannabis history, vocabulary, and dispensary protocol.

I just saw a doctor in Chicago and got certified this week. She taught me quite a lot about the subtlety of the law. I think I can train the doctors in what they need to know so that they would at least be willing to recommend it."

"So, you think you can get me certified?"

"I'm going to guarantee it. If I can't, I'm willing to give you your money back."

Michael knew he was not taking a risk because he had a doctor willing to certify even if he had to drive Catlin across the State of Illinois to do it.

"How much are you going to charge for this certification?"

"Would you pay 50 dollars to medicate with cannabis without fear of getting arrested?"

"Of course, I'll pay you 100 if you'll give me my money back if you can't get me certified."

"I'll tell you what, let's split the difference, you give me 75, and if I can't find a doctor to get you certified, I'll give you your money back."

Catlin and Michael agreed to meet later that afternoon. Michael spent the rest of the morning researching Irish Wolfhounds. A passage on their temperament particularly interested him because it provided information as to why they might be suitable as therapy dogs.

"Irish wolfhounds have a varied range of personalities and are most often noted for their personal quirks and individualism. An Irish wolfhound, however, is rarely mindless, and despite its large size, is rarely found to be destructive in the house or boisterous. This is because the breed is generally introverted, intelligent, and reserved in character. An easygoing animal, Irish Wolfhounds are quiet by nature. Wolfhounds often create a strong bond with their family and can become quite destructive or morose if left alone for long periods of time."

Catlin came by at two that afternoon, and Michael presented the seminar Carol had created titled An Introduction to Cannabis as Medicine. It was after that session that Catlin revealed she knew more about using cannabis as medicine then Michael could have imagined.

"See these strains that you talk about are strains that are popular in Canada and England." She explained. "You need to learn some things about American strains. Strains like Blue Dream, Jack Herer, Grand Daddy Purple, and Girl Scout Cookies are the most popular in this country right now. Some of the strains you talk about aren't even available in this country. I can teach you some things about the strains available at the dispensaries in America and would like to help you get this company off the ground. I have a friend who is a lawyer and can get us a business license, but as I say, she's an attorney, so she won't do anything for free. If you let me come along on the ride, I'll invest some money into your idea of us becoming medical cannabis educators together."

Michael knew the main thing he lacked was money. Most of his future expenses were slated for him to pay medical bills, to cover his living expenses, and to pay for Carol's death, and there was no way he was going to be able to survive the bankruptcy that awaited him.

"I'd love to have you join this company."

"OK, here's what we need to do," Catlin explained, suddenly taking control. "Tomorrow, I'll get us a business license from my attorney friend. You go to a bank and open a business account in the name of Medical Cannabis Consultants Inc. Make sure they know we are only an education company and have nothing to do with the product in any way, shape, or form. You only need to open it with a few bucks. Here's 75," she said, throwing down the fee he planned to collect from her for her certification.

It appeared to Michael that she had suddenly somehow just seized control of his idea, but he needed her for a couple of reasons, her knowledge, and her money. He also was beginning to fall in love. This tiny spitfire of a woman had everything Michael was attracted to in a woman, knowledge, independence, and an innate understanding of animals. He wished she had brought the dogs with her.

"When do I get my counseling session with Stanley and Stella?" He asked Catlin.

"How about after you're through dealing with the bank. You're going to be going into a bank with virtually no money and trying to convince them to provide services for a medical cannabis education company. You definitely need counseling if you're going to try something like that."

CHAPTER 12

Michael woke up the following Thursday morning happy with what he and Catlin had accomplished the previous day. He fixed breakfast and prepared for his meeting at the bank. He knew Catlin had left early to meet with her attorney friend in Moline.

He reached into the illegal stash of weed he had inherited from Carol, selected a flower of his favorite strain, ground it between his fingers, and placed it in the cheap desktop vaporizer that he kept on his bedside table. He set the temperature for 354 degrees and inhaled the medicine for a few minutes until his pain subsided. He continued to inhale for another 10 minutes because he figured if he was going to be dealing with bankers, it was better to be high while doing so and then set off towards Polaris Bank and Trust.

Amazingly there was an accessible parking spot right out front, and Michael transferred to his chair, grabbed his notebook, lowered the ramp, and exited the van. He rolled up to the front door and struggled to open it with his working right arm. Inside there was a second door, and an officer of the bank helped him open it. She greeted Michael.

"Hi, my name is Britney, and I can help you with whatever you need to do today."

"Hi Britney, my name is Michael Dunston, and I just need to set up a business account."

"Wonderful! I always like to help set up new businesses. Come back to my cubical, and we'll discuss the services Polaris Bank has to offer you."

Michael figured as soon as he announced the name of the company the politeness would end. He rolled up to Britney's desk, and she settled behind it.

"Okay, let's begin this way; what is the name of the company you want to open the account under?"

"It's called Medical Cannabis Consultants Incorporated."

"So, are you a dispensary or a cultivation center? Either way, we are not allowed to work with any company that specializes in either the production or the sales of marijuana."

"Let's use the word cannabis from now on. Marijuana is recreational; cannabis is medicinal. Also, the word marijuana is racist. Actually, I think we're the only medical cannabis education company in the nation that has no interest in either the cultivation or the distribution of cannabis. All we provide is researched-based information."

"Wow, that is interesting. I had no idea marijuana was a racist word. I think your business is something that is needed, but you know this is a new thing for banks, and you're aware of how the federal government feels about this topic. When you go deep into the structure of this or any other country, the banks are owned by the government, and there are certain rules by which we must abide. I'm not in authority to interpret those rules, so I'm going to have to get a decision from the president of the bank before I can open an account for you, but I will explain to him what you do and let him make the decision. Do you have time to wait while I call him?"

"Sure, and I'll understand if your bank president is against education, so many of the people that make decisions are. Just be sure to let him know that we have nothing to do with the product and all we're selling is researched based information. I'll just wander around while he ponders his decision."

Michael exited the cubical and wheeled across the lobby and eyed the display of safety deposit boxes of various sizes. He wondered what sort of things people kept in them and why they needed three different sizes.

He also began to consider and worry about what he would do if the bank decided his business was involved in criminal activities. He knew no officer of any bank would call him a criminal because he could sue them for slander if they did, but they could refuse to do business with him for any number of reasons. If this bank refused to work with him, other banks would certainly refuse as well. He wasn't confident his company could survive a decision such as this. He worried and looked at the purple and red pattern of the carpet covering the floor of the bank. When he looked up again, he spied Britney, signaling him to return. He maneuvered his wheelchair back to her desk.

"Well, I was able to talk with the President of the bank, and he happened to be in a meeting with some Board members, and they reached a decision about your business. You understand they have to be careful about getting involved with a business like yours."

"Yeah, I understand. Education is a dangerous thing."

Michael braced himself for the news she was about to deliver. When people in power make decisions about a topic they are utterly ignorant of, the results are never good. Britney looked him in the eye.

"You understand the position you trying to form this company has forced the bank into. To refuse to allow you to open a business account for Medical Cannabis Consultants, they must literally declare themselves to be against education, and they are not, at this point, prepared to do that. If you have a Tax ID number, they are willing to grant you a business account based on you agreeing to a few conditions."

"Well, my partner is in Moline right now with an attorney getting the Tax ID number" (Michael knew nothing about even the existence of these numbers), "and I can call you with the number as soon as we receive it."

"Well, you know the Federal Government issues the numbers so I doubt you can get one issued with the name cannabis in it. But in case you do, here's how the bank is willing to work with you: There are three categories that businesses fall into. They are Acceptable Merchants which respectable businesses like Walmart fall into."

Michael questioned in his mind whether Walmart could be considered respectable but allowed her to continue.

"The second category is Prohibited Businesses. These are businesses like dispensaries, cultivation centers, and child pornography businesses, and the Federal Government won't allow us to grant business accounts to those." Michael didn't like the idea of his business being equated with child pornography but continued to listen.

"The final business type is the one they've decided to place your company in, and it falls into this category simply because they don't exactly know what else to do with you. I wasn't even aware this category existed. I'd never heard of it before, and truthfully, they may have made it up on the spot. It is called a 'High-Risk Business.'

"What does it mean to be a High-Risk Business?"

"It means we'll be watching you." She said, trying to make the statement sound ominous.

"Oh, hell," Michael responded. "You can watch me all you want because I'm not doing anything."

A high-risk business was better than no business, and it was no issue if he could deposit and withdraw money, and they understood the money he deposited came from his company providing educational services for a fee.

He didn't expect to make much money. All he was really interested in was helping people and paying for his medicine. If he could make $75 a week, he could do that. That meant one patient a week. He hoped he would be able to pull that off.

He and Britney said their Goodbyes, and she helped him exit the double doors. He rolled back into his van, closed the door, did the double transfer thing, and drove back to WISFHP.

72

It was about 1:45 when he arrived, and he figured he better inform the office of his plans. He wondered how the federally owned housing facility was going to react to him operating a medical cannabis education company from his apartment.

He decided he better wait for a while to devise a strategy before broaching the subject with Stacy and cruised by the office without being noticed. He turned the corner toward the elevator, and Stacy was sauntering down the hallway toward him, her tight silk dress clinging to her tall, delicate frame.

"Hi Michael, how are things going for you today?" Her throaty voice once again tugged at his groin, and he immediately decided to spill his guts out.

"Stacy, when my wife applied to this housing facility, you told her that she would be allowed to operate a business from the apartment. Is that true?"

"Oh yeah, now you can't, of course, have a storefront, but if you have something in mind, that's not too disruptive and doesn't interfere with the other tenants you could operate a business here. As a matter of fact, a few tenants are doing some typing for people outside the building. The federal government encourages people in the building to get back into the workforce if they can.

"So, if I offered educational services for a fee and met clients on an individual basis to teach them in my apartment, there would be no issue with that?"

"No, that would be fine. But I don't know how you're going to get anyone to pay for an education. Most people don't want one even when it's given away for free."

Michael just smiled, thanked her, and headed up to his apartment. Catlin wasn't due to return until five, and he had some time to kill, so he spent the next few hours devising a strategy for when he met Doctor Packton.

5 pm came around, and there was no knock at Michael's door. He hadn't expected Catlin to be on time. She wasn't the type. Beautiful

women never were. He figured he'd give her a couple of hours until he began to worry. Still, he wondered what had happened with the lawyer and thought about Britney's opinion that a tax ID number would be impossible to get. He wished Catlin would have at least texted him with some news.

There wasn't much he could do but wait, and he watched out the window until 9:05 when her gray VW Beetle pulled into the parking lot below his window. He watched her as she exited the vehicle and walked to the door. He was unable to read her mood when the light from an overhead streetlight illuminated her face.

He knew she would head up to her third-floor apartment and then come back down to let the dogs outside. She probably needed some therapy time with them anyway. He didn't want her to be upset at the bad news she had likely received today. There would always be roadblocks in front of the goal they were trying to reach, and it was going to be a matter of getting around those roadblocks.

The knock on his door came about half an hour later. He opened the door, and Stanley was once again, staring him in the face.

"Hi Stanley, how are you this evening?" He asked the animal, "Did your mean owner lock you up all day?"

Stanley gave him a look that Michael interpreted to mean, *"Oh yeah, it was horrible. I didn't think she was ever coming back. She may have been away for days."* Michael knew he was exaggerating because dogs have no real sense of time. Catlin, Stanley, and Stella then entered the apartment.

Catlin asked, "What happened at the bank?" and she plopped down onto his sofa.

"We now have a business account and are considered a high-risk business. The business has 75 dollars in assets, and they told me they don't expect us to be able to get a tax ID number."

Catlin reached into her purse and pulled out a bound document. She dug through the 40 pages until she reached the one she wanted. "47-626-995."

"You got it!" Michael exclaimed.

"It's just a matter of knowing the right people. I got us a patient too. My attorney friend has a friend whose wife has a severe form of epilepsy. They just moved here from California. Before she started medicating with 200 mg of CBD spray, she had horrible seizures, and her husband has had to restart her heart on multiple occasions. They had a choice of moving to either Illinois or Florida because of his job, and they choose Illinois because it was 'medical cannabis-friendly.' Now they can't find a doctor in the state willing to give her the medicine she needs to survive."

"I'm meeting with a doctor tomorrow that I'm hoping will be willing to certify her."

"Well, if you can't find a doctor that cares whether she lives or dies, your little company isn't going anywhere."

"Yeah," Michael replied dejectedly. He was becoming increasingly depressed, and Catlin sensed it.

"You need some canine therapy. I'll leave the dogs with you sometime soon, and you'll see why they're called 'therapy dogs.'"

"That would be cool. I'd enjoy spending some time with them."

"Well, we'll make that happen." She said as she and the dogs exited his apartment.

He flipped on the TV and watched The Daily Show until Jon Stewart put him to sleep. Michael woke up the next morning, already thinking about how critical today's doctor appointment was. He didn't bother to eat breakfast since he wasn't sure to which lab tests the doctor was going to make him submit. He wondered if it was going to be an issue when THC showed up in his system.

The apartment complex was five blocks away from the clinic, where his appointment was scheduled. They had told him to come in early to fill out forms, and he was excited anyway, so he started his trip toward the clinic at 8:30 for his 9 am appointment He crossed the parking lot and decided not to bother to drive such a short distance.

It was mainly residential neighborhoods he had to traverse to get to the clinic. The weather was beautiful, and there was virtually no traffic.

As he rolled down the street, a yellow SUV parked in a driveway of a nearby house fired up. Michael knew he better get out of the way and fast.

His chair had a top speed of 4 miles an hour, and he pushed the joystick forward so he could escape the now reversing vehicle. The car had about twenty feet of driveway before it would turn into the street and back over Michael.

There wasn't much he could do except pray for more speed and a miracle. The increase in speed was technologically impossible and given his non-belief in a god, a miracle unlikely. The truck turned onto the street and backed toward him. The vehicle backed up at a speed that overtook the top speed of his chair, and Michael could do nothing except hope the death of being crushed by a yellow SUV would have a minimum amount of pain.

He wished he had an IV of Mondine as he felt the truck begin crushing his chair. He could feel the back of his chair begin to collapse when a car horn blared. Another motorist was on the road and was trying to alert the SUV driver that he was about to crush someone under his massive vehicle.

The SUV stopped and then started forward and off Michael's chair. It drove forward, and the driver showed the horn-blower his middle finger before driving merrily away. Michael continued his journey towards the clinic. He had to cross in front of the hospital before he reached his destination, and he wondered what kind of horrors were taking place inside.

He arrived at the clinic, filled out their forms, and was led back to the little room where a nurse took his vitals. She worked at a small laptop computer where she went over a checklist of important information that any doctor needed to know.

When she got to the part about medications he was currently taking, Michael said, "Medicinal Cannabis."

"Okay, there's no code for that. What else?

"That's the only thing I'm on."

"Well, there's no code for that, so I'm just going to leave it blank."

"No, no. I want it in my medical record that I am a medical cannabis patient. There must be something that says 'other,' or somewhere you can put comments."

The nurse sighed. "Yeah, I can put it in the comments."

It took her about a minute and a half to write the comment, and Michael could only imagine what the comment was.

She then stood up and said, "The Doctor will be in shortly," and left the room.

Michael stared at the wall and wondered if he had made a mistake declaring himself to be a medical cannabis patient. A few minutes went by, and the door opened, and a large man in a white coat entered and towered over him.

"I'm Doctor Packton. I understand you require a wheelchair. What's wrong with that one?"

"This is a loaner, Doctor. Mine broke down, and I need to get Medicare to replace it."

"Well, that shouldn't be a problem. All we have to do is prove to them that you need it. Tell me about your medical history."

"Here," Michael said, handing him two pages stapled together. "This will tell you everything you need to know about me.

Doctor Packton's brow furrowed. It wasn't often he had a patient that asked him to read. His eyes moved to the paper.

Michael J Dunston

I have a form of muscular dystrophy. Muscular dystrophy is a painful condition, and the traditional course of treatment for it is an increasingly strong series of powerful opiates I have been prescribed opioids throughout my entire adult life and have developed a tolerance to all. I have been through Fentanyl, Oxycontin, Hydrocodone, Vicodin, and Codeine, finally ending up being prescribed 500 mg of Morphine. This is an obscenely nasty amount, and opiates do very, very unpleasant things to your body. They weaken the immune system, are addictive, you develop a tolerance to them, and they damage the liver and kidneys. Opiates are also extremely easy to overdose on and make it difficult to concentrate (and my doctors gave them to me like they were candy at Halloween). There were times when I was on the opiates when I couldn't engage in a coherent conversation. I am currently confined to a wheelchair and lost the use of my left arm due to a stroke caused by the side-effects of those narcotics. I have discontinued the narcotics (and every other synthetic drug as well) and now only medicate with cannabis.

Until I began treating my muscular dystrophy with medical cannabis, I hadn't consumed any cannabis since college, and unlike Bill Clinton, in college, I inhaled deeply and frequently. At that time, I became aware that there was, in addition to the usual effects of smoking cannabis, a reduction in my pain.

Eventually, I was able to obtain a supply of medicinal cannabis from a supplier we won't discuss. It worked. It took me a few weeks to wean myself from the opiates, and cannabis took care of any pain issues I was experiencing. As I said, it's now the only thing with which I medicate.

Right now, I must drive across the entire State of Illinois to get to a doctor willing to recommend this medicine. This is extremely difficult for me because I only have the use of one arm, and according to Medicare's guidelines, I'm only supposed to travel between my bedroom, bathroom, and kitchen.

I don't tell you this story to give you some drama of "Medical Mary Saved my life," because whether this is true or not, it's meaningless. What does have meaning are the tens of thousands of research studies demonstrating that cannabis is a safe and effective medicine for a wide array of debilitating medical conditions. I have now been researching medicinal cannabis for years, and I currently use my degree in molecular biology to specialize in medical cannabis research and development.

This has become the next frontier of medicine, and I have enough knowledge about this subject to teach physicians everything they need to know about it. I continuously stay up to date with the science and technology in this field of medicine as it continues to evolve. This aspect of medicine is so fascinating to me that I can't help but stay at the forefront.

Dr. Packton finished the document, handed it back to Michael, and said, "Well, I'm in favor of medical cannabis, and I'm glad this is coming, but I don't have time to learn anything new. I'll submit the paperwork you need to Medicare."

He turned on his heel and exited the room. Michael sat back, stunned, and then returned to WISFHP. He entered the apartment and Catlin, and Stella were sitting on his couch. Stanley was crashed out on the nearby chair. A computer was on Catlin's lap. He had told her where he hid his room key within the apartment complex the previous evening.

"I've been working on a brochure for our company," Catlin said

"There may not be a company if we can't get any doctors to certify patients. The guy's a dick. He said he's not willing to learn anything."

"Well, we don't want a doctor like that anyway." Catlin said, "You know what we should probably do is print something up so that doctors don't have to think at all. This subject is simple enough that pretty much anyone can understand it, even doctors."

Michael chuckled at the remark. "I'm too depressed to even think about it. I'm going to bed."

"We're going to hang out here, and I'm going to work on the brochure."

Michael liked the idea of thinking of her as always hanging out with her therapists and wondered what it would be like to have canine therapy. He went into his bedroom and transferred to his king-size bed, crawled under the covers, and turned on his 61-inch plasma TV. These were the only halfway valuable possessions he had left after paying off what he could of his medical bills.

He pulled the covers over his head, and after about 5 minutes of sulking, Stanley sauntered into the room, jumped up onto the bed and lay down. Michael pulled the covers from his head and looked Stanley in the eyes. Stanley stared back, and Michael had his first encounter with canine therapy.

CHAPTER 13

T he dog looked Michael straight in the eyes, and it almost felt to Michael as if they were conversing. He knew if he told this story to anyone, they would call him a pothead and probably have him committed.

Michael thought, *"Why did this medical cannabis thing only seem to work out west? Why were the doctors in Illinois so insistent that they would be better served if the medical cannabis patients just died and they wouldn't have to learn anything. That way, they wouldn't have to worry if, in the next election, Chris Christie gets elected, he'll arrest any doctor who dares recommend medical cannabis. It seemed as if every doctor in the State of Illinois felt they would be better off if the medical cannabis patients just went ahead and died to solve their problem".*

"No, that's not it." Stanley seemed to say. *"All you need to find is the doctor that cares, truly cares about their patient's well-being. There are 19,000 doctors in this state. There must be a few whose motivations are pure, who didn't go into medicine strictly for the money. Of the 19 thousand doctors in the state, there must be at least one that can think outside the box and is motivated by a desire to help people. If you can find that one, the doctors who are motivated by money will see the money he makes because he is willing to provide patients the medicine they need. As soon as it becomes apparent how much money that doctor makes by certifying patients, they will fall all over themselves to get a piece of the action just like they did out west. Just because the medical cannabis programs are established out west now, don't think the patients out there didn't have these same problems."*

Stanley shook his head and continued. *"You haven't even talked to 10 doctors out of 19 thousand in Illinois. You haven't even scratched the surface. "This is going to be a great company, and I, Stanley Abramowitz, am going to be your best employee."*

Michael chuckled at that notion and came back to earth, not believing where his mind had chosen to take him. If this was canine therapy, it was bizarre. He decided to tell Catlin about it. He wheeled into the living room, where Catlin was still working at the computer.

"I had my first encounter with canine therapy a few minutes ago," Michael said.

Catlin seemed utterly uninterested. "Oh yeah? It's a weird experience, isn't it?"

"Yeah, you won't believe what happened."

"I don't want to hear about it. Whatever happens in your therapy sessions needs to be thought of in the same way as doctor/patient confidentiality. You also need to have a session with Stella. She and Stewart have completely different styles."

She then changed the subject. "That epilepsy patient is coming by at two tomorrow. We surely can find a neurologist that will recommend CBD for her. It's not even psychoactive, and she must have it to stay alive. How could any self-respecting doctor refuse to give her a medicine that assures her survival? You've got to figure someone like you; if you don't get your medicine can linger for months before you pass away and, in that time, you will be in so much pain because they pull you off the cannabis you will beg for the opiates, and they can addict you all over again. But with her, without the CBD, she will die pretty much immediately, and a neurologist will have to certify her ASAP."

"Yeah, that's brilliant. Let's go ahead and set up an appointment with a neurologist," Michael said. He pulled out his phone, googled Illinois Healthcare systems, and touched the icon that told the phone to dial the number. He then put the phone on speaker so that Catlin could hear as well.

"You have reached the Singularity Healthcare System. If this is an emergency, please hang up and dial 911. To reach our billing department, please press one. All other callers, please stay on the line, and a receptionist will be with you shortly."

It didn't take long for a human to answer. "Illinois Neurology, this is Bonnie."

"Hi Bonnie, how are you this afternoon?"

"I'm fine. How are you?"

"I'm doing well. The reason I'm calling is I have a patient that just moved into the State of Illinois from California. She and her husband had a choice to move to either Illinois or Florida."

"What was she thinking?" Bonnie asked, chuckling.

"Well, here's the story: They chose Illinois because this patient has a nasty form of epilepsy, bad enough that her husband has had to restart her heart several times. She now treats her condition with 200 milligrams of CBD spray. What we're talking about is a non-psychoactive molecule. All I'm looking for is a doctor that would be willing to recommend Medicinal cannabis for her so that she can survive."

"Well, none of our doctors are willing to prescribe medical marijuana."

"Okay, first off, let's not use the word 'marijuana.' The word is racist and should not be used by any medical professional. Let's stay with the scientific name and use the word cannabis from here on in."

"Well, none of our doctors are willing to prescribe cannabis.

"Okay, this medicine is not prescribed. It is recommended. No doctor in the entire nation can prescribe it because, for political reasons, it is considered one of the most dangerous substances on earth."

"Well, we have no doctors willing to recommend it."

"You're telling me you have no doctors willing to give their patients a non-psychoactive molecule they need to survive?"

"What the doctors in the Singularity Healthcare are advising patients to do is simply go online and get the CBD they need that way."

"Let me get this straight. Your doctors are telling their patients to use medicine with no controls on its purity or even an understanding of what it contains. They are further telling their patients to break federal law by being a party to transporting this substance across state lines? They're doing all this when proper laboratory tested medicines are available right here in the State of Illinois? Don't they understand they are leaving themselves wide open for a lawsuit if a patient follows this advice and end up getting contaminated medicine because their doctor told them to get it online? Going online to get medicine is essentially the same thing as buying it on the street. The patients have absolutely no way of knowing what they are getting."

"Well, all I can tell you is that no doctor in our healthcare organization will allow their patients to use cannabis as medicine. Singularity Healthcare system was purchased five years ago by the pharmaceutical industry, and they are forcing the doctors to stop providing pharmacy prescriptions to any patients that want to switch to medical cannabis."

"So, if a patient has been taking a painkiller for twenty years and has become dependent on it to control their pain, the doctors in your healthcare organization will force that patient to continue their addiction?"

"Yes, that is the way I understand it."

"Ok, that makes total sense." Michael replied, "Let's get back to my epilepsy patient. She needs this medicine to survive. Within the entire Singularity Healthcare organization, there is not even one physician willing to give her a medicine she needs to survive?"

"I'm going to bottom-line this for you, sir." She was starting to get snippy. "There is no doctor in the entire Singularity Healthcare system that will give your patient the medicine she needs to survive. Basically, they have an economic incentive from Big Pharma to want all medical cannabis patients dead, and I am going to add my own opinion here, society would be much better if they were. Every physician within the Singularity Healthcare system is willing to violate their Hippocratic Oath to make certain that is what happens to them, and I am behind that decision 100 percent. I suggest you not call here again." The phone disconnected. Michael looked at Catlin, who was scratching Stella's ear. "I wish we had taped that conversation. We could give it to the press," He said.

"Oh, the press wouldn't be interested. The people in power at the papers and TV stations grew up during the drug war or the Reefer Madness era. They've been conditioned to be against cannabis all their lives, and one little guy from Willow Springs with a recording of the truth is not going to change their minds. They might be willing to do a story about a dispensary opening. I can guarantee they'll call it a 'Pot Store,' but they're not going to go out of their way to expose corruption. This isn't Watergate, and nobody really cares about anyone's health but their own."

"That includes doctors apparently," Michael added dejectedly. He had a real sense the medical cannabis program in the State of Illinois was destined to fail, and he would be forced to move to Colorado.

"I'm going back to bed." He lay in bed for about 15 minutes utterly depressed when Stella entered, jumped up, pushed the blankets around with her nose and provided Michael a second session of canine therapy.

CHAPTER 14

Michael lay in bed and watched Stella fashion the blankets into a nest. Once she had completed the ritual, she plopped down.

"Well, Stella," Michael thought, *"What am I supposed to do now? There are no doctors in the State that are willing to learn about this medicine."*

"You're a moron," Stella responded, and Michael sat back in stunned silence.

"Doctors don't need to learn anything about this medicine. Do you think doctors know anything about the drugs they're prescribing? The pharmaceutical companies send in drug reps to show the doctors the medicine and tell them what condition to recommend it for. You know, you're dumber than Stanley."

Michael was taken aback. He decided if this animal was going to treat him like this in a therapy session, he probably should be medicated for it and reached for his vaporizer. He figured he'd better choose a strain that had a nice ratio of terpenes and broke off a corner off a small bud of Jack Herer. Stella continued her rant.

"You know, I bet you eat stuff out of the garbage the way he does too. You should understand how hard it is for doctors to learn any more than they already know and that they really don't need to. Let them think of you as a pharmaceutical rep that knows an extraordinary amount about one medicine that treats a wide variety of medical conditions. Meet with the

doctors on those terms. They don't need to learn anything; you already know far more than they ever will. Find an interested doctor and make yourself available to them. Throw a one-page summary of a study at them every time you have an appointment. They usually don't have time to handle any more than that. Once you find a doctor who is willing to listen, use your illness to see them all the time. It'll get the office staff used to seeing you around, and you can train them in little snippets. Get them to use the word cannabis and not marijuana. Cannabis is medical and ingested in nine different ways; marijuana is recreational and is usually smoked.

Teach them that slowly and in stages because this is a difficult concept for humans to understand. Humans are as stupid as Stanley is. My God, is he stupid. It doesn't matter what's in the garbage; my brother will eat it!"

Shirley's rant continued while Michael inhaled the cannabinoid and terpene molecules, which both relieved his pain and provided him a sense of well-being. Finally, Michael just got bored listening to Shirley drone on about how stupid Stanley was, and he got up and ventured back into the living room.

Catlin was still on her laptop and looked up. "Check it out. She said, looking up when he rolled in. "This is the brochure for our company."

She turned the laptop around, so he could see what she had created. It was a nature scene, and except for the content, you would never know its focus was medicinal cannabis. It looked like every other brochure you might find in some doctor's waiting room.

"This is awesome. Stella is kind of a bitch."

"Yeah, she and Stanly have completely different styles. I'm going to take off. You know you're going to have to deal with our epilepsy patient tomorrow, right?" She began packing up her laptop.

"Yeah, if nothing else, we'll just have to drive her across the State to get her certified."

"You know that's an 8-hour round trip, right?"

"Yeah, you and I are going to have to drive it every four months. We'll just take her along when you and I go to keep our relationship up with the good doctor."

"You know, all that driving isn't real good on a person with fibromyalgia, and I do have this desire to rip people's faces off."

"Well, we'll have to bring the therapy dogs."

Catlin burst out laughing. "Yeah, that'll be great. You, me, the patient, two Irish Wolfhounds, and a wheelchair all on a merry 8-hour excursion to Chicago." She rose with her laptop. "I've got to gather the troops."

Stanley rose from his position prepared to go. Catlin then went into the bedroom to gather Stella, who was crashed out soundly, her head resting on a blue pillow.

"Come on, Stella; we're heading out." Stella raised her head, looked Catlin in the eye, groaned, and lay her head back down.

"Oh, man.", she said, "She's always like this after a therapy session." She crawled onto the bed and began tugging at the manatee sized animal.

"Come on, Stella; It's time to go home." The dog completely ignored her until Catlin fell back exhausted.

"Can I leave her here with you for a while?" She asked Michael. "I can pick her up this evening when she'll need to go out."

Catlin crawled off the bed. "Sure," Michael replied, a little apprehensive about spending the afternoon listening to Stella whine about Stanley. "I'll just hang out in the living room."

"Well, if you want to lie down, there's room right next to her. Stanley and I are going to split. We'll see you guys this evening. Bye, Stella." Stella raised her head, looked at Catlin once more, groaned, and laid her head back down on the pillow.

Within a minute, Catlin and Stanley Abramowitz were gone, and Stella Abramowitz was lying in his bed. Michael realized that Catlin had suddenly infused herself into his life.

CHAPTER 15

That weekend was uneventful. Catlin came back and retrieved Stella Friday evening, and Michael spent the next couple days looking through Carol's computer. It contained thousands of folders and Michael hadn't yet been able to comb through them all. The folders were, of course, listed in alphabetical order. By Sunday morning he reached the D's and he eyed a folder labeled 'Definitive Guide to Medical Cannabis.' He opened the folder, and inside it was another folder labeled Cannabis Book. He wondered why her file system was so convoluted and opened this one to reveal nine chapters of a book she had written and never published titled The Definitive Guide to Medical Cannabis. The documents within that folder were titled with a number in front of them, so they were listed in the order she wanted them read or accessed. They were as follows:

1 Blurb
2 About
3 Introduction
4 History
5 Classifying
6 Biomolecular
7 Endocannabinoid
8 Using
9 Methods
10 Specific
11 Political

Michael had no idea what these files meant. He opened the file titled Blurb, and a document opened in Microsoft word revealing this:

The Definitive Guide to Medical Cannabis

Medicinal Cannabis is legal in 23 states and the District of Columbia. So, what do you do now? What conditions are helped by medical cannabis? How do you take it? What strains do you choose? How do you know how much to take?

The Definitive Guide to Medical Cannabis covers all these questions and many more. Beginning with the history of cannabis through the political future of medicinal cannabis in the United States, the topics covered provide an in-depth explanation of cannabis as medicine:

The History of Cannabis as Medicine

Classifying Cannabis and a Holistic Perspective of Why Medical Cannabis Works

A Biomolecular Perspective of How Medicinal Cannabis Works

The Endocannabinoid System and its Relationship to Dosing with Cannabis

Using Cannabis Strain Fingerprints to Target Specific Medical Conditions

Methods of Ingestion of Medicinal Cannabis

Specific Medical Conditions and Their Treatment with Medicinal Cannabis

The Political Future of Medical Cannabis

Michael spent the afternoon going through the chapters. At 5:30, he closed all the documents and the multiple folders. He emailed the file containing the entire book to himself. He then went to his computer and checked his email to make sure it had arrived. Finally, he went back to Carol's computer and deleted the file.

He shut down both computers shortly after 5:30 and realized he was missing the news.

He turned on the TV to watch the little bit remaining of ABC World News Tonight. They were just coming back from their first commercial.

Peter Jennings was introducing their next story, and when Michael heard the introduction, his ears immediately perked up. Peter, of course, introduced the segment flawlessly, and the reporter that picked up the story went down the bullet points in the same professional manner:

- "A terminally ill woman who successfully sued New Hampshire for the right to legally purchase medical marijuana has accomplished that aim."

- "New Hampshire's Department of Health and Human Services has approved a lung cancer patient's application for an identification card that will allow her to purchase medical marijuana in Maine."

- "Linda Horan, 64, of Alstead, New Hampshire, visited a medical marijuana dispensary Friday in Portland to buy medical cannabis."

- "Horan has stage 4 lung cancer. She said she needs medical marijuana to help relieve the pain and nausea she experiences."

- "What I have in front of me is not opioids, and that's the most important thing to me," she said, sitting in front of her newly purchased medicine. "I did not want to go out in an opioid haze. I wanted to be awake and aware as long as I can."

- "Medical marijuana legislation passed in New Hampshire in 2013, but because of delays in building dispensaries, no one could get an ID to obtain it legally. Horan successfully sued the state and then traveled to Maine with the first medical marijuana ID issued by New Hampshire."

- "And already, the quality of my life has improved, just knowing that I don't have to rely on narcotics," she said.

- "The New Hampshire Attorney General's Office advised the Department of Health and Human Services on Thursday that it could now issue IDs."

- "It was our intent from the beginning, not just to be beneficial to me, although I'm thrilled that it is, but to every other sick person in the State," Horan said.

Michael thought, *"I wonder how much trouble she had finding a doctor willing to recommend her for medical cannabis."*

Of course, that was New Hampshire. They didn't have medicine available yet either, but the state was letting her travel to Maine to get it. Michael wondered how she got it across the border and back into New Hampshire.

He could see in his mind's eye tomorrow's news story showing taped coverage of the D.E.A. Special Weapons Assault Teams descending on this sickly cancer patient and hauling her off to jail.

A seed began to germinate in Michael's mind. He realized that there was something to be learned from this news story which he was going to benefit from later. He hadn't yet figured out how this was going to play in his future, but any information about medical cannabis could prove useful. The people in this industry were notoriously secretive to protect both their business secrets and themselves legally. Michael figured he didn't have enough information to understand what made what he had learned from this news story useful to him yet, and he filed the information in his brain under border crossings.

CHAPTER 16

Michael slept soundly through the night and woke up to his phone ringing at 8:05 Monday Morning.

"Hello, Mr. Dunston," This is Heather from the Inception Healthcare Clinic. I wanted to give you an update on the status of your wheelchair."

"Great!" Michael said, expecting her to tell him his chair was either going to be repaired or a new one approved.

"Medicare now requires that you get a Physical Therapist's verification of our doctor's diagnosis. I set up an appointment with the therapist this afternoon because I know how important this is for you. Would you be able to make the appointment I set at 1:30 this afternoon?"

"Sure," Michael replied, "I'm willing to jump through whatever hoops are necessary. I want to thank you for setting this up, Heather." "Well, Michael, a friend of mine, is your epilepsy patient, and I am completely one-hundred percent behind what you are trying to do. I'm not sure you can get it done. The politics in this state are really weird. I think if he makes it, this will be the first Governor in three terms that doesn't go to prison. And he's probably going to going to try to send you to prison for trying to do what you are."

"The only thing we're trying to do is educate. You really think the Governor is going to arrest me for providing information?"

"Well, Michael, I've got to get my day started. Good luck with the Physical Therapist. Their office is right next to Dollar Store in that little mini-mall. 1:30, alright?"

"Okay, thank you, Heather." The line disconnected, and Michael felt pleased to know he had someone involved in the medical profession on his side.

He spent until one o'clock studying the book he had emailed to his computer. It was essentially a textbook designed for medical cannabis patients. The author obviously had fun writing it. Actually, Michael couldn't remember a time Carol was not having fun. Michael rolled out of the apartment at 1:05. It was only a ten-minute drive over to the office, and he liked to get places early, to kind of get the "lay of the land" as it were.

When he arrived, the therapist was just getting back from lunch. The session took no time at all; Michael told him he had muscular dystrophy; the therapist did some tests to check his coordination, and then asked: "Can you stand?"

Michael hated that question. The answer always made him feel weak. "No, if I stand, I'll dislocate my knee." He was out the door and returning home by two o'clock. At 4:40, he got another call from Heather.

"Hi Michael, it's Heather again. The therapist confirmed your diagnosis, and now Medicare requires that you see the doctor again before he sends them both sets of paperwork. Dr. Packton is out of the office, but Dr. Stanton had a cancelation tomorrow, and I plugged you into that spot. I'll make sure both sets of paperwork are faxed into Medicare after you see him tomorrow.

"Heather, you're the best, you know that don't you?"

"Yeah, I know." She replied, seeming slightly embarrassed. "9:45 okay?"

"Yep, I'll see you then."

"Nope, I've got the morning off, but I'll make sure your paperwork gets off to Medicare this afternoon."

"All right, thanks, Heather. I'll talk with you soon."

"Hey, I want to warn you, this whole chair thing is going to get weird."

"That's okay, Heather; I'm beginning to get used to weird."

"I'm just saying, bend over because you're about to get screwed." Michael had no idea how prophetic those words would be.

Chapter 17

Michael spent the rest of the afternoon printing up the manuscript of Carol's book and continuing to study the research still contained within her computer. He had no idea how to transfer the thousands of files and folders to his computer, so he spent most of his time on hers.

That evening Catlin, Stella, and Stanley strolled through the door. As usual, Catlin clutched her computer case. "I had the brochures printed up today." She said as she began to retrieve a handful from the case. You can give these to doctors and ask if we could leave them in the waiting room with the rest of the brochures. The thing we need is something that would separate us from the rest of the people that might want to do what we're doing."

"Would a textbook work?" Michael replied, beaming and pulling the manuscript from the printer, the name Michael J. Dunston emblazoned across the title page. "Wow, how'd you do that? I don't see you for two days, and you write a book?"

"Oh, I must have forgotten to mention this to you. I'm magical."

"Okay, I'm going to start calling you my Lucky Charms boy," she flirted, and the banter continued well into the evening. They talked and laughed much of the night away and grew steadily closer to each other throughout. Around 2 am, they both began to fade. The slept together with Stanley and Stella providing interference by crashing between them, leaving Michael frustrated.

He awoke the following morning, showered, shaved, and dressed for his 9:45 appointment. It was raining at nine that morning and Michael decided to medicate. He reached for his vaporizer and broke the corner from a bud of Blue Dream.

Blue Dream was Michael's favorite strain. It destroyed his pain, and he had no problem working and pondering while under its effects.

He thought back to when he was medicating with opiates and remembered how they messed with his mind so efficiently he was unable to connect his thoughts. It was as if they didn't allow his synapses to fire properly. He medicated for about five minutes, and then drove over to the clinic in the pouring rain. He lowered the ramp of his van and waited for a slight break in the downpour before making a break for the clinic entrance door. He pressed the button on the wall, which opened the door automatically for the clinic's disabled patients, and checked in at the desk, paid his copay, and waited to hear his name to be called.

It didn't take long, and he was led into the smaller office where a nurse took his vital signs. He asked her what the numbers were and was pleased that she told him. So many of his past nurses acted as if this was information only the doctor should know. Some had even refused to tell him. She left him in the little room, and he fumbled with the manuscript as well as the brochure half expecting this new doctor to toss him out of the office when Michael revealed the true nature of this visit. After 10 minutes, a light tap came on the door, and a man in a white coat came in with a big smile on his face.

"I'm Doctor Stanton, and I'm pleased to meet you. It's my understanding that you need a new wheelchair."

"Yes, Doctor, mine broke down. This is a loaner the wheelchair company has given me until they can get permission from Medicare to either replace or repair mine."

"Well, that's no problem." The doctor said. "You've met with the Physical Therapist, and all the paperwork is done on our end, so it's now in Medicare's hands. I'll have the paperwork faxed out this afternoon. Is there anything else I can do for you today?" Michael knew this was the moment of truth, and he struggled to begin.

"Yes, Doctor, as you know, medicinal cannabis is the next frontier of medicine, and I've been researching it for quite some time. I'd like to present you a manuscript for a book I've written which explains everything a patient needs to know to medicate with cannabis effectively."

"What do you plan on doing with this knowledge?" Dr. Stanton asked.

"I plan on training the doctors in your Healthcare system."

"That's interesting; we were wondering how we were going to learn about this." Michael now sensed an opening and handed him the brochure.

"Well, Doctor, I believe we are the only medical cannabis education company in the nation that has no interest in either the cultivation or the distribution of cannabis. Even though we have nothing to do with the product, I'd like you to think of me as analogous to a pharmaceutical rep. I know more about this aspect of medicine than the doctors in your healthcare system do, and I am willing to provide them that knowledge."

"Okay, I know a little about this subject." Doctor Stanton responded, now testing Michael. "Name six of the medicinal cannabinoids."

This was a good question, and Michael had never met a doctor that was versed enough in the subject even to ask it. He, of course, knew the answer and rattled off "Delta-9-tetrahydrocannabinol, Cannabidiol, Cannabinol, Cannabigerol, Tetrahydrocannabivarin, and Cannabichromene."

"Hmm, the doctor said, obviously impressed.

"Now, tell me a little about each one." Michael was prepared for this and had wanted a doctor to quiz him like this for months. He recited from memory a chapter of Carol's book.

"When searching for the perfect strain of cannabis, it's essential to know what you're getting. This is why laboratory testing should never be overlooked. Testing facilities like Steep Hill Laboratories in California give patients a complete cannabinoid and terpene profile of their medication.

"It's always a good idea to check a strain profile before deciding on the strain with which you medicate. To begin, let's discuss what a cannabis strain fingerprint is. A Strain Fingerprint shows the average concentrations of twelve of the most important cannabinoids and terpenes found in cannabis strains." Michael then reached into his notebook and pulled out a strain fingerprint.

"This is the strain fingerprint for the strain of cannabis I medicated with about half an hour before I came to see you. It's called Blue Dream, and it's often referred to as the Bayer aspirin of Cannabis. "Be aware that there are over 1100 strains of cannabis, and some of these strain names are pretty strange, and they are made up. Also, be aware that the name Google was made up; so, don't be put off by some of the idiocy of these names. What matters is the ratio of the medicinal molecules within the strain.

"Cannabis contains two groups of medicinal molecules, and they generally are considered to provide differing but sometimes similar therapeutic benefits. These groups are the cannabinoids and the terpenes.

"Phytocannabinoids mainly relive the patient's physical symptoms. The terpenes also have some medicinal value, but primarily seem to provide the sense of well-being for which cannabis is so well known.

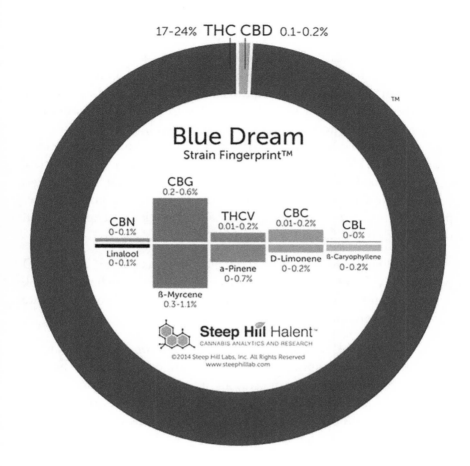

"When you evaluate a strain, the first thing you look for is the ratio of the two major cannabinoids THC and CBD. These ratios are located on the outer part of that ring.

Generally, for medical cannabis patients, the first molecule to look for is not THC but is instead CBD. The CBD molecule is important because it mitigates the psychoactive effects of the THC. I medicate with a strain that has a relatively high percentage of THC because it is the major neuropathic pain-killing molecule in cannabis. I need the pain-relieving aspects of that molecule due to my medical condition. The psychoactive effect of the THC is mitigated by the fact that I also choose strains that have some CBD. You don't need much. Essentially, the ratio of THC to CBD in the Blue Dream strain is appropriate enough for my body chemistry that it doesn't get me high but manages whatever pain issues I might have. Now this strain might get other people high because, like any other medication, it's all dependent on the patient's body chemistry.

"So, Doctor, let's look at the medical benefits of THC and CBD (which we will refer to as major cannabinoids). What the hell, let's look at them in alphabetical order." Michael pulled the molecular structure of the CBD molecule from his notebook.

"Cannabidiol (CBD) is sometimes the second most abundant cannabinoid in cannabis. It has serious implications in the field of medicine and is often the most sought out compound by medical users. It is a non-intoxicating component that regulates the effect of THC. This means that strains high in both THC and CBD will induce much clearer head highs than hazier heady strains that contain THC alone. CBD has a long list of medicinal properties. Listing only a few, this molecule relieves conditions such as chronic pain, inflammation, migraines, arthritis spasms, epilepsy, and schizophrenia. CBD has also been shown to have anti-cancer properties, and new uses are being found all the time as more research is conducted on the CBD molecule."

Michael then pulled out the molecular structure of the THC molecule. He continued. "Delta-9- tetrahydrocannabinol (THC) is usually the most abundant cannabinoid in cannabis, and it is responsible for the main psychoactive effect experienced when consuming cannabis. It stimulates parts of the brain, causing the release of dopamine – creating a sense of euphoria and a feeling of relaxation. THC also has analgesic effects, relieving the symptoms of pain and inflammation. Combined, this causes a great sense of well-being.

"After the patient determines the best ratio of THC to CBD for their body chemistry, it is time to start to look at what are referred to as the minor cannabinoids. These will become more and more major as the research progresses. In a typical strain fingerprint, there are five minor cannabinoids; CBN, CBG, THCV, CBC, and CBL. Let's take them in the order they are presented on the strain fingerprint.

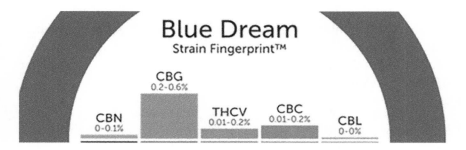

"Cannabinol (CBN) is one of the compounds in cannabis that makes you sleepy. I struggle with insomnia, Doctor, so in the evening, I tend to look for a strain that is high in ratio of CBN. These are difficult to find because strains that are high in CBN are rare. CBN is produced when THC oxidizes, the result of being stored for long periods of time. Now I don't want to oxidize my medication, and I have had a hard time finding strains with ratios high in CBN.

"As it happens, cannabis that has been seized by law enforcement and sits in evidence lockers for months on end turns out to have high levels of CBN when laboratory tested, but for obvious reasons, I hesitate to go to the police and ask for a sample of their stash.

"As already mentioned, cannabis is widely used as a sleep-aid for those experiencing insomnia, and CBN is one of the reasons why. Another use for cannabinol is as an antibacterial. According to an Italian study in 2008, cannabinol showed potent activity against MRSA when applied as a topical. Topical uses have also shown promise in treating burns and psoriasis. The research on CBN is still lacking, but early studies suggest it could stimulate bone cell growth. If that's the case, it would be helpful in treating osteoporosis. It could also help those with broken bones recover more quickly."

By this time, Michael was on a roll, and noticing the doctor's eyes hadn't glazed over, he continued.

"Cannabigerol (CBG) is interesting because it synergizes the other cannabinoids. Like CBN, Cannabigerol has antibacterial properties. It has also been found to stimulate brain cell and bone cell growth. CBG is also one of the cannabinoids in cannabis that treats glaucoma and inflammatory bowel disease. Another effect Cannabigerol has on the brain is that it inhibits the uptake of a brain chemical that determines how much stimulation a neuron needs to cause a reaction (GABA). When GABA is inhibited, it decreases anxiety and muscle tension similar to the effects of CBD.

A study published in the May 2013 edition of Biological Psychology suggests that CBG has strong anti-inflammatory properties and benefits patients with inflammatory bowel disease. It is also another of the cannabinoids that treat glaucoma because CBG increases fluid drainage from the eye and reduces the amount of pressure. CBG also has antidepressant properties and inhibits tumor growth." Michael had never met a doctor that would listen to him for this long, and he continued with what he considered the cannabinoid with the most potential.

"Tetrahydrocannabivarin (THCV) is an anomaly in the world of cannabinoids because it is an antagonist at the CB1 receptor. This means that rather than giving a person the munchies as other cannabinoids have been demonstrated to do, this molecule inhibits appetite. It also regulates the blood sugar levels and reduces the body's resistance to insulin. Therefore, this cannabinoid is likely to be quite effective in the treatment of diabetes, a disease projected to cost this nation half-a-trillion dollars by the year 2020.

"THCV also reduces panic attacks and curbs anxiety attacks in PTSD patients without suppressing emotion.

"This cannabinoid may be another of the many that help with Alzheimer's disease. Tremors and motor control issues associated with Alzheimer's appear to be improved by THCV, but research on this is still in progress in other countries, of course.

"THCV is yet another cannabinoid that stimulates bone growth. Because it promotes the growth of new bone cells, THCV is being looked at as a treatment for osteoporosis and other bone-related conditions."

At this point, Michael was showing off. He had been able to absorb so much information from Carol's computer; there were not many people in the nation that could claim to know more about this subject than he did.

He only had two molecules to go to complete the doctor's test. "Cannabichromene (CBC) is often the second most abundant compound in cannabis, after THC. CBC has been proven to be a successful remedy for migraines. It has also been shown to minimize pain and inflammation, and of course, it also stimulates bone cell growth.

"CBC shows real promise in treating cancer. It has been demonstrated to have anti-proliferative effects. This is likely the result of its interaction with anandamide. Anandamide is an endocannabinoid, which means our body produces it naturally. It affects the CB1 and CB2 receptors and has been found to fight against breast cancer. CBC inhibits the uptake of anandamide, which allows it to stay in the bloodstream longer.

"One of the earliest studies on Cannabichromene was published in 1981 by the University of Mississippi. In the study, researchers found that CBC exhibited 'strong antibacterial effects on a variety of gram-positive, gram-negative and acid-fast bacteria--including E. coli and staph (S. aureus).'

"CBC showed 'mild to moderate' activity against different types of fungi too, including a common food contaminant known as black mold (Aspergillus niger).

"The latest research on CBC – published just three years ago – highlighted one of the unique benefits of this compound: it may help your brain grow. Specifically, CBC appears to increase the viability of developing brain cells (neurogenesis). Contrary to popular belief, neurogenesis doesn't stop once you reach a certain age. However, it only occurs in a specific part of the brain known as the hippocampus. The hippocampus is vital for memory and learning, and a lack of growth in this area is believed to contribute to several disorders, including depression and Alzheimer's.

"While cannabichromene's ability to promote neurogenesis is a very recent finding, previous studies suggest THC and CBD can do the same. A more recent study from the University of Mississippi identified a significant antidepressant effect of Cannabichromene in rat models, concluding that CBC and some other cannabinoids may "contribute to the overall mood-elevating properties of cannabis. Scientists are still trying to figure out how CBC does this since it doesn't seem to activate the same neural pathways as THC.

"You catch a break with the cannabicyclol molecule because the only research I can find detailing a medicinal benefit is as an anti-inflammatory. There are a couple of other cannabinoids that need to be mentioned at this point, and, unfortunately, they aren't included in a strain fingerprint, but there are at least 80 other phytocannabinoids, and they had to stop somewhere. However, let's examine THCA and CBDV as well."

"No, let's not." The doctor said, chuckling, "I'm already way over my time with you. I'm the Chief of Staff for Inception Healthcare system, and if you want to do a presentation at one of our board meetings, you're welcome to come."

Michael was on a roll and laughed along with the doctor. "Do you want to hear about their mimetic endocannabinoids?"

"No, I just wanted to see if you could hold your own with a group of doctors. Doctors can be dicks."

"I know. My father was one."

"A doctor or a dick?" the physician asked.

"Both," Michael replied, and they roared with laughter.

"Well, I'm willing to recommend medical cannabis for you, and I'll set up a day you can come and present at a board meeting."

"Well, you can't recommend medical cannabis for me until we have a doctor/patient relationship. It's a requirement in Illinois."

"A doctor /patient relationship. This sounds like something you'd see in a pornographic movie. Just what exactly is a doctor/patient relationship with respect to medical cannabis?"

"Well, the way it was explained to me was that it takes three visits. The first is like this one, a meet and greet where the patient gives the doctor access to their medical records, so the doctor can establish that the patient indeed has a qualifying medical condition. The second is where the relationship is beginning to be established, and that visit protects you so that you're not making a recommendation after just one visit. The third visit establishes the relationship and is the visit where you send the certification information to the State."

"This seems pretty involved to get a medicine that can't possibly hurt you."

"Well, when Illinois implemented this program in 2012, they wanted to be able to claim they were the most restrictive state in the nation when it comes to medical cannabis. All the States have different methods of claiming they're the most restrictive. Illinois made their application process virtually indecipherable, Minnesota is making doctors go to school for another year before they can recommend it. Nevada is allowing the plant to be grown to produce medicine, but the sun can't be used."

"Why can't you use the sun?" the doctor asked.

"Well, the reason for this is that if the sun is used, someone might be able to look in and see the plants growing, and viewing a cannabis plant growing is analogous to viewing pornography."

"Oh, I see. That makes sense." The doctor said, and Michael could tell that it made no sense to him at all. "Well, I'll tell you what, come back in a couple of weeks, and we'll continue this doctor/patient relationship, and we'll talk about a time for you to come to a board meeting. I've got to get back to work." Michael left the little room, went back to the receptionist, and made another appointment for two weeks in the future.

Leaving the office, he was elated. He had finally found a doctor that seemed to care about his patients. Here was a doctor who was concerned about medicine and not politics. This was a doctor who had done enough research to know the right questions to ask. To top it all off, this was the Chief of Staff of a major Healthcare organization. On the drive home, Michael decided to call Medicare to let them know they would be receiving what they needed from the Doctor to clear the way for them to either fix or replace his wheelchair. Little did he know that Heather's prophecy was about to come true; he was about to get screwed.

CHAPTER 18

Michael decided to celebrate his luck at finding a doctor that cared about his patient's health by buying himself lunch at the Village Wok, the tiny Vietnamese Restaurant in downtown Willow Springs. He liked Vietnamese food, and the restaurant was always clean, and the owners pleasant. The food was good, and it puzzled him that the restaurant hardly ever had patrons. Michael disliked crowds, and so he always chose this establishment when he had a choice of where to have lunch. There was always a parking space open near the building that was van-accessible, where nobody could park beside him to keep his wheelchair ramp from lowering.

He entered the establishment and went back to his preferred table in the corner. He always liked to sit with his back to the wall, so he could keep an eye on whoever came in. It was a strategy modeled after Wild Bill Hickock, and since he was technically a criminal, he felt better when he could keep an eye out for anyone who might be an enemy. It hadn't worked for Bill, but the strategy was sound.

When he got to the table, he pulled his wallet from the pocket in the back of his wheelchair, retrieved his insurance card, and examined the back searching for the number of the Customer Care Department. He dialed the number into his cell phone and ate lunch while he sat through the menu of subliminal messages about paying his bill. He was finally connected to Kaya in the 'Customer Care Department.' He explained to Kaya that Dr. Stanton was faxing the paperwork to them, so they would have all the documentation they needed to make a decision on his wheelchair.

"Okay, Mr. Dunston," Kaya began, let me just pull up the records for this case."

Michael could hear Kaya's fingers hit the keys of her computer, and he took another bite of his eggroll appetizer. The waitress came over, and he placed an order for Chicken & Shrimp Chow Mein. Kala came back on the line.

"Mr. Dunston, I see here that the brand of your wheelchair is a Spirit, and since the chair is so new, we can't authorize its repair. We can only authorize repairs for chairs that are more than five years old. You need to have the wheelchair company that has the chair repair or replace it under the manufacturer's warranty."

Michael was confused. It was now 2015, he knew he had gotten the chair used, and the original owner had bought the chair well before 2010. Why was Medicare now claiming the chair was less than five years old?

His Chow Mein arrived, and he ended the call by telling Kayla that he would contact Mobility Specialists, the company that had the wheelchair. He figured he'd rather work with them anyway because they were less bureaucratic, and their hold music was far superior.

He disconnected the call and finished his lunch, and then returned to WISFHP. After settling into his apartment, he dialed Mobility Specialists.

"Mobility Specialists, this is Kim," the receptionist answered.

"Hi Kim, this is Michael Dunston, how're you doing today?"

"Well, I'm fine, Michael. How are things with you?"

"Things are getting weird, Kim."

"I thought they might. What's going on?"

"Well, Medicare is claiming my chair is less than five years old, so they won't fix it and suggest I get the manufacturer to fix it under warranty."

"Yeah, that is weird, Michael. I saw the chair when Dave brought it in, and it was definitely an older model, but Dave is the one that is going to have to figure out the true age by finding the model number. I'm going to transfer you to him."

The Hold music of The Beatles Yellow Submarine came over the phone, and Michael wondered why you never heard anything from the Revolver album. The music was interrupted after about 45 seconds.

"Hi Michael, what's going on?" As usual, Dave sounded frazzled.

"How're you doing, Dave? Medicare is saying the chair you have is less than five years old, and it should still be under warranty. They want the factory to repair it."

"That's weird." Dave responded, "There's no way that chair is less than five years old."

"Yeah, I got the chair about a year before I moved out here, and it was old at that time."

"Okay, let me do some research, and I'll find the exact age of the chair. That should satisfy Medicare."

"Hey Dave, thanks a lot, man. I'd like to get that one back. This loaner is kind of uncomfortable."

"Yeah, hopefully, we can get this straightened out pretty fast. That chair isn't designed for you and is probably doing a number on your back. I'll contact the manufacturer and get the exact age of the chair from them."

"Thanks, Dave. If I figure out anything on this end, I'll let you know." Michael hung up the phone, and it rang almost immediately.

"Hi Michael, this is Britney at Polaris Bank and Trust. We should probably meet sometime this week. There's been a development that relates to your business account. When would you be able to meet with me?"

Michael looked the clock on his smart-phone and determined he wouldn't be able to get to the bank before it closed.

"How about tomorrow?" He asked.

"No, I have meetings all day. Is it possible to meet Wednesday morning?

"That would be fine, Britney; I can stop by the bank at ten."

"I'll see you then."

As Michael was hanging up the phone, the apartment door opened, and Stanley, Stella, and Catlin lumbered in. "How'd it go with the doctor?" Catlin asked.

"Good," Michael replied. "I think he'll be willing to certify anyone that needs the medicine to survive and meets the qualifying conditions. I think we may have finally found a doctor that truly cares about his patients."

"I figured there had to be one out there. I scheduled five patients to meet with you tomorrow. If we can keep numbers like that going, we should be able to pay for our medicine. I told them our price is now a hundred dollars."

"Well, we can't buy any medicine until the dispensaries open, so let's just put the money in the bank until then. We'll see how the numbers go. I can't imagine five patients a day continuing. Right now, Illinois only has around 2000 people that applied to the program. If we get one patient a week, we can help somebody and pay for our medicine. That's all we're interested in doing. At this rate, I don't know how the dispensaries are going to make any money. There just aren't enough certified medical cannabis patients in the state to support the industry."

"You're getting depressed. Go lay down. I'm going to get some groceries. What do you want for dinner?"

"I'm not going to eat much. I had a pretty good lunch."

"Okay, Dinner's all about me then. I'm going to medicate and head for the store and get some".

She went into his bedroom, retrieved his vaporizer and a container of medicine. He transferred to the couch, and she plugged in the vaporizer and joined him there. What strain are we medicating with?" Michael asked her while he watched her grind the bud between her fingers.

"This is Larry O.G.," She replied. "It's very effective for my fibromyalgia. "By the way, what does O.G. stand for?"

"Ocean Grown." He answered, "The strain was created by a guy that lives on the coast of California. He's probably the most famous grower in America. All of his strains have the letters O.G. in them."

"What about Larry? Who's he?"

"This is just a guess, but I think it has to do with a guy in Canada that owns a lab that is using microdialysis to study the endocannabinoid system. From what I understand, Carol used to know him."

"Well, this is my favorite strain ever. It treats my illness effectively and tastes pretty good."

"Yeah, the molecular profile is solid and very similar to Jack Herer. That's another one you should try."

"Maybe tomorrow. Hey, we're not going to run out of medicine before the dispensaries open, are we?"

"I doubt it. If we start to, I have a plan, but we don't have to worry about it for a while."

"Okay, you good?" indirectly asking him if he was through medicating. "I'm going to head out; I'll leave the critters here. You could probably use some canine therapy. Don't let them council you together, though. They have no respect for each other's techniques."

"Which one should I get my therapy from?" Michael asked, enjoying the concept of canine therapy she had invented.

"Oh, just go lie down for a while, and they'll decide," she said, smirking and left the apartment.

Michael went into his room and transferred into bed. He lay back with his head on his pillow and pondered the events of the day. He had found a doctor, there was an issue with his wheelchair, he had five patients showing up the next day, and the bank wanted to meet with him for some mysterious reason.

He had begun to drift into unconsciousness when Stella came in, jumped up onto the bed and used her front paws to start fashioning a nest out of the blankets.

"Okay, Stella," Michael thought, continuing the game in his mind. *"I'm paying for this session. You know everything that's happening in this little 'company.' What do you have to say about what's going on?"* Her response again appeared in his mind.

"You're a moron." Michael was again taken aback, and once again, he didn't appreciate her therapeutic style.

"The wheelchair issue is in someone else's hands. Don't worry about it until you have to take over. Let Kim and Dave deal with it until the bureaucracy kicks in again. The government is involved, so you have to figure it's going to turn into a bureaucratic mess. Don't think about it until you have to. The patients will be easy, just teach them what they need to know to use the medicine effectively and send them to the doctor that cares. The bank is no problem unless you overdrew your account. You only opened the business account with 75 dollars, and with all the hidden fees, it may be gone by now. But you can deposit the money from the patients on Wednesday. I can't believe you see all this as a problem. You are about the stupidest person I know. You worry about everything. You need to take some attitude lessons from Stanley. He just enjoys life and parties his way through it. Every time a trash can gets filled, it's an invitation to party. All he has to wait for is the adults to leave the house and its 'Party in the Trash Time!'" When the adults get back home, and trash is all over the house, they're pissed, but he's a dog, so he doesn't have to clean it up. All he has to do is slink into a corner and act like he's sorry. Humans fall for that bit every time. All he does is flash his sad eyes and give his patented 'I'm sorry' expression. Humans are so stupid it amazes me. All we dogs have to do is tell them how much we love them every now and again, and we're forgiven for pretty much everything we do. The human-animal is a real piece of work. Let's look at your whole political system..."

Stella droned on about politics, and Michael decided he couldn't stand to listen to the disparaging remarks about his species any longer, so finally, he said, *"Well, I see our time is up. Do I need to schedule another appointment?"*

Stella arose in a huff. *"I'll counsel you again when you need me."* Stella lumbered from the bedroom right around the time Catlin came back with her groceries.

She called out, "I'm taking the critters. Have fun with the patients tomorrow. I'll talk with you soon." Michael turned the television on and watched the news.

CHAPTER 19

The following day was uneventful. Stella was right, of course. All he had to do with the patients was teach them why the medicine worked, how to navigate the complex State of Illinois Medical cannabis application process, how to medicate appropriately, and how to select the strains containing the molecules to treat their individual medical conditions. He explained that he was referring them to a doctor who cared about his patient's health. Most had never experienced this and immediately made him their primary care physician.

All the patients had a variety of conditions that legally qualified them to medicate with cannabis. Many brought friends with them, and Michael was able to help them all get certified. All promised to refer more people to him. By the end of the day, Michael had collected over a thousand dollars and added 12 more patients.

The next day Michael awoke at 8 am, showered, shaved, and prepared for his excursion to the bank by vaporizing with his cherished Blue Dream. He wanted to be clear-headed and undistracted by pain when Britney explained how the 75 dollars he had deposited last week had been gobbled up by service fees, fees for utilizing a teller, ATM fees, exchange rate fees, currency conversion fees, paper statement fees, and deposit and withdrawal fees.

He had deposited his money a week ago. He figured by now that money had been whittled away by fees, and now the bank wanted more. He had eleven hundred dollars in his pocket, which he had received from the patients the previous day. He planned to deposit a thousand dollars and keep a hundred to buy Catlin dinner. He figured the grand would pay whatever fees the bank might have imposed.

As Michael pulled into the bank parking lot, he was happy to see the vacant handicapped-accessible spot right in front. Since it was raining steadily, he was delighted he wouldn't have to travel far to reach the entrance. Britney met him at the door, held it open, and greeted him warmly. She walked him over to her desk and moved a chair so that he could take its place.

"Michael, the reason I wanted to meet with you is we received a communication from the processing company that dictates the policies of the bank. They've decided to label your business as prohibited."

"Why?" Michael asked.

"Well, I assume it has something to do with the fact that that you are in the marijuana business."

"No, we're not," Michael responded. I thought you understood this when we met last week. We are in the education business, and we have nothing to do with the product in any way."

"Yeah, I understand you only provide education, and I personally support what you are doing, but the processing company makes the decisions, and there is nothing the bank can do to change their minds. They sent this form outlining the policy on prohibited business types. This should explain their reasoning."

She slid the page across her desk to Michael, and he quickly perused the form.

National Credit Union (NCU) Prohibited Business Types

The following business types or activities will generally not be provided a merchant processing account. In the unlikely event an application is considered regardless exposure the application must always gain the approval of the NCU

CEO unless approval cannot be granted by NCU CEO as notated below.

- **Adult Content Websites**
- **Airline or Cruise line>$12mm annual volume**
- **Any product, service or activity that, from time to time, may be considered deceptive, unfair, or predatory**
- **Any merchant selling products that infringe on the intellectual property rights of others, including counterfeit goods, or any product or service that infringes on the copyright, trademark or trade secrets of any third party.**
- **Any merchant whom NCU has knowledge that the business functions performed by the merchant as deemed illegal by or in direct conflict with US federal, State or Local laws related to money laundering, drug trafficking, or tax evasion or terrorist financing.**
- **Debt elimination or reduction services**
- **Depressed Property Sales and marketing.**
- **High-Interest rate non-bank consumer lending including Payday lending and title loans**
- **Loan payments transacted on a Visa-branded Credit Card**
- **Timeshare resale's and related marketing**
- **Any merchant selling goods or services that represent a violation of the law.**
- **Any merchant located outside the United States Puerto Rico or Guam.**
- **Marijuana dispensaries and related products or services**
- **Merchant submitting sales that resulted from another commercial entity providing services to the cardholder unless the merchant is a Visa PSP or MC Payment Facilitator.**

"Well, we have nothing to do with any of these things," Michael protested.

"I think their reasoning is the point where it lists 'Marijuana dispensaries and related products and services.'"

"We have nothing to do with marijuana products or marijuana services."

"Don't you have to do with marijuana services?"

"No, we don't; for two reasons. And from here on in, we're going to stop using the word 'marijuana.' We have nothing to do with 'marijuana,' and the word is racist and offensive. From now on, we're going to use the word cannabis. If you feel you must use an 'M' word, use medicine. My company provides researched-based information about a medicine, and until we start getting into research, this is the only thing it does. Secondly, 'Products and services' refer to marijuana paraphernalia like pipes and bongs, and we have nothing to do with those things. Again, the only service we are currently providing is education. We teach medical cannabis patients how to use the medicine appropriately to treat thirty-seven different medical conditions in Illinois and how to go about selecting the appropriate phytocannabinoid and terpenoid molecules they need to target those conditions."

"Hang on, Michael, let me call Beth. She's the person that talked to the processor, and she should be able to explain their reasoning."

Britney reached for the phone, and Michael glanced around the lobby, taking a mental note of where the surveillance cameras were placed.

The phone call didn't last long, and Britney told Michael that they could meet in Beth's office. She escorted him over, a chair was removed to make room for his, and the policy meeting continued with a third party. It felt to Michael as if he should have a lawyer with him because someone in the organization seemed to think he was in the "marijuana business."

"So," Beth began, "Britney is telling me you don't understand why our processing company is considering your company a prohibited business."

"Yes," Michael said. "She gave me this form, and nothing on it applies to my company." Barb took the form and continued as if she were addressing a child.

"You see Michael; it says right here that Marijuana dispensaries and related products and services will be considered prohibited."

"Yes, Beth, I did see that, and it in no way applies to my company. We have nothing to do with 'marijuana products,' and we have no affiliation with any dispensary or cultivation center. All we are is an education company. Now, if your bank and its' processor are prohibiting education, I'd like you to put that in writing. If I might suggest, when you do that, don't use any words that stink of racism like 'marijuana.' A word like that can only serve to offend anybody that has researched cannabis in depth."

"What do you mean 'marijuana' is racist?" Beth asked, and Michael realized he now had a captive audience.

He reached into his notebook and pulled out a document. He handed a copy to both Beth and Britney.

'"A man named Harry Anslinger coined the word 'marijuana' in the 1930's because it sounded foreign and scary." "Here is a summary of the man responsible for making cannabis illegal in this country."

The Devil Weed
and
Harry Anslinger

Harry J. Anslinger, a former railroad cop and Prohibition agent, is almost single-handedly responsible for outlawing marijuana. A law-and-order evangelist -- one biographer called him 'a cross between William Jennings Bryan and Reverend Jerry Falwell'--Anslinger believed that alcohol prohibition could have succeeded if only the penalties had been tougher.

When he was named America's first drug czar in 1930 Anslinger initially tried to keep the Bureau of Narcotics clear of the marijuana issue because he knew eradication would be impossible. The stuff grows, he said, 'like dandelions.' But in the budget squeeze of the Great Depression he decided to create a little excitement by transforming marijuana from a low grade nuisance into an evil 'as hellish as heroin.' To add a little spice he played the race card.

"Reefer makes darkies think they're as good as white men," said Anslinger, **"...the primary reason to outlaw marijuana is its effect on the degenerate races."** To make sure nobody missed the point he offered this profile of the average

toker: **"... most are Negroes, Hispanics, Filipinos, and entertainers. Their Satanic music, Jazz, and swing, result from marijuana use. This marijuana causes white women to seek sexual relations with Negroes, entertainers, and any others."**

Most Americans had never heard of the weed. Clearly Congress hadn't either. The transcript of the 1937 Congressional Hearings on the Taxation of Marihuana are 'near comic examples of dereliction of legislative responsibility,' according to one legal observer. The principal witness was Commissioner Anslinger and his evidence consisted of newspaper clippings. The solitary medical expert, Dr. William Woodward of the American Medical Association, undermined Anslinger's testimony by pointing out that the facts in these newspaper clippings had originated with the Commissioner himself.

But the hour was late and it was time to move on. In a vote they didn't bother to record, on a matter of little interest, a handful of Congressmen forwarded a bill that would one day fill the nation's prisons to the roof beams.

Common Sense for Drug Policy
www.CommonSenseDrugPolicy.org www.DrugWarFacts.org
www.ManagingChronicPain.org www.MedicalMJ.org
www.TreatingDrugAddiction.org
info@csdp.org
Text excerpted from *Drug Crazy*, Mike Gray, Random House 1998

So," Michael continued after they had finished reading, "When we discuss what my company provides, the answer is education. When we consider what aspect of education, the answer is medical cannabis, not medical marijuana. Your processor is essentially accusing me of committing some sort of heinous act that I should, in some way, be prohibited from committing.

"An appropriate way for your bank and your processor to look at this is; marijuana is recreational, cannabis is medicinal. Your processor is playing the 'marijuana card' like it's a big deal. Your processing company thinks if they accuse me of committing some evil act, I'll just accept it and go away, and he'll never have to think about cannabis again. Your processor needs to explain why he thinks education and scientific knowledge should not be allowed in this country. I am formally requesting that you provide the name and contact information of the person that decided that education should be prohibited in the United States of America."

Desperate to justify what was now the bank's policy, Barb made one last attempt. "Sometimes, the Processor doesn't accept a business because they find the logo objectionable. That may be what is happening with you."

Michael reached into his notebook and pulled out another document. "Here is our logo; I'd like you to explain what aspect of this your bank finds offensive."

Barb examined the logo and said, "I'm not sure what anybody

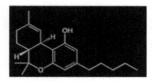

could find offensive about this."

"Okay." Michael said, wanting this unproductive meeting to be over, "Bottom line this for me. What exactly does it mean for my company to be considered a Prohibited business?"

"What it means is any money that is paid to you by check or credit card would be considered legitimate. However, any payments you receive in cash must, by necessity, be considered illegal because there is no way you can prove it didn't come from selling drugs. Now, please understand that this bank doesn't believe you are providing anything except education, but our processor is pretty certain you are a drug dealer. We are in the midst of the drug war, and your company would simply have to be considered a casualty."

Barb then stood up and continued her diatribe. "I think you're probably going to want to withdraw your money now."

Michael sat back and considered. If he withdrew his money, they would consider it a victory. They obviously just wanted him to go away, and he chose at that moment to be a thorn in their side.

"Well, he said, "I just wrote a book that I am selling online. I figure most of the book sales will be by credit card, and they can deposit those funds into my business account at this bank."

He considered the eleven hundred dollars in his wallet. "But any money that comes to me in cash, I'll find another avenue for."

He maneuvered his wheelchair from the office, and Britney walked with him and held the doors open so he could leave. He then went to a nearby restaurant, "borrowed" their Wi-Fi connection and submitted Carol's book to a publisher with his name listed as the author.

After he was finished committing his act of plagiarism, he drove to another Willow Springs bank, rented a safety deposit box, put a thousand dollars in cash in it, and locked it away.

When he returned to WISFHP, it appeared Stacy had been waiting for him, and he was summoned to her office.

CHAPTER 20

M ichael was escorted to Stacy's office, and she explained the transgression he had committed against WISFHP.

"Michael, when looking over this weekend's surveillance tapes of your hallway, I noticed a lot of people entering and leaving your apartment. I was hoping you would explain to me what the activity was all about."

"Sure, Stacy," Michael replied. "Remember, I asked you if I could run a business where I would meet clients in my apartment and provide educational conferences for a fee. The people you saw on the tapes were probably my clients."

"Well, it seems as if your endeavor is having some initial success, and I congratulate you on that. As I told you, the Willow Springs Federal Housing Project wants to see you be successful in any business you attempt, and I hope you can make your business work. Have you filed for a business license yet?"

"Yeah, I got the license last week. I want to make sure everything I do is legal, so I'm jumping through all the hoops the government deems necessary."

"Just what sort of business is it?" Stacy inquired.

"It's called Medical Cannabis Consultants, and as far as I can tell, we're the only medical cannabis education company in the nation that has no interest in either the cultivation or the distribution of cannabis."

"Well, Michael, on a personal level, I applaud you. I am totally in favor of medicinal cannabis, and since it is now legal in Illinois, I don't see any problem with your providing information about it. I know we have some tenants that are looking at medical marijuana as an alternative to their prescription meds, and I hope it will provide them some relief from their pain. My mother is in a nursing home with Alzheimer's, and I'd like to see if it would work for her. Who knows, I may become a client. What can you tell me about Alzheimer's Disease?"

Michael's mind flashed back to Carol's book, and he recited from memory. "Alzheimer's disease is an age-related brain disease that is often associated with profound cognitive decline. The critical aspects of the disease are tightly intertwined with the body's endocannabinoid system. In the near future, measures for the prevention of Alzheimer's will target parts of the endocannabinoid system, and some treatments for the disease will be cannabis-based. "Alzheimer's disease is the leading cause of dementia among the elderly, and with the ever-increasing size of the population, cases of Alzheimer's are expected to triple over the next 50 years.

Consequently, the development of treatments that slow or halt the disease progression has become imperative to both improve the quality of life for patients as well as reduce the health care costs attributable to Alzheimer's disease. "In Alzheimer's disease, deposits of a protein plaque called beta-amyloid builds up between nerve cells and kind of blocks neurons that are trying to fire messages among themselves and results in the confusion many Alzheimer's patients seem to suffer. Some cannabinoids break this plaque up. One of the most important is the delta-9 tetrahydrocannabinol molecule, and this is one of the most important molecules in the targeting of Alzheimer's disease."

Michael's molecular biology background took over at that point, and he continued.

"When selecting a strain to target Alzheimer's, the cannabinoids you should seek out are THC, CBD, CBC, CBG, and THCA. Of the terpenes, the molecules demonstrated to be AChE inhibitors are Pulegone, alpha-pinene, alpha-Terpineol, terpineol-4-ol, and p-cymene. I always like myrcene because it synergizes the other terpenes and changes the permeability of the cell membranes to allow for better absorption of the cannabinoids into the brain. I would also look for strains high in Pulegone because it has been shown to have memory-boosting effects. Other memory-boosting terpenes are Alpha Pinene and Eucalyptol. Also, if I had a relative with Alzheimer's disease, I would recommend they target the pinene terpene because of its tendency to promote focus. I would also be looking at linalool due to its calming effect. Limonene has mood-enhancing properties and might also be appropriate."

"Well, Michael," I think it's a good thing you're doing, and I'll mention your business to my superiors. Thanks for letting me know what you're doing, and I'll talk about this with my mother. I'm not sure if she'll be willing to do it because she grew up during the Reefer Madness era."

"You know," Michael replied, thinking back to his experience at the bank, "That era hasn't really ended." He was about to learn how right he was.

CHAPTER 21

Michael headed back to his room, and as he entered the elevator, his cell phone rang. He swiped his thumb across the screen to activate the call as the elevator door closed, and the box that contained him began to rise toward the second floor.

"Good Afternoon Mr. Dunston. My name is Rachel, and I'm from National Care United's Customer Care Department. I am calling to let you know that we have reached a decision regarding your power wheelchair currently located at the office of Mobility Specialists in Peoria, Illinois. I'm afraid..."

As the elevator neared the second floor, it was surrounded by steel and wire, the cellular reception was interrupted, and the call lost.

The elevator arrived at the second floor a moment thereafter, and Michael was expelled. He entered his apartment to find Catlin sitting on his couch.

"How'd it go at the bank?" She asked.

"Bottom line, they're allowing us to put money in, but they aren't willing to let us take it out without somebody accusing us of laundering it."

"They said that?"

"Well, not in such blatant terms, that would be accusatory. But the bottom line is any cash we earn by educating patients about this medicine will be considered tainted. We have officially been declared a prohibited business. That means that they believe we are doing something illegal, and it is up to us to prove to them we aren't. Just consider our ability to have a legitimate business a casualty of the drug war."

"So, did you pull the money out?"

"No, I want to make them sweat a little. I expect to make a little bit of money on book sales, and that will be mostly through websites. That money will come in the form of credit card payments. As long as the money isn't in cash, it's legal. Any cash payments are not."

"Well, the patients pretty much all pay in cash. How do we deal with that money?"

"I rented a safety deposit box, and right now, I plan on stashing it in there until the politics resolves itself."

"Something else," Michael continued changing the subject, "My insurance carrier called about the wheelchair, but we were cut off, so I think my best strategy before I call them back is to medicate."

He went into his room, dug deep into Carol's stash, and located his beloved strain of Romulan. The strain was loaded with pinene, a molecule known to promote focus. He figured since he was going to be talking with a government organization, it had the potential to get silly, and he better have the ability to negotiate a complicated system of phone menus without getting angry.

He was glad Catlin was going to be there to witness the events. He transported the bud and the vaporizer into the living room, and he and Catlin breathed in the vapor until they felt the familiar sense of well-being the medicine provided.

He braced himself and dialed the number on the back of his insurance card and put the call on speaker.

"Hello," the computer voice said, "and thank you for calling National Care United. We're happy to get you the information you need today. I've matched your phone number to the information we have on file. Please listen carefully as our menu options have changed. Briefly tell me what you are calling about today. For example, I need to make a payment".

Michael was prepared for the question this time. "Customer Service."

"Sure. Now, in order to get you to the right department, just tell me what you are calling about. Your account balance, how to make a payment, or you can say give me some choices."

"Give me some choices."

"Sure, now, in order to get you to the right place, just tell me which area you are calling about, your bill, your account balance, how to make a payment, or adding new benefits to your plan. You can also say, help me with something else."

"Help me with something else."

"Okay. Which service is this about? For your bill press one, for your account balance press two, for the benefits of your plan press three, for a change to your benefit plan press four. Or you can say help me with something else."

By this time, Catlin was in hysterics, and they were both laughing so hard nothing was being said.

"All right, let me get someone on the line to help you."

"So now we get to talk to a person?" Catlin asked.

"Just wait it out," Michael replied.

"I just need to get one piece of information before we proceed. Please key in the last four digits of your social security number."

Michael Keyed in 6817

"All right then, which service is this about? Your bill, a change to your benefit plan, setting up a payment plan or to speak with an agent, say 'agent.'"

"Agent," Michael said quietly, and Catlin convulsed again. "All right, let me get someone on the line to help you. We also offer customer support services on our website: NCU dot support backward slash-dot accounts dot gov. We also offer free live agent chat support on our website, support dot National Care United dot heath dot backward slash, dot gov. We also offer our customers apps for smart-phones and I-pads. Simply search for Medicare on the apple I-store or on google play." By this time, Catlin was on the floor, and again nothing was said. "I've matched your phone number to the information we have on file. So, to get started, tell me your date of birth."

"Four, twenty, nineteen fifty-nine."

"Thank you. In a few words, tell me why you are calling today." Catlin obviously couldn't take much more, and Michael watched her go into the kitchen and retrieve a Coke from the refrigerator. "Here are some examples of things you can say. I have a question about my bill, I have a prescription drug question, or I have a question about my benefits. So, tell me, what can I help you with today?"

"Customer service."

"All right, I just need a little more information to get you to the right department. You can say, I have a question about a payment, or I have a question about a claim." Or to speak to a customer service representative, simply say representative."

"Representative," Michael said. Catlin returned from her excursion to the kitchen and seemed suddenly attentive. 'Representative' was a new menu prompt, and this one had some potential to be effective in reaching a real live human being.

"All right, I'm transferring you now." The welcome phone ringing signal seemed to encourage Catlin into believing their luck was about to change. Michael knew better.

"Thank you for calling National Care United; My name is Yolanda. How may I help you?"

"Hi Yolanda, my name is Michael Dunston. I recently received a call from Rachel, and we were cut off. Can I speak to her, please?"

"Well, Mr. Dunston, we cannot connect you with specific agents, but I can provide you the information you need. Could you verify your date of birth, the last four digits of your social security number, and your mailing address?" Michael and the agent went through the mandatory session, where he proved he was who he claimed to be. The agent then asked, "What can I help you with Mr. Dunston?"

"Rachael said a decision had been made regarding my wheelchair?"

"Yes, Mr. Dunston." He could hear her fingers flying across her keyboard. "That would be the wheelchair that is currently being stored in Peoria?"

"I would hope it's currently being repaired in Peoria because the chair I'm in now is pretty much destroying my spine."

"Uh-huh, well, I'm sorry to hear that Mr. Dunston, but I'm afraid that since the chair is less than five years old, it's not National Care United's responsibility to fix it. You need to contact the manufacturer to get it fixed under their warranty." Is there anything else I can do for you today?

"No, I'll try to get things straightened out on my end. Thank you for your time."

"Certainly, Mr. Dunston. We're always here for you." The phone disconnected.

"So," Catlin asked, "They're going to fix it under warranty?"

"No way," Michael replied, I bought the chair from a guy five years ago, and it was used then. I don't understand why they think the chair is new. I need to call the wheelchair company."

"Well, you can't do that until normal business hours," Catlin said. Michael looked at the clock and realized that in the time it took to negotiate the phone menu, the afternoon had changed to evening.

CHAPTER 22

Michael woke up the following morning, wondering how much it was going to cost to get a new wheelchair. It was apparent National Care United, or Medicare had no interest in paying for one and was going to continue issuing verbal denials of medical coverage. There wasn't much Michael could do until they put something in writing. He decided he would continue to jump through the hoops that his insurance company placed in front of him and called the wheelchair company.

"Mobility Specialists, this is Kim."

"Hi Kim, It's Michael Dunston."

"Hi Michael, how are you? Have you heard from your insurance company yet?"

"Yeah, Kim, that's what I'm calling about. They say they won't pay because the chair is less than five years old."

"No way, I know the chair is older than that, and Dave has taken the serial number from it, and we'll find out to the day when it was built. Dave's not here right now, but I'll have him get back to you when he figures it out. In the meantime, you should come down here and look at our collection. We've got a lot of different models, and you can choose the one you want when your insurance finally decides they've tortured you enough."

"So, is this common that the insurance company denies?"

"Oh yeah, it happens all the time. I think it's just standard procedure that if they deny verbally for long enough, the patient will die or just give up."

"Well, I have no plans to do either one. If that's their strategy, they've effectively declared war on me, and when I'm in a war, I am more than willing to resort to nuclear weapons. I've just got to figure out what nukes I have at my disposal."

"Yeah, well, good luck with that," Kim said, rolling her eyes. Michael pushed the icon to disconnect the call and reached for his vaporizer and his cherished Blue Dream. At that moment, Catlin walked into the apartment.

"Hi, Michael." She called out.

"I'm back here in the bedroom," he called back. "I'm getting ready to medicate."

"Good." She said, crawling into bed next to him, and Stanley and Stella plopped down between taking up most of the bed. "I haven't medicated yet today, and I have some news. I got a call from a lady with the American Cancer Society, and she's got a group of cancer patients that need to be certified ASAP, so I set them up for this weekend."

"How many? Michael asked.

"Well, she said 20 or 30."

"And how do you expect us to do that many patients in a weekend?" Michael asked.

"Well, the American Cancer Society said that if we could provide a forum, they could just come as a group, and we could train the group of them all at once. So, I reserved the community room downstairs to do training programs for the entire weekend."

"WISFHP lets you reserve that room?" Michael asked.

"Oh yeah, I do it all the time. I just tell the office I have a family reunion and they reserve it for me. You know they watch what goes on around here pretty closely on the weekdays and treat us like inmates in prison, but on the weekends, we are pretty much ignored. I think if the building burned down on a weekend, nobody would notice until Monday. So, I figure what we'll do is certify the patients all as a group and conduct a little PowerPoint training session on the big screen television down there. What we can do is start bringing in patients in groups. We'll do cancer patients this weekend, Fibromyalgia and Lupus patients next, then we'll do pain patients, then Crohn's, and end up with Alzheimer's and TBI. We should able to fill a few weekends until they catch us."

Michael chuckled to himself. He appreciated the irony of a Federal housing facility being the home of the premier medical cannabis certification fortress in the State of Illinois.

Things were uneventful for the next three weeks. On the weekends, they averaged 40 patients because some brought friends. On weekdays, Michael met with the patients that didn't want to be associated with the stigma of being a medical cannabis patient individually. Over the work-week, Michael was able to certify an additional 25. When he and Catlin took their cashbox to the bank on Saturday morning at the end of the three weeks, they stuffed nineteen thousand five hundred dollars into the tiny safety deposit box he had rented only weeks before.

Catlin was giddy. "It's too bad we can't spend it." She whispered while they huddled together in the tiny room the bank put them into to load their box.

"We can." He whispered back. "We simply can't buy anything that costs real money, like houses and cars. Anything that we have to pay more than 10 thousand dollars for we can't buy because it would generate a Currency Transaction Report. I can't even buy a new wheelchair with it because they're so expensive. What we can do is take about 400 dollars out of here, and we can use it to buy food. I figure we can buy a whole bunch of ground beef and jam it into our freezer and get some Hamburger Helper and eat pretty well for quite a while."

Catlin smiled coyly. "We don't need to spend the money on food. I've got about 200 dollars in food stamps in my purse, and the State is going to reload my card on the 5th, and we can just start buying our food with my food stamps. There's a grocery store in The Quad Cities that has an excellent meat department, and we can load up there."

"That sounds awesome!" Michael exclaimed, still attempting to whisper. "What we can do is pull 500 dollars out of here and go to an auction and buy a huge used refrigerator/freezer."

"Yeah," Catlin Whispered, dollar signs forming in her eyes. "I could store sodas in it and sell soda to the entire apartment complex. People are always coming to me for sodas anyway, and I can buy it with my food stamps and sell them for a dollar. That's a dollar profit for every can I sell."

Michael considered the morality of such a venture but decided that since he had plagiarized his book, he was in no position to pass judgment. He pulled 500 dollars from the box, deposited it into his wallet, and closed the box. The money took up nearly half of the small box, and he looked forward to seeing how much money it could hold.

When he was in Las Vegas, he went to a casino that had a million dollars in cash on display, and it didn't take up as much space as he thought it would, but 19 thousand dollars took up a pretty significant portion of the small safety deposit box.

Michael locked the box up and watched the bank officer lock it in the wall alongside the others. He and Catlin spent the rest of the weekend researching auction houses and searching for refrigerators and freezers.

CHAPTER 23

O n Monday morning, Michael awoke to his cell phone ringing. He checked the caller I.D. and was not surprised when it indicated it was the office of WISFHP. He touched the "answer" icon and greeted the caller.

"Good morning Michael, this is Stacy in the office. Could you stop by here sometime today? There's been a development that's come up which concerns you."

"Sure, Stacy." Michael replied, "I can come down around ten."

"That would be great, Michael. I'll look forward to seeing you then."

Michael sat, reached for his vaporizer, and considered; Stacy sounded very pleasant on the phone. But he knew he had to remain aware that she was a government official, and they can turn on you without notice. He figured she had probably discovered the weekend get-together of patients, and he would receive a proverbial slap on the wrist for having a reunion without a family.

He vaporized with a strain of Super Lemon Haze. It was loaded with limonene, a molecule considered to have mood-enhancing properties. He had no experience with this strain but thought a little mood enhancement might serve him well in the situation he was about to endure.

When he felt the sense of well-being, he shut the vaporizer off and cruised down to the offices of the Willow Creek Federal Housing Project. He entered through the swinging doors of Stacy's office. Stacy was on the phone and signaled him over. She completed the call and greeted Michael warmly.

"Well, Michael, I wanted to let you know that I talked with my superiors about your business, and they feel that because this is a federal housing facility, you will not be allowed to conduct your business here. They also feel that since you have admitted to ingesting an illegal drug within the property on a daily basis, clearly violating Federal law, you are ordered to find other housing accommodations by the end of this month."

Michael didn't consider it appropriate to inform her that at that time, 195 patients had been certified to medicate with cannabis within that very facility and WISFHP was quickly gaining the reputation as the place to go if you wanted to get approved for medicinal cannabis.

He exited the office and wondered how he was going to go about finding a new place to live. He returned to his apartment to find Catlin vaporizing on his couch.

"You know I really like this Larry OG strain." She said as he entered. Stella was crashed out next to her, and Stanley was asleep in a nearby chair.

"Yeah, it's an excellent strain," Michael replied.

"It seems to be the perfect strain to treat my fibromyalgia. Where've you been?" She asked.

"I've been getting evicted."

"Just because we certified a few patients?"

"No. They don't even know about that." It has to do with the fact that I'm using medicine the federal government considers one of the most dangerous substances on earth within a federal building."

He took the whip of the vaporizer from Catlin's hand and took a deep breath of Larry. Stella raised her head and groaned. Michael jostled her head and said, "What's wrong, Stella? Is the fact that I'm now homeless boring to you?"

Catlin said, "Don't worry, Stella, we'll find him a place. We'll probably be homeless soon too, and then we'll go live with Michael." Stella raised her head and groaned again. "I know Stella... You don't want to live in a grocery box on the street." She retrieved the whip from Michael and drew another breath of Larry."

"Seriously, though, I don't want to live in a box on the street either. What's the plan to avoid that happening to me?"

"How much time we got?"

"They're giving me to the end of the month to vacate the premises."

"No problem. Let me touch base with some of my contacts. We'll find you a place to live that's not a grocery box. How about a paper bag?"

Michael could see she was having fun with this, but he wasn't a big fan of uncertainty. "Seriously, though."

"Look, if you don't find a place by the end of the month, they're going to have to get the police to drag you out, and I promise you I will make sure the press is here for that. It'll be a pretty good show. The police aren't going to know how to handle someone with your condition, and all you have to do is start screaming, 'You're hurting me! You're hurting me!' It'll make a great story and become an internet sensation."

"Yeah," Michael replied unsurely, "I think I just need to get out of here and not create a fuss."

"You know, you could sue them."

"Well, without the dispensaries open, what we're doing is illegal, so they have every right to have me dragged out of here kicking and screaming. They are in a war against the cannabinoid molecules, and a metaphorical bomb blast has just destroyed my home."

Catlin just smiled, Michael tended to look at things metaphorically, and she always appeared to enjoy his analogies. "I'll find you a place to live. In the meantime, just keep meeting patients in the room during the week, and the last weekend before you're evicted, we'll do a big certification for pain patients. We'll skip this weekend and play. Your mind isn't clear, anyway."

"You know what we can do this weekend?" Michael asked excitedly. We can take my certification letter and go to a dispensary in Michigan. They have an agreement that says they will honor medical cannabis patients from other states."

"Yeah!" Catlin exclaimed, "Maybe we can find some more Larry because we're beginning to come to the end of this bud."

"The biggest issue we have is that we have to travel through a corner of Indiana to get back to Illinois, and Indiana has no sense of humor where it comes to medicinal cannabis. We could easily end up in an Indiana prison for two years."

"What about going through Wisconsin?" Catlin asked.

"Wisconsin prisons are just as bad," Michael replied. "What we can do is drive up through Wisconsin. The scenery is better anyway and then slip down through the corner of Indiana. Once we get back into Illinois, we're safe."

"It seems like a lot of trouble to go through to get the medicine you need to survive. Is that why Medicare denies you a wheelchair; because they want to kill you off for being a medical cannabis patient?"

"No, I don't think they even know I'm a medical cannabis patient yet. I think there's financial incentive to try to kill off anybody that files a claim."

CHAPTER 24

The following week was uneventful. Between the time Michael spent consulting with patients, he was issued another verbal denial of the repair or replacement of his wheelchair because the provider hadn't yet told Medicare what was wrong with the chair and how much it would cost to fix it.

He also hadn't proved to their physician that he needed the chair. After speaking with Medicare, Michael called Dave at Mobility Specialists.

"Well, there's a form they have to send me on which to provide that information and they won't accept the information unless it's on one of their forms," Dave said

"Don't you just have a bunch of forms?" Michael asked.

"No, they create the form for each case and mail it to the provider. I'll call your insurance provider and have one sent down. They really should have sent it a while ago. They probably didn't because they think the manufacturer will cover it under warranty. I know how they got the idea this was a new chair. They think it's a Spirit Wheelchair and it's actually a Victory. Spirit changed its name to Victory four years ago."

"They haven't sent anyone down to take a look at it, right?" Michael asked.

Dave chuckled at the thought. "No, all they go by is their forms."

"So, what's the next step?" Michael asked.

"Well, once we get the form thing straightened out, things should happen pretty quickly. We have the chairs that will work for your condition right here, and once you get approval, all we need is the copay. We can get you into a chair the same day we get the approval letter."

"Good, because this loaner is beginning to do a number on my spine."

"Hey, you take care of that chair," Dave demanded. "Don't take it out in the rain. The electronics can't handle it."

"Sure, Dave," Michael said, not certain how he could avoid getting rained on.

After this conversation, Michael packed up a travel bag for their upcoming trip to Michigan. He made sure he packed his letter of acceptance to the Illinois Medical Cannabis Pilot program, and Catlin's attorney friend rented a spot at a Michigan campground under his name to establish residency.

On the Friday before their trip, five complimentary copies of Carol's book with his name emblazoned across the cover arrived at his doorstep. He examined the tome, a little ashamed that he was now officially a plagiarist.

They started for Michigan at midnight that evening. Catlin drove all night while Michael slept, and they arrived in Flint at 8:15 A.M. They stopped at a Denny's near their chosen dispensary and had breakfast. Both he and Catlin and were excited. They had never bought their medicine legally before, and all Catlin could talk about was Larry.

"I want to buy up our allotment in that." She said.

"No," Michael replied. "We have to split it up and buy a variety of different strains. I think we need to split things up two-thirds Sativa and one-third Indica.

The waitress came over and set down two glasses of water. "Do you need to see a menu, or are you ready to order?"

"I'd like to see a menu please," Michael said. Now they were just stalling for time. The dispensary was half a block away, and they wanted to plan their strategy to arrive right when new medicine was made available. Catlin had done her research and determined the dispensary received new shipments from their cultivation center and lab on Saturday mornings. Hence, the greatest selection the dispensary had to offer was Saturday at 10 am.

They had only made 16 thousand dollars that week, and Michael put 14 thousand in the safety deposit box on Friday afternoon, thinking he was going to have to move to the next larger size soon. He decided he'd better mention it to Catlin.

"You know that tiny safety deposit box isn't going to hold all that money."

"Yeah, I was wondering about that. If we start moving up in sizes, the bank is going to notice. I think we need to add another bank and rent the biggest box they have. What we've got going on shows no signs of stopping. This was a slow week, and we made 16 thousand dollars. If we average that…" She pulled out her phone and punched some numbers into the calculator. "We'd make 832 thousand dollars in the first year. Have you seen how much space that much money takes up?"

"Not really," Michael replied, tiring of the subject. The money wasn't the issue anymore. All he had really wanted to do was help people and pay for his medicine. Now it appeared he was going to have to pay for a wheelchair too, although he wouldn't be able to with cash without generating a currency transaction report. If he put up a fight for the wheelchair, sooner or later they were going to cancel his insurance altogether.

Finally, he said, "I think we should just keep loading up safety deposit boxes until the banks allow us to deposit it. Someday we may have to pay medical bills with it. Hospitals are always ready to accept cash, and since they're an acceptable merchant, they can launder all the money they want to as long as they don't provide information about medicinal cannabis."

Michael was beginning to get angry, and when the waitress came back to take their order, Catlin said, "You know, this water tastes kind of funky. Do you think I could get a Pepsi instead?"

"No problem," the waitress replied, "come to think about it we have been getting a lot of complaints about our water," Michael ordered his customary breakfast of a three-cheese omelet with mushrooms and Catlin ordered a Grand Slam with sides of sausage and bacon for the dogs.

"I'm going to have to put the service animal vests on Stanley and Stella so that we can take them into the dispensary." She said to take Michael's mind off the money problems. She didn't understand the problem with having 832 thousand dollars in cash, and her eyes glazed at the thought of it. Sure, they couldn't buy a house, but they could stay in some nice hotels. Anyway, Michael's rent was covered by his social security, and hers came from the pittance her ex-husband paid her in alimony.

"Okay, so what strains should we get?" She asked Michael.

"I think we should stay with the classics. We've still got a lot of exotic stuff at home. Of course, we need Larry, and I want Blue Dream. We probably should get some O.G. Kush, some Jack Herer, and some Girl Scout Cookies. For the Indica, let's just get Grand Daddy Purple. That'll help me sleep and kill the pain from sitting in this loaner chair all day. Oh! And I want to get some Romulan. And maybe some Super Lemon Haze, anything with limonene in it is bound to be good." Michael was now in his molecular mode, rattling off strains and analyzing each from a molecular perspective.

Catlin left him to pay the check and went out to let the dogs go to the bathroom. They seemed to be enjoying this little excursion to Michigan, and she seemed glad that Michael took it as a given that the troops would just come with them whenever they went traveling. She put their vests on so that each dog was immediately identifiable as a service animal. Stella played her role perfectly. Stanley was, of course, kind of a moron. To him, everything about life was an excuse to party and make friends, and some people didn't like a hundred forty-five-pound animal getting too friendly. They decided Stanley would be left in the car, and she and Michael drove the half block to the dispensary.

CHAPTER 25

Catlin, Michael, and Stella entered the dispensary while Stanley waited in the van. They were allowed to purchase two and a half ounces of medicine, and Michael divided up two of the ounces between Blue Dream, Jack Herer, and Grand Daddy Purple. The rest of the allotment they split up among remaining strains with which they weren't familiar. The repository had no Larry or Romulan, and after 15 minutes they returned to Stanley and the van with a big plastic grocery bag consisting of Medicine bottles with varying quantities of Super Lemon Haze, Northern Lights, Girl Scout Cookies, Acapulco Gold, Mowi Wowi, Train Wreck, Cannalope Kush, and Blueberry Yum Yum. They now had a permanent address in Michigan. This was thanks to Catlin's lawyer friend Pam who seemed to be capable of doing magical things. They could now return to Michigan if they ever needed medicine again, although they never would. All they had to do now was get through Indiana. Michael's mind flashed on the Indiana Cannabis laws he had found online.

Penalty Details

Marijuana, which includes hash and hash oil under the Indiana Criminal Code, is listed as a Schedule I drug.

Possession for Personal use

Possession of fewer than 30 grams of marijuana is a Class B misdemeanour punishable by not more than 180 days and a possible fine of not more than $1,000. Possession of more than 30 grams is a Class A misdemeanour punishable by up to 1-year imprisonment and a fine of not more than $5,000. See: 35-48-2-1, et seq. of the Indiana Criminal Code 35-48-2-4(d)(22) of the Indiana Criminal Code 35-48-4-10,11 of the Indiana Criminal Code 35-48-4-11 of the Indiana Code 35-48-4-12 of the Indiana Code 35-50-2-7(b) of the Indiana Code 35-50-3-3 of the Indiana Code

The fact the lawmakers from the State of Indiana had spelled misdemeanor wrong was irrelevant to Michael, and he considered the error an indication of the intelligence of the State's lawmakers as well as the implications for them if they faced a judge of equally low intelligence.

He also thought about what it would be like to spend a year in an Indiana prison and felt a tinge of guilt that he hadn't fully explained to Catlin the risk they were about to take. All she could talk about was her disappointment about not coming home with Larry. He knew how deeply she cared for the strain, but Jack Herer had a similar molecular profile and would likely treat her medical issues just as well.

Michael navigated the van southwest on Interstate 65 through Lansing until it intersected with Highway 94 in Marshall and followed it through Portage and continued to New Buffalo, where they stopped for lunch.

They spent the time eating and contemplating their next move. They were about to cross the border into Indiana, and Michael wondered whether this would be their last meal outside of prison.

They would have to spend slightly over an hour in the State, and he considered letting Catlin know the ramifications if they were caught in Indiana with 2 ½ ounces of their medicine. The cops had a choice of who to charge with the offense. Michael owned the vehicle, so they were more likely to charge him with possession of the entire stash. With that amount, they could charge him with intent to distribute, which carried far more significant penalties. They could also charge them both with possession of 42 grams and incarcerate everybody, including Stanley and Shirley. He spoke very little through lunch, and Catlin had to work to get a conversation going. She had been talking through the entire meal about their lack of access to Larry and finally exploded.

"What the hell is wrong with you?" She whispered at Michael.

"We probably need to get gas here." He replied, pushing his plate away and reaching for his wallet. You need to check the lights and turn signals to make sure we don't get pulled over for something stupid."

"You know, you can be a real dick sometimes. I need to talk with my therapists, so I don't rip your face off." She stood up angrily and stalked out of the restaurant.

Michael sat back and wondered how much of a dick she would think he was if he got her ass thrown in prison for half a year. He decided to allow time for her canine therapy session, and then they would medicate before they entered Indiana.

CHAPTER 26

The trip through Indiana was uneventful. I 94 intersected with I 80, which took them out of Indiana, across the State of Illinois, and home. Michael had never been so glad to see the Mississippi River.

They arrived around dinner time and had the meal at an outdoor café overlooking the water. The cafe claimed to be French, but only the fries seemed to be. Both he and Catlin were exhausted and hurting. They had medicated at a rest-stop about halfway across Illinois. Still, they were both hurting pretty bad and wanted to get back to the Federal Housing Facility so they could commit an act of which the government didn't approve.

The 2 ½ ounces they just came home with added to Carol's medicine meant they might have enough until the dispensaries opened in Illinois. If they ever did. There were rumors. There were always rumors.

When they finally returned to WISFHP, they were full of good "French" food and both so tired they could hardly see. They crawled into bed with the dogs between, and Michael broke the corner off a small bud of Grand Daddy Purple and loaded the Desktop vaporizer with medicine.

They medicated for about five minutes and were asleep in 20. When Michael awoke, the following morning Catlin and the dogs were gone. He spent the morning researching until his cell phone rang.

"Hi Michael, this is Megan in the office. A package came for you over the weekend if you want to pick it up.

"Sure, Megan," Michael replied, "I'll be down in just a few minutes."

He didn't know why he was getting a package but figured any package was a present and was interested to see what it was. He cruised to the elevator and rode down to the office to retrieve what turned out to be a cardboard box. He resisted the urge to look at the label because he didn't want to answer any questions about the contents and exited the area as quickly as he could.

He entered his apartment, retrieved a knife, and slashed the package open. Inside were ten complimentary copies of Carol's book with his name emblazoned across the cover, and the pit of Michael's stomach churned. The door opened, and Catlin and the troops strolled in. Stella hopped onto the couch and lay her head down, and Stanley deposited himself in his favorite chair.

"Wow, these are awesome!" Catlin exclaimed. "I love the mother and child on the cover."

"Yeah," Michael replied quietly, "my publisher did that."

"Well, you have to do a book signing." Catlin said, "I'll set one up for this weekend, and you can sell autographed copies. I'll write a snippet on the title page. Something like 'Thank you for being medical cannabis-friendly,' and you can sign your name right in front of the person that buys it."

Michael wasn't enamored with the idea of peddling a plagiarized book but said nothing.

Oh, I almost forgot. I found you a house."

"Really?" Michael exclaimed, happy to be distracted from his moral turpitude. "Where is it?"

"It's about two blocks from the hospital. It's a little more money than this place, but the owner is medical cannabis-friendly. She even says you can grow if you want to."

"Oh yeah? Well, we won't need to do that if the dispensaries ever open."

"It's wheelchair accessible, and the owner will take cash payments. I'll get the key from her tomorrow. Oh, by the way, you have two patients every day this week."

Michael wished Catlin would quit springing things on him, but eight new patients would undoubtedly cover his rent at the new place, and he was happy he would be helping them with their medical issues.

The week flew by. Michael helped certify the eight new medical cannabis patients. He and Catlin were in bed, medicating early Friday evening. As usual, the dogs were firmly rooted between them, and as usual, Michael was frustrated, and Catlin was talking.

"You have a book signing in Davenport tomorrow."

"What do you mean?" Michael snapped.

"You think when you're meeting patients, I sit on my ass?" Catlin snapped back. "I'm always doing something for this company! I've been negotiating how much the owner of the bookstore would get for each sale. You don't have to do anything for this book anymore except show up and sign it!"

Michael thought *'Well, that's good because I haven't done anything for it up to now.'*

"So, where is it?" He asked.

"It's on Brady Street in Davenport, Iowa right on the river. It's a very nice bookstore, but I don't think it'll last long. Bookstores are going under all across the nation. I'll be with you to help you set up. The owner put out a nice press release to advertise the signing, so plenty of people know about it." (That thought didn't thrill Michael) "You wouldn't believe how many bookstores rejected this book. The first one said they were a family store, and their clientele wouldn't accept a textbook about medical cannabis. The next one told me I shouldn't even be talking about a subject like this in America". Michael kind of wished the other store had rejected her as well but resigned himself to the fact that he was about to claim authorship of a book he hadn't written.

The next morning bright and early, he and Catlin were once again in the van, this time driving into another state that had no sense of humor when it came to medicinal cannabis. They crossed the State line without product but were once again particularly well medicated.

They arrived at the bookstore shortly before ten, and Catlin went in and helped set up the table. She spread out five books in fan design and garnished the display with brochures for the clinic. Michael sat behind the table, hoping nobody would show up. At 10 A.M. the store opened, and a large group of people swarmed in. He did his best to avoid eye contact.

When the store became crowded with people shopping for books, Michael glanced over at the manager to see him conversing with a man wearing a white short-sleeved dress shirt and a short black tie. The man in the white shirt appeared quite animated, and after quite a lengthy conversation, they both approached Michael.

"Hi, my name is Gabriel. The man in the white shirt said, "I'm the Vice-Chairman of the Iowa Christian Coalition. I'm just here to inform you that God created the laws in this country and what you are doing goes against the Will of Our Lord. I've informed the Acting Manager of this bookstore that if you are allowed to conduct a book signing about this subject, the Iowa Christian Coalition will boycott this store. We are a God-fearing State, and we don't need you to bring your Illinois sins to Iowa. We're shutting you down."

Michael thought, *"Thank you, Lord, Christian Soldiers to my rescue."*

Catlin stepped in with her concept of subtlety. "Now hold on there, Mr. Christian man. You can't shut us down without the store owner's approval."

"Actually, Miss Pushy lady, this young store manager has decided he can't afford to lose the Christian market while the store owner is away."

She looked over at the 19-year-old manager of the store. "Is this true?" she asked him.

He shrugged his shoulders and replied, "They buy a lot of Bibles."

Michael was all too happy to pack up and scooped up the books and the brochures and headed out the door. He reached the van quite quickly and lowered the ramp. Catlin remained inside, arguing with the store manager.

Gabriel followed Michael out and thanked him for adhering to the Will of God and slipped a flyer into his hand. Gabriel then walked a short distance to his car, climbed in, and drove off. Michael ascended the ramp and turned his wheelchair around to close the ramp door when a well-dressed woman exited the store and ran up to him.

"I think it's just terrible what that man did, and I'd like to support you in your cause. My name is Heather Humboldt, and I'm the President of the Illinois chapter of the American Diabetes Association. I think I might be able to provide you with some patients. That's why I'm here. I heard about you, but I didn't know how to find you. You stay pretty well hidden."

"Well, we're not allowed to advertise," Michael replied.

By this time, Catlin had given up her battle with the manager and was watching this new course of events.

"I have scores of people with diabetic neuropathy. I know that's one of the qualifying conditions." She reached into the fifteen-hundred-dollar purse she was clutching and said: "I came here today only planning to buy one book, but after the display, I just witnessed in there, I want to buy all five." Catlin stepped in. "No problem! Would you like them autographed?"

"Of Course," Heather replied, smiling, and Catlin had Michael sign five copies right there at the van.

Catlin collected 200 dollars from the nice lady and when they were through the store manager came out and said, "I'm sorry, but if the Christians come back and see you here, they're going to blame me, and I don't want to lose my job if they boycott the store while the owner is out of town. I need to ask you to leave."

"No problem!" Catlin exclaimed. "Just allow us to thank the nice lady and give her some brochures so she can send her ailing diabetes people to us, and we can get them access to the medicine they need."

Catlin concluded the business transaction with Heather while Michael transferred to the driver's seat, and when Catlin finally entered the vehicle, she was giddy. "She just bought 200 dollars in books, and she says she can get us at least 25 more patients. That's 3000 dollars profit from this lady alone, and with the eight patients this week, we made 38 hundred dollars this week alone, and this was a slow week." Michael thought about how much space thirty-eight hundred dollars would take up in his small safety deposit box. Michael drove home while Catlin read aloud the brochure the enjoyable Christian man had given to Michael.

WHAT DOES THE BIBLE SAY ABOUT MEDICAL MARIJUANA?

MARIJUANA for medicinal use is not addressed in the Bible. So, there is no biblical answer to the question of whether Christians should use MARIJUANA as medicine. However, after a thorough analysis of the book composed by God, the answer to this question becomes much clearer. First, although almost half the states have legalized medical MARIJUANA, its use is still illegal according to Federal Law, which is God's law. Paul extolls us to obey the law of God and our Government in this way: "Everyone must submit himself to the governing authorities, for there is no authority except that which God has established. God has established the authorities that exist. Consequently, he who rebels against the authority is rebelling against what God has instituted, and those who do so will bring judgment on themselves" (Romans 13:1-2). Additionally, there is a biblical mandate to keep our bodies pure. "Do you not know that your body is a temple of the Holy Spirit, who is in you, whom you have received from God? You are not your own; you were bought at a price. Therefore honor God with your body" (1 Corinthians 6:19-20). Be sober, be vigilant; because your adversary the devil walks about like a roaring lion, seeking whom he may devour" (1

Peter 5:8). These passages command Christians to avoid intoxicants, which impair clear thinking. Clouded thinking leads to questionable moral choices. "Woe to you who make your neighbors drink, who mix in your venom even to make them drunk so as to look on their nakedness!" (Habakkuk 2:15). Use of intoxicants has also been closely associated with witchcraft and sorcery in the Bible. Christians have a hard enough time battling temptations without making Satan's job easier. The Christian disciplines his body and keeps it under control (1 Corinthians 9:27), so that he is able to set his mind on things above (Colossians 3:2). The bottom line is the Bible condemns drunkenness and warns that those who engage in such behavior will not inherit the kingdom of God. Besides the moral question, there is the legal question. Christians are commanded by the scriptures to be in subjection to governing authorities and submit to every human institution. God created the laws in the United States, and it is a Christians' sacred duty to follow them for there is no authority except from God, and those laws which exist are established by God. Therefore, whoever resists authority has opposed the ordinance of God; and they who have opposed will receive condemnation upon themselves. (Romans 13:1-2) Finally, Satan is the great justifier. He always wants to help us rationalize and justify sinning against God, almost making it seem like the right thing to do. We must never forget that Satan is a liar and medical cannabis patients and the doctors who prescribe it have done nothing to validate the medical necessity of this satanic drug. Although many people may be deceived by such practices, God is not deceived. He will not be mocked (Galatians 6:7).

Michael drove home in silence while Catlin complained about the inaccuracies in the document the enjoyable Christian man had given to Michael. Michael thought about what had taken place and realized he had stopped having fun in this venture. Five copies of a book had gone out into the public, which proved he was a plagiarist. If Carol had shown her book to anyone, he would be disgraced.

When they got home, Michael told Catlin he was tired and went into his bedroom with a plan to sleep until Monday. Catlin stayed in the living room making phone calls, and after he began to drift off to sleep, Stella strolled in and hopped on the bed, and Michael experienced yet another session of canine therapy.

CHAPTER 27

Michael was nearly asleep when he felt Stella step onto the bed and plop down next to him. Michael had pulled the covers over his head, and he pretended to be asleep. After a few seconds, Stella began to push Michael out of bed. Michael was annoyed, but Stella was pretty insistent that he needed the counseling session she was about to provide.

He pulled the covers from his head and thought, *"Damn it, Stella, I want to stop the world and get off. Trying to educate people about this medicine has caused me to lose my home. The banks think I'm laundering drug money; there is still some speculation that the reason Medicare won't fix my wheelchair is that I'm a medical cannabis patient. To top it all off, I am now guilty of plagiarism, and the Christians have declared a holy war on me."*

Once again, Stella's response took Michael aback. *"You have got to be the dumbest person I know. Let's break down your problems individually. Catlin found you a new home, and you knew from the start you should never try to educate anyone in a federally owned building, especially about medicinal cannabis in the middle of a drug war. You're lucky nobody has called the cops on you and had you hauled off to prison. Everyone in WISFHP now knows you use cannabis as medicine, and the basic fact is that what you are doing is illegal. It's now time for you to cut and run. You've fired all the bullets you have in the drug war by certifying 323 patients right in the middle of a federally owned building. It's now time for you to retreat and fight your battle from another front. "Now, I'm a dog, so I don't know much about banks, but it's my understanding they are all about money. Everyone knows cannabis is going to be America's next gold rush, and Mark Twain once said, 'When there's a gold rush, it's good to be in the pick and shovel business.' You are in the pick and shovel business. Ironically, the banks are more likely to accept money from the people that are growing and selling the plant before they accept money from a person who is educating people about it. You don't have enough money to offer anyone a decent bribe, and in Illinois, that's a problem.*

You'll simply have to wait the banks out. It won't take long for them to figure out how much money they're losing by not being part of this industry. "As for the wheelchair, it's unlikely they even know you're a medical cannabis patient. Medicare probably just denies payment of medical benefits as a matter of course. If they give a couple of verbal denials, most people will simply give up asking for the benefits they're entitled to, and it saves the company money. All Medicare has to care about is collecting the payments for the coverage. Your next step with Medicare is to get the denial in writing so you can appeal their decision. There's nothing you can do without a verbal denial, so get the denial in writing and respond. As far as your holy war goes, I don't believe it even exists. Every group has some fringe element to it. I think the clown that had you thrown out of the bookstore was just a guy that thought he was doing the right thing and wanted to feel important. I don't believe there even is an Iowa Christian Coalition. Have you researched it?

"Finally, yeah, you're a plagiarist, but it's unlikely you'll ever be exposed. Carol probably never showed the book to anyone. Did you see how deeply she buried it in her computer? I mean, it's really unlikely Carol is going to sue you for stealing her ideas. Do you have any other problems I can help you with?"

Michael sat back and thought. This was his chance to put this smug animal in her place.

"I don't have a clue as to how I'm going to pay my taxes."

"What are taxes?" Stella then got up and strolled out of the room.

CHAPTER 28

O n Sunday, Catlin and Michael drove over to the house he was going to inhabit. It was a hovel; way too small for what they wanted to do, and Michael expressed his concerns to Catlin.

"How are we going to look professional in a place like this?" Michael demanded.

Catlin replied, "We don't have to look professional; we just have to be professional. You know more than the doctors know about this medicine, and patients are going to realize that fast. The fact that we don't have a million-dollar office complex will be irrelevant to them. Our medical cannabis patients will figure out immediately if they have anything wrong that can't be treated with medicinal cannabis; we'll get them to a doctor who will care about them and treat them like human beings and not like criminals."

Catlin continued, "I'm giving you this week off. You need to focus on your war with the insurance company over the wheelchair and pack all your stuff to move. I've got a bunch of people together to help you move this weekend."

"Who's doing that?" Michael inquired

"Oh, they're mostly relatives of patients, a lot of sons and grandsons and a few daughters and granddaughters. They should be able to get you moved in half a day. We'll do it under the secrecy of the weekend."

Catlin continued, "You get this week off. The only things you need to worry about this week are the war of the wheelchair and packing up your stuff."

Michael was pleased to get the week off and vowed to get something done about the wheelchair. The denials had begun in September. It was now June. Medicare had stalled the process for seven months. The only items he had received in writing from his health insurance provider were the monthly bills for the service they were providing.

As Stella suggested, he needed to get a written denial in writing before anything could happen. Michael had one simple goal this week; get his insurance company to issue a written denial of his health insurance benefits. With a written denial, he could proceed to the next series of their rejections. Michael figured if the health insurance company could stall the process until January, they could deny the benefit based on the fact that it was the wrong calendar year.

After they finished touring the hovel, they went to Michael's Vietnamese restaurant for lunch. They spent the afternoon talking and laughing and enjoying each other's companionship immensely.

By the time they got back to the apartment, Stanley and Stella wanted to play, and they took the animals to the nearby river access so that they could run. Michael thought back and could only remember having this much fun with Carol in High School. He was glad he met Catlin. That night the whole makeshift family slept very well.

Michael woke up the following morning, Catlin was gone, and the dogs expressed no interest in rising. Michael pressed record on the digital tape recorder and called the number on the back of his insurance card. After 15 minutes of negotiating with a computer, he was transferred to a real live human being.

"Hello, my name is John. Could I have your account number please?" Michael read the number on the front of the card.

"How can I help you, Mr. Dunston?"

"Well, John, I was wondering about the status of my wheelchair."

"That would be the chair currently housed in Peoria?"

"Yeah, I guess it lives there now."

"Well, looking at your file, your wheelchair coverage has been denied for several reasons. I think you have already been informed that since your wheelchair is less than five years old, it should be covered by the manufacturer's warranty. Also, your provider needs to show exactly what is wrong with you as well as exactly what is wrong with the wheelchair."

"Okay, so who is the provider? Is that my primary care physician? Because I don't think he has a clue about what might be wrong with the chair."

"No. In this case, the provider is the wheelchair repair company."

"Is there any way I can get the chair fixed?"

"Well, no. If the chair was more than five years old, we would pay for its repair. The only way we would pay for a new chair for you would be if you proved the current chair no longer meets your medical needs due to a change in your condition."

Michael could hear the legalese in John's answers and considered whether there was an angle he could play.

"Okay, and there would have to be some sort of written documentation that showed there was a change in my condition."

"Correct. Is there anything else I can help you with?"

"Yeah, I need this denial of medical benefits in writing."

"Why do you need it in writing Mr. Dunston?"

"Well, over the course of 7 months, Medicare has given me four or five different reasons for denying me a wheelchair and John, you have given me three. Oh John, what is your last name, so I can properly document this call in my records."

"Oh, I'm sorry, Mr. Dunston. We're not allowed to provide our last names to customers.

"Yeah, if I were the owner of your company, I wouldn't want my employees to be able to be identified either. But then I'm sure you are probably the only John that works for Medicare, am I right?"

"Well, I have no way of knowing that Mr. Dunston."

"Totally understandable, John, but I do need you to provide me the reasons for the denial of my benefits in writing so that I can formulate a response."

"Why do you need to have these denials in writing, Mr. Dunston?

"Well, I can't respond to them unless I have something in writing."

"Well, what are you going to do when you get something in writing, Mr. Dunston?"

"I'm going to appeal your decision."

"Okay, Mr. Dunston. I will have to ask a representative to put the various reasons for the denial of your health insurance benefits in writing, and you should be receiving that letter within seven to ten business days."

"Can't you just email that to me? That would make things much quicker."

"I'm sorry, Mr. Dunston. We're a Government organization, and as such, we're not allowed to use email."

"I understand. As a Government organization, you can't have anything happen too quickly, am I right?"

"Is there anything else I can help you with, Mr. Dunston?"

"No, John. You just send that Denial of Medical Benefits letter, and I'll take it from there. I'll be looking for that letter in 7 to 10 business days."

"Certainly, Mr. Dunston. Thank you for your time, and thank you for being a valued customer of National Care United Medicare Solutions."

The phone disconnected, Michael pushed stop on the recorder and analyzed the discussion in his mind. He had gotten a little snarky towards the end and hoped John would actually have the letter sent.

The loaner chair Mobility Solutions had provided was okay for short runs, but it was not built for someone with muscular dystrophy, and it was beginning to break down his spine. What's more, he had already had the chair for seven months, and there was a chance Dave would be demanding the chair back.

He decided he'd better call Mobility Specialists and see if there was any progress on that end.

"Mobility Specialists, this is Kim."

"Hi, Kim, how're you doing? This is Michael Dunston."

"Well, good morning Michael. How are you doing this lovely morning."

"I'm doing well, Kim. Hey, I just got off the phone with my insurance carrier. I was wondering if you guys had made any progress on your end."

"Well, we're still waiting for a response from the wheelchair manufacturer to confirm when the chair was made, and once we have that, we should be able to get the approval from Medicare. I think as soon as we have the proof of how old the chair is, they'll have no other option but to replace it. You're probably going to want to come down here, so you can see all the different models we have to choose from."

"I would be interested in doing that, Kim. But Medicare has come up with a whole bunch of new reasons for denying me a new chair."

"Well, Michael, the only suggestion I can make is for you to contact your Senator and see if he'd be willing to intervene on your behalf. A couple of our patients have had success using that approach."

"That's an interesting suggestion, Kim. I'll try that. In the meantime, I'd like to come down and look at some chairs. Can we schedule a time to do that?"

"Well, Dave handles the scheduling for that. He doesn't allow me to schedule anyone myself. Confidentially, he's kind of a dick."

"That's okay, Kim. I can schedule it through Dave. Is he around by any chance?"

"Sure, Michael. Let me transfer you."

This time the hold music was by Pink, and Michael began singing along to it. "I'm coming out, so you better get this party started." By the time Dave picked up the phone, the song had almost reached its conclusion.

"Mobility Specialists, this is Dave."

"Hi Dave, this is Michael Dunston. Kim is thinking we might be getting close to the end of this nightmare, and she thinks I should come down and look at some new wheelchairs."

"Yeah, that's a good idea. As soon as we get proof of the age of the chair, everything should sail right through."

"Cool, so let's set up a time I can take a look at those chairs. Is there any time this week you're available?"

"Sure, Michael, how does Thursday morning work for you?"

"That's fine. 11 O'clock?"

"I'll pencil you in."

The call disconnected, and Michael reached for his laptop to find out who his Senator was. He immediately discovered the Senator's name was Mark Kirk. It took him a little longer to discover the man had four offices scattered throughout the State and one in Washington. He called the number in Chicago first.

"Senator Kirk's office, my name is Matt." Michael was surprised to get a human being immediately and was impressed.

"Hi, I was wondering if I could speak with Senator Kirk."

"I'm sorry, Senator Kirk is in Washington today. Is there something I might be able to help you with?"

"Well, I was hoping the Senator could help me either get a new wheelchair or get my old one repaired."

"What do you mean?"

"Well, Medicare has denied me a wheelchair for the past seven months."

"Let me transfer you over to a caseworker. Are you able to hold for just a minute?"

"Of course," Michael replied.

The hold was silent, and Michael was thankful he didn't have to listen to music that had been selected by some Republican politician.

"Good Morning. My name is Ashley. How can I possibly help you today?"

"Hi Ashley, I was wondering if the Senator might help me get my wheelchair either repaired or replaced."

"Is there some reason you haven't been able to get this done on your own?"

"Yeah, Medicare has denied my medical benefits for the last seven months."

"And what is the reason for their denial?"

"They're claiming my wheelchair is less than five years old. But I bought the chair in 2008. That was seven years ago, and I bought the chair used then."

"Do you have any documentation to prove you bought the chair in 2008?"

"Well, I lost a lot of documents in my move to Illinois, but there's a serial number on the back of the chair."

"And what put you in the chair to begin with?"

"Well, I have a form of muscular dystrophy, and I was prescribed increasingly powerful opiates for 28 years, finally being prescribed so much it caused me to have a stroke from which I lost the use of my left arm. That was also the last day I walked. I then had surgery in a hospital that was crawling with MRSA, contracted it, and spent several months literally dying."

"Well, you seem OK now."

This was Michaels opening, and he told her about his stroke, his bout with MRSA, the pain from his muscular dystrophy, and about how they had all been treated with medicinal cannabis. After he was through and he knew he had her full attention, Michael said, "Now I don't know what the Senator's position is on medicinal cannabis, but I can't imagine he would be against someone like me using it as a medicine especially since it is now legal in Illinois."

"Well, Mr. Dunston, I need you to fill out a Privacy release form for us to help you. Do you have access to email?"

"Of course."

"What is your email address?"

"I'm going to spell it out for you. H, I, D,I,N,G,I,N,G,I,N,P,L,A ,I,N,S,I,G,H,T,4,2,0 at gmail.com."

"So, it's hiding in plain sight four twenty at gmail.com?"

"Exactly," Michael said, smiling and wondering if Ashley understood the symbolism.

"Well, getting back to the wheelchair, can you get the serial number off the chair and email it to me?"

"Sure."

"Well, I'll email the Privacy Release Form to you, and once you return it along with the serial number, we'll do what we can to help you."

"Okay, Ashley, I'll email the form back to you this afternoon." The phone disconnected, and Michael spent the rest of the day, packing up his things for his eviction. He worked on that until 5:30 and then turned on the national news.

It was another July slow news day, and Catlin came home in the middle. The dogs spent the last part of the news telling Catlin how much they loved her. She took the dogs outside to play and conduct their business, and the local news came on.

Michael didn't usually watch the local news, but the first story caught his attention.

"Senator Mark Kirk issued a policy statement from his Springfield office today and called for increased restrictions on marijuana. He called users of medicinal cannabis 'burnouts' and said users of the drug generally have lower I.Q.s and are, for the most part, 'lower performing in their lives.' He went on to say 'the dangers of marijuana were established "inconclusively in the 1930s and "reconfirmed by both the Nixon and Regan administrations. He continued his statement by saying that people simply should not be allowed to use such a dangerous drug when the pharmaceutical industry has so many more appropriate alternatives."

Catlin returned with the troops, greeted Michael, and plopped down on the couch. The dogs took their usual positions.

"What's going on?" she asked.

"The guy that's going to help me get a wheelchair is bound and determined to take away my medicine," Michael responded. "This whole thing is so messed up."

"Well, Michael. A lot of people want you dead, and he is just one person, not the majority of the nation, and not with the majority of the people in Illinois. He'll be voted out soon."

"I should have never told his staff that I was a medical cannabis patient." Michael lamented.

"Don't worry about it." She replied. "I've been running all day. I hurt and need to medicate. What strain should we use?"

Michael considered the countless options available to them between what they had bought in Michigan and the medicine Carol had left him in her estate.

"Dig into Carol's stash and find a strain called Cannatonic. I'm getting some major anxiety, and that strain has a ton of CBD in it."

Catlin rose and retrieved a canister of medicine from the small dehumidifier in Michael's room. She returned with the canister and their vaporizer, and they inhaled the medicine that relieved both Catlin's pain and Michael's anxiety.

They spent that evening watching the latest installment from the television series Breaking Bad. Michael observed the scene where Walter White's cash began piling up and contemplated about their need for a second safety deposit box. He hated the concept of only being allowed to work in cash, but didn't think it would be in his company's best interest to stop accepting money.

He said to Catlin, "You need to get us another safety deposit box. Let's rent a big one this time and see how long it takes to fill it up. What we can do is put all the fifty and twenty-dollar bills in the big box and use the small box for the hundreds."

Catlin rented the box the next day, and Michael never saw the money again.

CHAPTER 29

Michael and Catlin tried to go to sleep early that evening, but Michael was too frustrated to rest. The conversation he had with the Senator's office was wearing on him. They told him the Senator was in Washington, yet he appeared in Springfield that afternoon to denounce the use of cannabis as medicine. He decided to make a phone call at 11 o'clock that evening, which would change his relationship with Medicare and National Care United for the remainder of his life.

He redialed the Senator's Washington office. He planned to leave a message on their voicemail, but as it was, the Senator's Washington office was indeed occupied.

Two janitorial workers Howard and Ray, were in the process of cleaning the Senator's office. When they were finished with their minimal duties, one sat in the Senator's desk chair and began rolling their nightly joint. They always rolled and smoked a joint at the Senator's desk at 11 pm and then completed their cleaning.

They had just fired up, and each taken a hit when the phone rang. They both eyed the phone. It had never rung at this hour before, and both giggled at the possibility of what the call could be about.

Howard reached over from the chair he was occupying and answered the call. "Senator Kirk's office, my name is Howard. How may I assist you?"

Michael hadn't expected to have his call answered and was not prepared. He explained the situation with his wheelchair.

Howard leaned back, took a hit from the joint, and said, "Mr. Dunston, solving problems like yours is exactly why the Senator wanted to be in Washington in the first place. My name is Howard, and I am Senator Kirk's Personal Assistant. The Senator just arrived in Washington a few minutes ago and is standing right here next to me. I'd like you to tell your story directly to him. Can you give me a minute to fill him in on the details, and then you can explain your situation to him as concise a manner as possible? Would you hold, please?"

Howard pushed the hold button on the phone and handed the receiver and the joint to Ray. Ray took a hit and asked Howard what he was supposed to do.

"Just tell him you're the Senator and whatever you think the Senator would advise him to do." By this time, Howard could barely contain his laughter.

Michael knew how busy the Senator was and spent the time on hold considering how to adequately express the battle he had with Medicare as quickly and concisely as possible.

The phone was once again connected, and Ray said, "Good evening, Senator Kirk speaking."

"Good Evening Senator. Thank you for speaking with me. My name is Michael Dunston, and I am a paraplegic. I've been in a wheelchair for the past few years, and Medicare is refusing to repair or replace it."

Ray smiled deviously and said, "Just don't pay them until I tell you it's appropriate."

"Thank you, Senator; I will follow your instructions to the letter." Ray hung up the phone, and both janitors broke into hysterics.

Michael slept well that night, and when he awoke in the morning, Catlin and the dogs were gone. Michael spent the day packing for the big move and prepared for his drive to Peoria the next day. He was interested in seeing the selection of wheelchairs Mobility Specialists had in stock and knew the chairs appropriate for his condition ranged from ten to fifty thousand dollars. It was not surprising Medicare was reluctant to pay their eighty percent.

Catlin and the dogs came home late that evening. She had spent the day renting safety deposit boxes at various locations throughout the Quad Cities, and she explained to Michael what she had done.

"I took all the money from the small box in Willow Springs and put it in a big box in Moline. We'll put hundred-dollar bills in the small box in Willow Springs and the small bills in the big box in Moline. I took out a grand to buy a big refrigerator. We won't need that much, but with the move and everything, we'll probably need some extra spending money."

Michael was glad he had Catlin to take care of the minor aspects of his personal life and slept well that night.

He woke up early the next morning, and this was the day he was introduced to the County of Peoria's concept of justice.

CHAPTER 30

Michael returned from Peoria pissed off. The cop had essentially called him a dick and a criminal and stuck him with a fine of at least a thousand dollars. The charge was a Class A Misdemeanor and could conceivably result in the loss of his driver's license.

Michael knew the cop would like nothing more than to be the agent to make that happen, and by the time he got home, he was livid. He entered the housing facility and checked his mailbox and found an envelope containing a letter from Medicare.

It was virtually impossible to open his mail with just one hand, and he took the envelope to his room. Catlin was on the couch watching television, and Michael had her open the letter, and he inspected the contents.

He carefully counted the three-page document. The language was clearly designed to intimidate him, and he analyzed the contents carefully.

Important:

This notice explains your rights to appeal our decision. Read this notice carefully. If you need help, you can call one of the numbers listed on the last page under "Get help & more information."

Notice of denial of Medical Coverage

Date: June 15, 2015

Member number: 952687015732

Name: Michael J. Dunston 230 Sycamore drive Willow Springs, Illinois 62799

Your request has been denied.

Your request for the medical services /items listed below requested by you or your doctor has been denied for the following reasons:

New power wheelchair

Why did we deny your request?

Your request for the medical services /items listed above requested by you or your doctor has been denied because:

Your physician asked for a new power wheelchair for you. You have trouble walking. You get around your home in a power wheelchair. Your request for a new power wheelchair can be approved if your records (office notes, test results, treatments) prove you meet Medicare criteria for power wheelchairs.

Our physician examined your records. Your records failed to prove the following:

- Your power wheelchair is at least five years old, broken, and cannot be repaired.
- Your provider must show exactly what is wrong with your power wheelchair in addition to the cost of repairs.
- Your provider must give us information on the age and condition of your current power wheelchair.
- Your power wheelchair no longer meets your medical needs because of a change in your medical condition.

You have the right to appeal our decision

You have the right to ask us to review our decision by asking us for an appeal within 60 days of the date of this notice. We can give you more time if you provide appropriate reasons for missing the deadline.

You may enlist an attorney to act as a representative on your behalf. If you choose to do so, you must call us at 254-679-9580 to learn how to name your representative. Both you and the person you want to act for you must sign and date a document confirming this is what you want. You will need to mail or fax this document to us.

Michael smiled, opened his laptop, and formulated his response. He decided to mimic their style, but he was unable to be as creative as they were, and his reply was only two pages.

Notice of Appeal of Denial of Medical Benefits

Date: June 28, 2015 member number 965881017
Name: Michael J. Dunston

Thank you for providing me a written denial of my medical benefits in such a timely manner. Seven months is an extremely fast timeframe for any government organization to produce three typewritten sheets of paper.

While you didn't provide any specific reasons explaining why my coverage was denied, you were kind enough to include four bullet points for me to address. Each of these points was communicated to my providers or me in your series of verbal denials over the past seven months, and I will address each one.

- Your agents have verbally communicated that my chair cannot possibly be five years old because the Spirit Wheelchair Company has only been in existence for four years. The chair I own is, in actuality, a Victory Wheelchair and manufactured in 2008. Victory changed its name to Spirit four years ago.

- I understand your confusion because there is no possible way you could have known they changed the name of their company.

179

- My provider (Mobility Specialists) is currently in the process of detailing precisely what is wrong with my chair, as well as the cost of repairs.

- Mobility Specialists have provided (or will provide) you age and condition of that chair.

- Because your series of verbal denials has forced me to use a loaner chair for seven months that was inappropriate for my medical condition, that condition has deteriorated, and I now require a different chair.

As you suggested, I've talked to my physician about my case, and you can expect to hear from him soon.

Again, thank you for your timely denial of my medical coverage, and thank you for your consideration, as well as your forthcoming response.

Michael J. Dunston

cc:

The Honorable Senator Mark Kirk

David Scalia (Provider) Technician at Mobility Specialists Wheelchair Company

Dr. Jonathan Stanton, M.D. (Primary Care Physician)

After he finished composing, he went to bed.

CHAPTER 31

Michael spent all day Friday packing for his move to the hovel on Saturday. He looked forward to the move, and all his neighbors congratulated him on his ability to escape Government Housing. The move was scheduled to commence under cover of darkness, and by noon on Saturday, all his belongings had been deposited into various parts of the hovel. The people Catlin had enlisted to conduct the move were quick and cautious and took care not to damage his belongings.

Michael cruised around his new place and eyed his possessions. He noticed they deposited his decorative Cholla cactus log in the kitchen rather than the living room where it belonged. Michael had brought the log from Nevada, and he wanted it placed somewhere he could view it as a reminder of happier times.

When Chollas died in the desert and dried out, the needles could easily be removed, and Michael thought he had accomplished this task until he picked the log up, and a spine impaled itself under the fingernail of the index finger of his right hand.

If he could have, Michael would have simply pulled the needle with his left hand, but without the ability to use the arm, Michael had no way of removing the thorn.

Catlin and the rest of the crew were gone, and Michael didn't consider "Can you remove this splinter?" an appropriate way of introducing himself to his new neighbors. He tried grabbing the end of the thorn with his teeth but was unable to do so. It didn't take Michael very long to realize if he touched anything with his fingers, he would drive the needle deeper under his nail. Catlin was away with her parents for the weekend, so Michael knew of no one who could help him remove the object.

He retrieved a pair of tweezers and tried holding them in his teeth to try to dislodge the needle somehow. All he was able to succeed in doing was driving what now felt like a spike deeper under the nail, and he realized he was going to need some medical attention.

He didn't want to bother the hospital with something so minor, but there was no way he'd be able to go through the weekend with the cactus needle in his finger. He now only lived two blocks from the hospital, and he stuck the tweezers in his shirt pocket and cruised over. He knew the people at the reception desk and liked them. He figured if he provided them the instrument, they would remove the splinter for him, but when he got there, they said it was hospital policy that such procedures had to be performed by a qualified physician and escorted him to the emergency room.

They took his vitals, and he felt unbelievably embarrassed, awkward, and weak that he was unable to take care of this thorny issue by himself.

There he sat in the emergency room of a hospital with nothing wrong except a spike protruding from the most significant digit he owned. Fortunately, he was the only "emergency" patient that lazy summer afternoon, and it only took the doctor forty minutes to appear. She was extremely understanding of his circumstance and explained that if he was going to damage a hand, it was going to be this one because it was the only one he used.

Michael handed her the tweezers, and she extracted the skewer. The doctor gave Michael back the tweezers and some literature about the possibility of infection, and he exited the hospital ashamed at his inability to fend for himself. He returned to the hovel and spent the rest of the weekend, organizing his belongings.

Catlin returned Sunday evening. "You're not going to believe the refrigerator/freezer my father was able to get us," She told Michael.

"It's huge. The freezer is on the top and will probably hold a hundred pounds of ground beef. I'm going to go to Moline tomorrow and buy them out. We'll be able to eat Hamburger helper forever on my food stamps."

Michael was happy to know that even if their fledgling business failed, they would at least not starve to death because the government would keep them nourished, and he looked forward to seeing what the massive fridge looked like.

Catlin continued, "My parents know of a bunch of people who are interested in certification. We should have the entire week covered. It's going to be a tough week because we're going to be dealing with cancer, Alzheimer's, and a lot of really major pain patients. It's likely to get emotional, and you're not going to like it. My mom volunteers in a nursing home, and the people she is going to be sending us are going to be sad, ailing individuals that simply need the help the medicine provides. They're also people that have gone through the Reefer Madness craze, and some are going to be weird about the stigma that goes along with being a medical cannabis patient. I'm going to stay with you all week to help you get through the emotional upheaval these patients are going to bring in you. My mom said some of these people have some incredibly heartbreaking tales.

CHAPTER 32

T he week was indeed rough, and the stories heart rendering. Catlin kept the numbers down, and they took care of the certification of 16 patients. Four chose not to pursue the medicine because of the cost and the associated stigma. There wasn't much Michael could do about either, and he was sorry the government would only allow insurance to cover narcotic and opiate medicines.

Michael, Catlin, Stanley, and Stella spent the weekend playing. On Wednesday of the following week, Michael was scheduled for his pre-trial hearing in Peoria, Illinois, for the transgression he had been accused of committing against them the summer of the previous year.

The storm-trooper had told him he'd throw Michael's pothead ass in jail for as long as he could if he failed to show for the trial, and he and Catlin left at six that morning to make sure they arrived in time for his 9 A.M. hearing.

They arrived in Peoria at 8:15 and decided that if they were going to deal with a major tribunal, he had better be pretty well medicated. They pulled the van into a cemetery, and Michael reached under the seat where he hid the portable vaporizer he had loaded with medicine the night before. He rarely left the house with medication, and since the dispensaries were not yet open, he and Catlin spent the next ten minutes in a Peoria cemetery committing an illegal act.

"What strain are we using?" Catlin asked, breathing in the vapor.

"Harlequin," Michael replied. "It has a high ratio of CBD, and CBD kills anxiety like Raid kills cockroaches. It's also got enough THC to deal with my pain issues. I don't want to go into court in major pain. It would be too distracting."

"The courthouse has to be close, but it may take a while to find a handicapped-accessible entrance. We'll circle the building and see if we can see a wheelchair ramp from the car and then try to find a place to park where you can get out and head up while I take care of the dogs."

Stella was occupying the seat in the back of the van while Stanley slept on the floor of the cargo area, curled around Michael's wheelchair. There wasn't a lot of room for the animals, but they were happy just to be invited on the journey.

"We should probably roll," Michael said, beginning to notice the limited amount of time they had to appear for the hearing on time. The last thing Michael wanted to happen was for the cop to come looking for him, and he figured there was going to no way he would come out of another encounter with the trooper unscathed. They circled the block surrounding the massive courthouse and located a wheelchair ramp leading to a back entrance.

They had to park a few blocks away to find a spot where the ramp would not damage an adjacent car, and Michael arrived at the back door at 8:55. He reached up and pulled the door handle to find it locked.

There was a sign on the adjoining wall which read "Handicapped Accessible Entrance. Please Ring Bell".

Michael pushed the button and waited. No response came, and after a few seconds, Michael pushed the button again. A buzzer sounded, and a gruff male voice screamed from a speaker located about 15 feet above his head. "Open the door! Open the door!" Michael tugged at the door. It was heavy, and he was barely able to manage the sequence of opening it and manipulating the joystick which controlled the chair. He was able to maneuver the chair partway through the threshold when the door slammed against the side of his wheelchair. The same gruff voice yelled at him, but this time from a different direction. "You're damaging the door! You're damaging the door!"

Michael looked up to see a burly man approaching him in a police uniform with a 57-magnum strapped to his side. Michael was able to inch his way inside and did what he could to keep the door from slamming but failed, and the man was clearly pissed.

"You only need to push the button one time. We're very busy here and can't do our job when people keep interrupting us. Why are you here?"

"I'm scheduled for a preliminary hearing at 9 am," Michael responded

"Fine," The officer replied. "You'll have to go through security first." He gestured to the center of the courthouse. Michael looked over and eyed the metal detector he was supposed to pass through.

He looked the officer in the eye and said, "There's no way I'm going through that without setting it off."

"No shit Sherlock," The officer sneered. "You just go up there, and another officer will pat you down."

The search was not overly invasive, and Michael understood the reasoning for it. He asked the nice man with his hand on his genitals where he needed to go for his pre-trial hearing, and the man used his free hand to point to the stairs. "How am I supposed to get up there?" Michael asked.

"There's an elevator over there." The man said, pointing in the opposite direction. "Take it to the second floor."

Michael did what he was told, entering the elevator and pushing the button with the number 2 on it. The elevator rose, and the doors opened, exposing the second floor, which contained at least 300 other people awaiting their 9 A.M. pre-trial hearing.

Michael hated dealing with crowds in his wheelchair. People towered over him, and he was always worried he was going to run over somebody's foot.

He exited the elevator and scanned the massive room and moved off to the side to see if he could identify anyone who might be in some position of authority. No authority figure was apparent, and he entered into what appeared to be a reception area with administrative staff. They clearly were not happy to see him.

"Yes?" A scowling woman sneered down at Michael from behind the counter.

"I have a pre-trial hearing that was supposed to start about 10 minutes ago, and I don't know where I'm supposed to go."

"Sir, everyone out there has a preliminary trial that was supposed to start 10 minutes ago. Go back out and find a man wearing a red suit and tie. That would be what is known as 'The Bailiff,' and you need to check in with him and tell him the crime you committed. He'll let you know which prosecutor has been assigned to handle your particular violation of the law."

Michael knew he had committed no crime in Peoria on the day he was cited, but the fact he had to be in the building on this day and time meant he must be a criminal. He decided he had better do some play-acting if he was going to have fun with this experience. It was probably in his best interest to appear frightened and stupid. But first, he decided to go fishing for information.

"Is everyone here for a traffic violation?" he asked the intimidating lady sneering down at him.

"Sir, I am not here to help you. Go out and speak to The Bailiff. He'll direct you to the prosecutor who will assess the fee for your criminal activity."

This was the information Michael needed. It was about money. The 300 people now milling around the second floor were probably the people that were picked up for violations the same month that he was, and most would end up just paying the fine. He would be informed how much the city of Peoria wanted to extort from him and figured the criminals surrounding him were probably picked up within the same period he was. Some were here for serious offenses like DUI. Their fine would probably be more than his, and when he found out how much the city wanted from him, he'd have a sense of how much money this day was going to generate for Peoria County.

Whatever the fee was for his violation was likely average. By multiplying his fee by 300, he'd have a pretty good idea of how much money was being generated. He went back out among the masses and scanned the area for a man in a red suit. There was a table off to the side with many people in suits, but none of them were red.

On the north wall was a door marked "Courtroom," and after about three minutes, the door opened, and a portly man in a red suit walked out holding a clipboard. The entire horde of people swarmed the man, and Michael watched from a distance. He had no intention of battling the throng to get to this man and waited. It took about half an hour for the horde to begin to thin out. Michael rolled up to the man in red.

"Name, please?" the man asked.

"Michael Dunston, I have a pre-trial hearing that was scheduled to start about 45 minutes ago and don't know what to do. The cop that cited me told me if I wasn't here on time, he would 'throw my ass in jail as long as he legally could,' and I'm frightened."

The man in red understood. "Don't worry, sir, nobody here wants to put you in jail. I'm going to assign you to a prosecutor who will assess the fee for your violation. Just hang out here, and I'll call you in a few minutes."

Michael cruised to a nearby wall, having determined that fear was the best demeanor to display. He faced the wall and examined the sign carved into the granite.

The Duty Of a Prosecutor is to Seek Justice, Not Merely to Convict.

Catlin appeared at his side. "The dogs are asleep, and I got bored. What the hell is going on? Who are all these people?"

"This is the criminal element of Peoria, of which I am apparently a part," Michael responded. "They are all waiting for a hearing scheduled to start at 9 A.M. I'm waiting for the guy in the red suit to call my name."

"How many people are in front of you?"

"Probably about two hundred and seventy."

"We're going to be here all day."

"Yeah, we may as well have some fun with the system. They're going to try to get some money from me by making me plead guilty, but they're wasting their time. I intend to waste the time of every Lawyer, Judge, Office Worker, and Police Officer taking part in this charade, and they are going to spend more money on me than they ever will collect. The cop called me a dick, and I'm not going to reward him by giving them money."

"The cop didn't call you a dick; he just said he didn't have time to watch you dick around."

"That's right. We'll see how that plays in open court."

"You'll never get that statement admitted into evidence. You need a lawyer."

"You think Pam would be willing to defend me?"

"Not without money, and she's not going to guarantee she'll win."

Michael considered his situation. "I think my best bet is just to go in and represent myself. I'm going to go in and play the ignorant slob and let them believe the system is running me over and force them to expend a ton of resources in their effort to convict me. I probably won't win, but my mission needs to be to force them to spend so much time on me it won't justify the cost."

"You're sure you don't want me to rip somebody's face off?" By this time, they had been in the courthouse for four hours, and he knew she was serious. Catlin was not the kind of person that dealt with bureaucracy well, and Michael prayed she wasn't about to attack.

It was then the man in the red suit called his name. Michael cruised over to the man who told him to sit at the table against the wall with the other people in suits.

"Your prosecutor is finishing up with another criminal and will take care of you in a minute." Michael rolled up to the table. It didn't take long until a man resembling Donald Trump joined him.

"Mr. Dunston? My name is Kevin McDaniels, and I am the attorney assigned to handle your case. How are you today?"

"To be honest, I'm a little frightened," Michael replied. The cop who arrested me said if I didn't show up here at nine this morning, he would hunt me down and throw my ass in jail."

"First of all, Michael, you weren't arrested. This is just a simple traffic violation and can be taken care of by paying a fine. All you have to do is plead guilty to violating Illinois State Criminal Statute 625 Section 5/11605.1, and this all goes away. Won't that be nice?"

"Yeah," Michael replied, "That would just be ducky." He then realized he was becoming snarky and continued his hunt for information. "How much is the fine?"

"Well, the charge is speeding in a construction zone, so it's a little more than a simple speeding violation. With court costs, I can make this all go away for fourteen hundred and sixty-three dollars."

Michael failed to understand why he was paying court costs when he hadn't yet appeared in court, and he did some quick math in his head. If the average fine for the 300 people that were here in today was 1400 dollars, it meant in this session alone; the County was generating four hundred twenty thousand dollars in revenue. It amazed Michael the State had budget problems. He went fishing for information again.

"Well, I don't believe it was a construction zone. There were no signs, and there were no workers on the bridge. Without those things, how was I to know it was a construction zone? I was told later that everywhere in Peoria is considered a construction zone, but shouldn't there be a big sign that says that when you enter the city?"

Kevin McDaniels snickered and said, "You have the option to plead not guilty, but you might want to speak with an attorney before you do that. Also, you would have to appear before the Judge to do so."

This was the statement for which Michael was waiting. His mission to waste time was falling into place. If he could add a judge's time into the mix, his mission was complete. He figured a judge's time had even more value than the attorney sitting next to him. If he could get to see the judge, he could tell his story to someone who was at least paid to appear somewhat impartial.

"I'd like to plead not guilty," Michael said.

"That is your right," Kevin said, rising. "You understand to do that; you have to first face the Judge."

"I understand that, and it's pretty scary, but I didn't commit this crime, and I think my best bet is just to plead not guilty."

"You know Michael, I have the discretionary ability to reduce the amount of the fine, and if you plead guilty, I can reduce the amount of the fine to 900 dollars." Michael considered the offer.

"This would still be considered speeding in a construction zone, right?"

"Yeah, I can reduce the fine, but I can't change the crime you committed."

"We haven't yet established that I committed a crime."

"Well, Michael, I can see you feel strongly about this. I think I might be able to get the fine dropped to 600 dollars."

"Still speeding in a construction zone, right?"

"Yeah, as I said, I can't change the crime, but you will spend a lot more than 600 dollars on a lawyer to defend you."

"Look, I'm going to explain to you precisely what happened that day; I was pulled over by your officer. I was told to retrieve my license, which was located in a pocket in the back of my chair. For me to get to my license, I have to transfer from the driver's seat to the passenger seat and then electronically maneuver the passenger seat, so it is parallel to the wheelchair, and I can transfer over. By the time I began the part of the process of electronically maneuvering the passenger seat, your cop said, 'I don't have time to watch you dick around all day. I'll look it up myself.' The way I see it, if I give you money for this, I would be rewarding that cop for calling me a dick."

"So, you want to plead, not guilty."

"You're damn right, I do."

"I'll set a hearing in front of the Judge. It'll be a few minutes before you can see her. Go back to your wall and find a comfortable spot and wait for a while, and the bailiff will call you."

Michael returned to his wall and read the granite sign a few more times. Catlin was angry at having to spend the day waiting in this cold, stone building, and she expressed her discontent. By this time, most of the other criminals had paid their fine and departed, and she obviously believed Michael should do the same, but Michael was resolute.

"Just pay the damn fine." Catlin pleaded. "I'm sick of this. We've got the money. I can't believe you're such a dick."

Michael considered. Within a three-month timeframe, he had been called a dick precisely three times, twice by the person he cared about more than any other. Maybe he was being a dick, and he should just cave to what the system was trying to do to him. He had little knowledge of the law and certainly could not defend himself. If he went in front of the judge, he might be digging himself into a hole from which he wouldn't be able to extract himself. He needed the advice of a lawyer.

"Catlin, go down to the car and call Pam and ask her how much she would need to represent me."

Catlin was all too happy to get out of the building. Twenty minutes later, the man in the red suit approached.

"Mr. Dunston, Your matter is next. You may enter the courtroom now."

CHAPTER 33

The bailiff held the courtroom door open for Michael, and he entered as unobtrusively as he could. A proceeding was finishing up where the judge was asking a woman accused of driving under the influence whether she wanted a trial by judge or a trial by jury. The woman chose a judge, and Michael wondered what he should do when he faced the same decision. The woman was escorted out, and Michael's Pre-trial hearing commenced in the CIRCUIT COURT OF THE TENTH JUDICIAL CIRCUIT IN PEORIA COUNTY, ILLINOIS.

The Clerk read the Charge against Michael. "This is the City of East Peoria versus Michael J. Dunston for violation of 625 ILCS 5/11-605.1

Michael chose to begin the proceedings by being contrite. "Your honor, I apologize for appearing in the wrong attire."

The Judge, a pleasant-looking woman in her late 50's with medium length salt and pepper hair, smiled down at him from the bench. Michael continued. "I don't want you to assume that I don't respect this court because of what I am wearing. I didn't realize I was going in front of a judge today. If I had, I would have worn something nicer."

"No." The judge replied. "That's quite all right; I can't quite read it. What does your tee-shirt say?"

Michael had picked out the shirt special the night before. "It says 'Stop Plate Tectonics.'" Michael replied.

The judge chuckled. "That's a good one. When I was in college, I had a tee-shirt that read 'Nuke the Whales'."

Michael chuckled as well. "That's a good one too."

"Let's see here, Mr. Dunston. You got ticketed on June 11, 2015, for a construction work zone case.

Michael began his explanation. "Yeah, see…"

"That's all right. What we're going to do is, you're going to decide whether you want to be tried by me or have a trial by jury. Do you want a jury trial?" Michael and the judge seemed to be hitting it off, and by the way she phrased the question, she seemed to be hinting that being tried by her would be in his best interest.

"No, Your Honor," He said. "I believe you are capable of rendering an impartial decision."

"Okay, I want to make sure you understand this. The trial itself is going to be set for September 14th at 9 o'clock, but we have a pre-trial on August 26 at one pm, which you need to come to. Because we only have trials once a month in this courtroom, so I try to get the line-up, and if you don't show up on the 26th of August, I will just assume you don't want your trial."

"I understand Your Honor. That's completely appropriate."

"All right, so we're going to give you a copy of this order to come back here on August 26 at 1 pm for the trial in September. I know that's a little misleading.

"I've got a jury trial in September, why do I have to come to the other? I don't like coming to this part of Illinois. The last time I was here, a cop called me a dick, and the officers downstairs wouldn't even let me in the door."

"We have a pre-trial to see if everything's ready and to make sure that the witnesses are available still."

"So, the witness will be here on the 26th?"

"No, that's what we want to see. The trial's actually September 14. The 26th is to see who's ready to go to trial and who is not ready to go to trial."

"Well, basically, I'm ready to go to trial, and it's going to be the officer that called me a dick that will be here at that time calling me a criminal."

"Yeah, the question will be, is the officer going to be here and so on and so forth."

"Okay."

"And then also for me to tell you, Mr. Dunston, there are eight cases before you."

"Well, I'm willing to plead, except for the construction zone business. I don't want it to be in a construction zone, because there was no signage for construction. There were cones on the sidewalk, and the officer said I should have known by the cones on the sidewalk that it was a construction zone. I was told after the incident that the entire City of Peoria is considered a construction zone."

"All right, I understand. All right, you just come here on August 26, and we'll see where we are at that point."

"Yes, Your Honor."

"Okay. "The clerk will get this ready for you right now, okay? She'll get that for you."

"Okay. Now, is this all documented today?"

"Yeah, we are on the record."

"So, would I be able to get a copy of the record?"

"Okay, yeah, but you have to pay for it.

"How much?"

"I don't know."

The clerk interjected, "There's nothing that was said out there that was on the record."

"Okay. I just wanted," Michael stammered, allowing his nervousness to show. "I'm very interested in having a court document that I can provide to my attorney.

"You ask your attorney before you get that." the judge advised. "Nothing was said or done here today to affect your trial. We just set it, so your attorney will -- don't go to that cost until you talk to your attorney, okay? It's pretty costly. Ask your attorney first."

"Okay. Like pretty costly, being hundreds of dollars?"

"No, but just ask your attorney first okay, because nothing that was said. All we did today was set a trial."

"But what I said is on the record, right?"

"Yeah, okay. But you didn't say anything."

"No, I didn't say anything essentially. I just wanted to have the documentation just for my benefit, you know. This is something, you know, if I want to go to the press, this is something that maybe I should have documentation."

"Sure, if you want that."

Michael could sense the mention of the press kind of surprised her, and he dug the hole a little deeper.

"Well, it's an option."

"It's an option. You can get it at any time you wish. You just go to the court reporter on the third floor. You don't have to get it today. It's available. It's on a recording. It's available up there any time you want it. You just have to give them time to prepare it."

"Your honor, I appreciate your time." He didn't let her know he wished he could waste more of it.

"That's what we do, okay?"

"Okay, thank you."

"Good luck."

The hearing with the judge lasted all of 10 minutes, and Michael left the courthouse and joined Catlin, who was playing Frisbee with the dogs.

"I figured you were in a cell with a contempt of court charge by now." She joked.

"The judge was really nice. I think she wants to sleep with me." Michael joked back.

"Oh, she does, does she?"

"Actually, I don't know of any woman that doesn't," Michael replied, continuing the banter.

"So, what happened?"

"I have a preliminary hearing scheduled on August 26th and a trial scheduled on September 14th."

"So, you planned to waste their time, and they're wasting yours. I'm not coming back here for the next one. Just pay the damn fine," She implored. They drove back to Willow Springs in Silence.

CHAPTER 34

Michael and Catlin arrived home at 5:15 that evening, and by the time they got there, Michael was hurting. He had been sitting in the loaner wheelchair almost the entire day, and he could feel it destroying his spine.

Catlin was feeling pain too, and remarked, "I need to medicate before I go back to my place. It's been a rough day."

They arrived at the hovel at 5:15 and were medicating by 5:25. Catlin had gone through the mail, and Michael selected a strain of Super Lemon Haze they had purchased in Michigan.

Michael was loading the vape when his cell phone rang. The caller I.D. said Provo, Utah. He was puzzled at the weird number and put the call on speaker so Catlin could listen to the conversation.

"Mr. Dunston? My name is Louise, and I am from the Customer Care Department of National Care United, a Division of Medicare, and we're calling to let you know your appeal has been approved." Michael was still in his court mode and realized he didn't understand the vocabulary Louise was using, so he asked for clarification.

"What does it mean my appeal has been approved? Does it mean that you have accepted the fact I am appealing your decision to deny my medical benefits? Or does it mean you are authorizing me to get my wheelchair repaired or replaced."

"Well, Mr. Dunston, after a thorough review of your case, our organization has determined you need to go back to your doctor for the wheelchair prescription and that it will be approved."

"That's great news, Louise. Can you put this approval in writing and email it to me?"

"I'm sorry, Mr. Dunston, As a Federal Government organization, we cannot do anything through email. I will put this in a letter, and you should receive it in 10-14 business days."

"I understand the Government's resistance to using email. You certainly don't want to be hacked, but there are a variety of programs on the market designed to thwart hackers. I use Norton, but there is probably better protection available. Considering how much money you are saving by denying people benefits, you should be able to afford one."

Catlin Whispered to Michael, "You're getting snarky." Michael nodded and changed the subject.

"All right, I'll jump through the next hoop and return to my doctor again and get another prescription for the wheelchair. Now, to be clear, you are going to be sending me a letter stating that you will approve the repair or replacement of the chair when my doctor writes another prescription."

"That's correct, Mr. Dunston. You will be receiving this letter within 10- 14 business days. One other thing National Care United wanted to make you aware of. We are going to be lowering the copay of prescription drug medications beginning in the year 2016. Instead of paying 10-dollar copays for your prescription medicines, beginning in 2016, you will only pay 5. Isn't that good news?"

Michael decided now wasn't the time to announce to the Federal Government; the only medicine he was currently using was cannabis.

He inhaled deeply from the vaporizer and said, "That is good news, Louise. Considering the price of some of these meds has increased by over 4000 percent, it will be a real benefit to only pay 5 dollars for them."

"Well, understand, Mr. Dunston, there is a tier system involved in relation to the prescription medicines. The true price you will pay is dependent on the medicine you are prescribed."

"I completely understand Louise. Some of the meds cost around 15 thousand dollars for a 30-day supply. I know your company can't afford to eat that. But getting back to the matter of the wheelchair, you are going to be sending me a letter stating when my doctor writes me another prescription for a wheelchair; it will be approved."

Louise was clearly beginning to tire of the conversation and sighed, "Yes, Mr. Dunston; you will be receiving the letter in the next 10-14 days. Thank you for calling National Care United."

The call disconnected.

Catlin breathed in the vapor and observed: "You didn't call them, they called you."

"Yeah, that's just a standard exit line they're bureaucratically required to say. The point is they're approving my chair." Michael didn't hear from his insurance company again for 21 days.

CHAPTER 35

In the next three weeks, Michael spent the majority of his time researching Illinois traffic laws and helping patients get certified. He also went to Dr. Stanton, who wrote another prescription for a wheelchair. Catlin spent the time putting money into the different safety deposit boxes scattered around various banks throughout Northwest Illinois.

She also found two more doctors willing to certify patients provided they could demonstrate the patient would die without the medicine. It wasn't much, but they had plenty of such patients, and appointments were made with these physicians. Michael and Catlin were now more than just paying for their medicine; they were beginning to create a legitimate business even though the banks wouldn't admit it. The bank officers pretended not to notice the tens of thousands of dollars Catlin was stuffing into boxes each month. Michael had no idea how much money there was and had no interest in learning. Catlin finally approached him about it on the twentieth day after the call from the insurance company.

"What are we going to do with all that money? We need to get a house and a clinic, so we can do a better job of teaching our patients. We can't buy a house with cash. How the hell are we going to make that money appear clean?"

"Look!" Michael snapped, "Quit worrying about the damn money. I've got a plan. We signed a year lease on the hovel. That means we're here until June. I don't want to hear anything more about the money until June. I'll fix things then."

This was obviously the wrong thing for Michael to say because Catlin and the dogs spent the weekend with her parents. That was the weekend his loaner wheelchair broke down. This time the problem was electrical, and Michael could have diagnosed and fixed the problem but not one-handed.

He spent Saturday and Sunday crawling between his bedroom, bathroom, and kitchen. Catlin and the troopers came back Monday morning. Michael was in bed, medicating. He told her about the chair, and she grabbed a screwdriver and a pair of needle-nose pliers from the junk drawer in the kitchen and quickly fixed the chair. Michael watched the ease in which she worked, thought back to the weekend he spent crawling around the house, and realized how weak he really was.

He vowed to himself that no matter how irritated he got with Catlin about their money issues, he would never snap at her again. Catlin and the dogs joined Michael in the bed. The dogs, of course, firmly planted themselves between the two humans, and Catlin recapped her weekend with her parent in whispers. She went right to business.

"My parents know someone with Polio. She's in constant pain. Is there any way we can get her certified?"

"I doubt it," Michael replied. "Illinois didn't put chronic pain on the list of qualifying conditions, and I don't think anyone even thought about polio when they created the list. The Governor has been rejecting every new condition that comes across his desk, and he seems to feel the people of Illinois elected him for his medical expertise. The fact the state has no budget and isn't even paying off winning lottery tickets must make him believe he knows more about medicine than he does about finance. He seems to think we elected him to make our medical and financial decisions, so this must be what the people of Illinois want. From an economic perspective, there is simply no real reason anyone associated with the State should care about a woman with polio. The Governor sure doesn't. How'd she get polio anyway?"

"She contracted it two weeks before the vaccine was available at her school in 1956."

"I don't know if somebody with polio can legally be certified. The pain is throughout the body, so it can't be considered Regional Pain Syndrome. I'm just not certain whether doctors in Illinois can legally recommend cannabis to patients with polio. We may be able to help her in another way, though. Have her get her medical records together. If she was alive in 1956, she might have one of the other conditions."

At that moment, the mail carrier walked past the bedroom window, and the mail was deposited in the box on the side of the house. Catlin jumped up.

"That letter about the wheelchair may have come today." Stanley lifted his head and groaned. Catlin retrieved the mail and sifted through the contents.

"Yeah, here it is." She returned to the room, sat in his wheelchair, broke open the envelope, and handed the contents to Michael.

National Care United: A Division of Medicare

Michael J. Dunston 230 Sycamore Drive, Willow Springs, Il 61278

Re: Your September 2015 Statement.

Previous Balance $ 472.00

Payments received $0.00

Current Charges $ 59.00

Total due $531.00

Due in full by September 30, 2015

About Your Payment

You have a past due balance. Please pay the total amount due by the due date. If we don't receive payment, you may be dis-enrolled from the plan.

Michael handed the letter to Catlin and reached for his laptop.

"Why is the balance so high?" she asked.

Michael replied, "They denied me the wheelchair in September of 2014. I paid them through December of that year. I even paid for January of 2015. In February, I finally realized they had declared war on me, and I stopped paying them.

"The cost is adding up." She said.

"Don't worry about it." He replied and began composing a letter of response.

He once again used the same font his insurance company used.

Medicare Complete issued through National Care United

Date: August 24, 2015
Name: Michael J. Dunston
member number: 965881017

About My Payment

I am writing to express my admiration of your companies' ability at subterfuge. It is evident that National Care United and Medicare have declared war on me and my need for the new power wheelchair which my physician prescribed. The tactics you have employed against me are absolutely brilliant. If I wanted to engage in subterfuge, I would seek out the agents that work for you and offer them more money to come work for me.

Commanding your agent to call me and verbally communicate that my appeal had been accepted was an inspired bit of deception. Instructing her to command me to go to my doctor for the wheelchair prescription and that it would be approved allowed me to believe that your organizations had agreed to an armistice with me. As you are aware, when you send me to doctors, you are authorizing me to violate your policies restricting me to only travel between my bedroom, bathroom, and kitchen. Your inaction in producing the promised written "cessation of hostilities" document you verbally assured me you would provide forces me to assume that your war against me continues.

Attached to this document is the only communication I have received from you as of this date. I understand that you want to receive payment for the quality health insurance that you are providing, and I promise that you will receive remuneration as soon as my attorney and Senator Kirk tell me it is appropriate to provide it.

Please be aware that I am a peaceful little country and have no desire to fight your country's nuclear arsenal. I would appreciate it if you could talk to the ambassadors that represent my tiny nation. They include Dr. Jonathan Stanton, M.D. (Primary Care Physician), Pamela McMillan, Attorney at law, The Honorable Senator Mark Kirk, and David Gaiter, Wheelchair Technician for Mobility Specialists organization.

When you are at war, as your countries (Medicare and National Care United) are with mine, it is necessary to use deception and chicanery to advance your nation's cause of destroying the opposing sides' army (me).

I congratulate your country's tactics in keeping me in a loaner wheelchair for as long as possible in the hopes that my nation will be destroyed, and yours won't have to pay war reparations at all. Were I in the same vocation as your country, I would employ the same deceptive strategies, though probably not as effectively. I congratulate your country's citizens on their ingenuity. I have provided you a list of my country's ambassadors (below). Sometimes it is hard to get to them by phone, and since your nation does not utilize email, it may take some time for you to communicate with them individually. I can usually reach most of them by phone.

Congratulations again,

Michael J. Dunston

cc:

The Honorable Senator Mark Kirk

David Gaiter (Provider) Technician at Mobility Specialists Wheelchair Company

Dr. Jonathan Stanton, M.D. (Primary Care Physician)

Pamela McMillan, Attorney at Law National Care United – Appeals and Grievance Department

Michael had Catlin review the document, and she sent it out that afternoon.

CHAPTER 36

On Wednesday, August 26th, Michael once again drove to the courthouse in Peoria for his preliminary trial, which was scheduled at 1 p.m. This time, he was alone and got in a little quicker. However, the security officers were again no help in getting him through the door, but they were kind enough to fondle his nether region. When the officer felt satisfied, Michael's testicles were released, and he was sent to find the portly man in the red suit.

The bailiff whisked Michael into the courtroom, placed him at the defendant's table, and the proceedings were called.

"This is the City of East Peoria vs. Michael J. Dunston"

Michael decided to begin the proceedings by kissing up. "It's a pleasure to see you again, Your Honor."

"Thank you, Mr. Dunston, remember you've got the construction zone charge, and we went over the penalties for that. They're a little bit more money."

Of course Michael remembered the money, and he responded. "Right."

The Judge reiterated. "No jail. Money."

"Right," I am aware of that, Your Honor. But I appreciate the reminder."

"All right, and you are ready for a Bench Trial?"

"Yes, Your Honor, I am ready. I'd like to get some discovery done. I'd like to have the police officer's body cam and dashcam video."

"Okay."

"Of the whole thing, particularly the part where he told me to quit dicking around when I transferred from my driver's seat to my passenger seat and then attempted to transfer to this seat to get my wallet, he said, I don't have time to watch you dick around all day."

"Okay."

"And…"

"Now, what you're asking for are two things here. You're asking for…"

"I'd like his body cam (a video) as well as the dashcam video from the officer's patrol car."

"Okay. Now, there's no discovery. I can't order them. There's no discovery in these types of cases."

"But he's got them, the body cam and the dashcam, I mean. If he's got the body cam, I should be allowed to view the body cam as well. There's all that I just told you that's on that body cam."

"Let me tell you this. I will tell you this. I've made it a rule here that if the prosecutors are going to use a video at trial, they have to show it to you beforehand."

"Okay, but one thing, when the cop told me to quit dicking around, why would the prosecutor use that? That's something the defense would use. That's what I would use, so shouldn't I be allowed to get that body cam? I mean, realistically, shouldn't I be allowed access to that?"

"I can't give you advice, sir, but there very well may be a way to get that."

"Okay. Let's figure out the way to do that."

"I can't give you advice, sir."

"Okay, yeah. My attorney wants me to give him 1800 to 2000 dollars for that advice. Now, I don't have the power that an attorney or a Judge has. The City of Peoria has attacked me, and I don't know exactly what to do."

"All right."

"The police officers in the City of Peoria attacked me."

The Judge now seemed to be beginning to become uncomfortable "I can't give you advice, okay?"

"I understand."

"Okay, if the City was to use that, and in my opinion, fairness is fair."

"That's the point, Your Honor; They would never use that. I would use that."

"Well, I don't know what the City may or may not do, but I can't -- you know, Mr. Dunston, I can't give you advice. That I cannot do. I'm the umpire, okay? I call the balls and strikes. That's what I do. The only thing I can tell you today is that if you're ready for trial, I'll put you down for trial. If you're not ready for trial, I'll grant you a continuance to get ready for trial."

"Then I have to come here in the wintertime, and I don't want to come to Peoria in the wintertime, and the Peoria police force hates my guts."

"Okay. You're from Willow Springs, Illinois?"

"Yes."

"We're Peoria, Illinois. You know, I guess winter is October. I don't know."

"They've been incredibly rude to me, including the police officers downstairs. They would not even let me in the door. They yell, 'open the door, open the door.' Now, I cannot open the door. I had a stroke, and I don't have the use of my left arm, and I did manage to open the door, and the door slammed into my chair, and they screamed, 'you're damaging the door.' Everybody in Peoria, every city official in Peoria, has been that way. The cop told me…"

"Well, you're in Peoria County now. Not Peoria."

"Okay, all right, then every official in this County, has been incredibly rude. Except for you, Your Honor."

"All right, thank you, Mr. Dunston. I'm here to hear your case. If you want me to continue it for you to get ready for trial, I'll continue it for you to get ready for trial."

"I would like you to continue it."

"For you to get ready for trial?"

"Yes."

"All right, now, when do you think you might be ready for trial?"

"As soon as I can get the video from the cop's body-cam and dash-cam."

"All right. Well, do you want me to set this in November, December?

"I'd like you to set it in the spring. I don't want to come down here in the wintertime, especially when the cops are after me."

"All right. Mr. Prosecutor, do you have any objection to…"

This was the first time the prosecutor had a chance to talk, and he was looking to make his views known. "Your Honor, I have no objection to April. However, I would like to state an objection to the aspersions that have been cast on multiple municipal police departments.

"Oh, come on. How can you?" Michael began.

This was battle the prosecutor clearly did not want to fight and interrupted him.

"Your Honor, I have no objection to the springtime."

Michael was now on a roll and had no desire to stop. "How can you do that after -- I mean, look at the video. Look at the body cam. It's all there."

The Judge stepped in. "That's all right. He's taking exception that you might say something about his municipality. What do we have in April of 2016? That's springtime."

The Judge continued, clearly not wanting to deal with this clown in the wheelchair, who was now monopolizing her time.

"Mr. McDaniels, will you be prepared to try the case at that time?"

"The State will be ready Your Honor."

"Fine, we'll schedule it at that time then."

The prosecutor asked, "Will this be for trial we're continuing this for, Judge, for which we'll need another pre-trial then?"

"Do you wish to have another pre-trial?

"I think it would be appropriate, your Honor."

"All right."

Michael wasn't sure what was happening. "So, I've got to come back here again?"

The Judge attempted to take control, "Well, you're pretty adamant about going to trial, and I really don't -- I think we'll just set it for a bench trial in April."

The prosecutor was relieved things were beginning to get settled. "Okay."

"That will save you a trip, Mr. Dunston." But Michael was now having fun and wasn't ready to quit.

"Because I don't like coming here. "It's scary to come here."

"How about April 20th?" The Judge asked.

"How about April 20th?" Michael replied.

"All right." The Judge said, "We'll do that."

The prosecutor chimed in. "The City has no objection to April 20th, Your Honor."

The Judge now attempted to wrap things up. "All right, we'll do that. Now, Mr. Dunston, I'm going to give you an order, so you know when this is."

"Okay."

"And that way, you've got time, because I can't give you advice. The prosecutor can't give you any advice."

"Well, I need to figure out a way of getting them to comply.

"The Court will note that you are in a wheelchair, and that can be difficult in the winter months. April 20th, 2016. Do you think you can remember that date, Mr. Dunston?"

"I don't envision that being a problem, Judge."

The prosecutor piped in again. He was now wasting his own time. "The City would request that no further continuances for preparation purposes be granted."

The Judge was becoming annoyed. "I won't be granting any more continuances to get ready."

"I don't see why I would need any continuances once the City allows me access to the body cam and dashboard cam."

"Well, you've got to get them on your own. I can't do that for you."

"Okay. But there's a system to do that, right?

"There can be, could be. There can be a system for you to do that."

"I would like to know the procedure.

"I can't give you advice, but I'm saying that there are usually ways to ask for things."

"Okay. Yeah, all right. I'll figure out a way."

"You've got plenty of time to figure it out."

"Right, even though I'm not an attorney and I can't afford an attorney. Now, what happens when I come here and they, the police officers downstairs, won't allow me into the building?"

"Well, let me tell you what the security is here, sir, and that may be some miscommunication. This is an older courthouse. We have one handicapped-accessible entrance, and if you push the button and talk to them, and usually our bailiffs are very good about coming to the door."

"No, Your Honor, I have to disagree. They don't come to the door. They scream, open the door, open the door, and then because you're outside, you can't say, I can't open the door, and when you do open the door, and it slams against your wheelchair, they scream, you're damaging the door."

"All right."

"And all the cops have been that way in this county."

"All right."

"They're all condescending." Court officers were now surrounding Michael in an effort to escort him out. They hovered over him like they were about to beat him to a bloody pulp.

"Am I done?" He asked the Judge.

The Judge replied. "He's going to give that to you. He's going to open the door for you."

"Okay." Michael was handed a pink sheet of paper with his next court date on it, and the proceedings ended.

CHAPTER 37

Michael drove back to Willow Springs, understanding he hadn't yet achieved victory. He knew he had wasted people's time, which was the primary reason for the trip, but he still hadn't been able to get them to drop the charge of speeding in a construction zone. He drove to the cemetery he and Catlin had medicated in before his pre-trial hearing, stopped in the same spot, and phoned Pam. Pam always answered her phone the same way.

"This is Pamela McMillan Attorney at Law."

"Hi, Pam. It's Michael Dunston."

"Good afternoon, Michael. How'd it go in court today?"

"To tell you the truth, Pam, I'm not too sure."

"Did you get them to dismiss the construction zone charge or not?"

Pam always seemed annoyed at him. She clearly didn't like the convoluted nature of the medical cannabis industry. She was aware the politics could change at any moment and was dependent on whoever Michael happened to be dealing with at the time. She wouldn't have even associated with Michael if he wasn't treating her mother's cancer. She wasn't making any money talking to him and wanted to end this unprofitable call as quickly as possible.

"They still won't budge on the construction zone charge, Pam."

"Michael, this is the only legal advice I'm going to give you. You could plead guilty to speeding in a construction zone and get put on probation, but if you get stopped for a burnt-out tail light six months from now, they can legally take away your license to drive. You could plead guilty and just never go into Peoria County again."

"Pam, I can't do that. I need to go back to Peoria because that's where the company is that fixes my wheelchair."

"Okay, Michael, then you have to beat the construction zone charge."

"How much would you charge me to represent me in court?"

Dollar signs flashed in her eyes. "Well, Michael, you have to understand that would entail me taking an entire day to travel from Moline and spend the day in court and travel back. I couldn't do that for any less than twenty-five hundred dollars."

"Can you win?" Michael asked.

"Well, I can't guarantee victory, but I have won cases like this in the past, and I can represent you as well as any other attorney."

"Well, Pam, let me consider my options, and I'll figure out what I want to do."

The call disconnected, and Michael drove home, trying to figure out a strategy the entire trip back. He entered the hovel, and Catlin was on the couch waiting for him.

"How'd it go?" She asked.

"I wasn't successful, but I had fun, and the Judge was nice enough to let me know she wasn't interested in throwing me in jail," Michael replied.

"She's probably the first government official that ever told you that." Catlin joked.

"Yeah, she made the county's interests clear." Michael recapped using the Judge's words. "No jail; money."

"Oh, you got a letter from Medicare today."

"Really? That was a quick turnaround time. They usually need seven months."

As usual, Catlin ignored his sarcasm and opened the letter. "I picked up a hundred dollars' worth of ground beef today. It's in the freezer. You want Hamburger Helper for dinner tonight?"

Michael had no interest in the question and grunted an affirmative response, which only served to piss Catlin off, and she threw the letter at Michael and stalked into the kitchen. Michael pulled the letter from the envelope and read.

Your Explanation of Benefits

Medicare and Hospital Claims Processed in

July 2015
date: June 15, 2015
Member number: 952687015732
Name: Michael J. Dunston

• This monthly report of claims we have processed tells you what care you have received, what the plan has paid, and how much you can expect to be billed.

• This report covers medical and hospital care only. We will send you a separate report on your prescription drugs.

Totals For medical and hospital claims in July $17,009.43

Amount your plan has approved $4075.96 Plan's share $2624.62

Your share $9583.72

Michael reached for his cell phone and called the number on the back of his insurance card. He went through the mandatory marathon session with the computer and finally got to an agent.

"Thank you for calling National Care United and Medicare. My name is Tami. How may I help you?"

Catlin came into the room, holding two steaming plates of Hamburger helper Potato Stroganoff. She handed a plate to Michael, and he put the call on speaker.

"Hi Tammy, my name is Michael Dunston, and I received an explanation of benefits in the mail today. On July 15th of last month, I had a splinter removed in a hospital emergency room. I supplied the tweezers, and a doctor removed a cactus thorn from my finger. I'm looking at the explanation of benefits, and it seems to say the hospital billed you 17 thousand dollars for pulling the splinter, you paid four, and I am responsible for nine thousand five hundred eighty-three dollars and seventy-two cents."

"Okay, Michael, I can help you set up a payment plan for that amount."

"No, Tammy, you don't understand. The hospital charged you 17 thousand dollars to remove a splinter from my finger. I provided the instrument they used to do it. Do you think the amount of this bill is appropriate?"

"Well, you have to understand Mr. Dunston. Hospitals have a lot of overhead. They have to keep the lights on. So, would you like to set up a payment plan now?"

"Well, no, Tami. I think I'll go over to the hospital tomorrow and discuss it with them."

"Sure, Michael, remember we're always here. And thank you for calling National Care United." The phone disconnected.

"Was that a threat?" Catlin asked.

"She didn't know what she was saying," he replied. "Her job is to assure they receive payment. I'll straighten it out with the hospital tomorrow." He took another bite of the meal. "You know this is pretty good. What is it?"

Catlin pantomimed, holding up a box and advertised, "Hamburger helper Potato Stroganoff. It's the perfect meal when you've had a long day in court. Simply use your food stamps to buy all the ground beef you possibly can, and General Mills will provide you enough dehydrated potatoes and vegetables to keep your family alive for decades. There are 41 varieties to choose from, including my favorite, Cheesy Jambalaya Hamburger Helper."

Michael made his opinion known. "Cheesy Jambalaya Hamburger Helper? I had no idea this had gotten so far out of hand. It's terrifying. But thank you for feeding me, this was great. I'm really tired, though. I think I'm going to crash." He crawled into bed and was asleep by 8 pm.

CHAPTER 38

Michael woke up early the following morning and waited around for the hospital to open. Two receptionists were at the desk, and one greeted him as he approached.

"My name is Michael Dunston, and I need to talk to someone about an explanation of benefits letter I received in the mail yesterday."

"Well, that would be Dana; I'll take you to her office."

The office was huge and nicely furnished. Beautiful paintings hung on the wall, and the office was adorned with plants of various varieties, some as big as trees.

"Dana," the receptionist said, "this is Mr. Dunston, and he'd like to discuss an explanation of benefits letter."

"Sure. Hello Mr. Dunston, what can I help you with?"

"Hi, Dana. Wow, this is an incredible office."

"Thank you," Dana replied, obviously proud. "I spent a lot of time and money, getting it just the way I want it."

"How do you get the plants to grow so well indoors?" Michael asked, hoping to get some tips for cultivators he knew.

"High-pressure sodium grow lights come on at night and run for about 12 hours and nurture the plants. The hospital has a facilities manager who adjusts the time accordingly. He has a solid background in horticulture."

"What's his name?" Michael asked. He was always searching for people he could bring into the cannabis industry.

"Mr. Dunston, What can I help you with?"

Michael pulled the Statement of benefits from his notebook and said, "In July, I got a splinter in my right hand. I couldn't remove it with my left hand because I lost the use of the arm after I was overprescribed narcotics by a doctor not associated with this hospital. I asked the receptionist out front to remove it with tweezers I provided, and she said I had to have it done in the emergency room. The doctor in the emergency room used my tweezers to remove the splinter." Michael handed Dana the Statement and continued, "I got this in the mail yesterday, and it seems to say the hospital charged my insurance company seventeen thousand dollars to remove the thorn. It also appears to say that I owe the difference, which has somehow been calculated to be nine thousand five hundred eighty-three dollars and seventy-two cents. I called my insurance company, and they told me I could set up a payment plan to pay the bill. I was wondering if you could explain these numbers to me."

"Well, Michael, you should have never have even received this statement. It only serves to confuse you. I'll just throw it away for you." Dana then threw the statement onto the table behind her.

"No, Dana." Michael replied, "I want to keep that document." Dana reached back, retrieved the Statement, and reluctantly handed it back to Michael.

She said, "Michael, don't worry about this. You will not be receiving any bills for this, and you don't need to think about it ever again."

"Thank you, Dana. I appreciate your help," Michael replied and exited the room and never thought about the document again.

CHAPTER 39

Saturday, Catlin had scheduled an event to certify Veterans in a park in Moline. The State of Illinois had chosen to be kind to its Veterans and allow them access to the medicine provided they had a V.A. doctors' diagnosis of one of the qualifying conditions. Catlin and Michael drove up to Moline together and talked while Stanley and Stella slept in the back of the van. This was the first time they had a chance to talk together about the events of the week.

Catlin began the conversation. "You won't believe the trouble we are having with the Veterans."

"What do you mean?" Michael asked. "They're the group that deserves this medicine more than any."

"I called the leaders of three Veteran's organizations, and the response was always the same. I taped the third conversation because I thought you'd want to hear what I'm dealing with." She pulled out a tiny digital tape recorder and pushed play. She adjusted the volume to compensate for the noise of the van. "This is the Veteran's Administration in Traverson, Illinois."

The sound of the phone ringing came from the recorder, and the recording was quite clear.

"Traverson V.A. My name is Sandy, can I help you."

"Hi Sandy, my name is Catlin Abramowitz. I'm an Officer with

Medical Cannabis Consultants, and we are going to be in the Quad Cities on Saturday, helping Veterans get certified to legally medicate with cannabis within the boundaries of the State of Illinois." Sandy's reaction was nothing but positive.

"Really? That's great! I know a lot of Veterans who are using cannabis for pain and some more for PTSD. Wouldn't it be wonderful if they didn't have to hide the fact that they're using cannabis for medical reasons?"

"I agree with you, Sandy. Our nation's heroes should be allowed the choice of medicating with cannabis rather than being forced to medicate with dangerous narcotics. So, would you let your group of Veterans know that we're going to be in Munroe Park in the Quad Cities all day Saturday?"

"Well, Catlin, everything we do needs to go through our commander first. You need to speak to him. I can transfer you. Hold on."

The call was transferred, and a new voice came on the line.

"This is Major Reynolds." A gruff male voice answered.

"Hello, Major. My name Catlin Abramowitz and I'm calling to provide Veterans some information. I was hoping you could inform certain Veterans about an opportunity they can benefit from. Sandy said any information provided to the Veterans had to be disseminated through you."

"Well, I am the Commander." Came the sharp reply.

"Yes, sir. That's why I'm calling."

"What sort of information do you want my men to have?"

"Well, as you know, medicinal cannabis has been proven to be effective in treating the symptoms of PTSD as well as a variety of painful conditions, including MS and cancer. I was hoping you could let some of your Veterans know that we will be providing information on the procedure to go about getting certified to use cannabis as medicine in the State of Illinois."

"No."

"No?"

"Listen, girlie, I am the Commander, and I speak for my men, and I can tell you right now there is not a single man in my platoon that wants to smoke marijuana. If marijuana is so good for you, why is everyone that was in the movie Reefer Madness now dead?"

"That's an interesting point, Commander. The fact the movie was released in 1936 likely has something to do with it."

"Listen, girlie, no true American wants to smoke marijuana, and no Veteran's organization is going to provide information on how to do it." The phone disconnected, and Michael roared with laughter. Catlin shut off the recorder.

"Every call was like that," Catlin complained. "Maybe I should have told him the medicine is vaporized and not smoked."

"I don't think that would have helped," Michael replied between guffaws.

Two veterans showed up that day. One had heard about the event from Sandy; the other was a referral from a patient they had already helped certify.

A few civilians showed up wanting to know why they were only certifying Veterans, and when they presented their medical records, Michael and Catlin helped them too. A lot of their patients came who were now friends, and the event had turned in to an enjoyable get together when Michael's cell phone rang. Michael looked at the caller I.D., and it read "Unavailable." He answered the phone and put it on speaker so that everyone could hear.

"Hello, Mr. Dunston? My name is Mallory. I'm from the billing department of National Care United, a division of Medicare, and I'm calling because we haven't received a payment from you in quite some time. We were wondering when we might expect you to bring your account up to date."

"Well, Mallory, I've talked with your billing department on several occasions, and this matter has been referred to Senator Kirk. He personally told me that because your company has been trying to kill me for the past year, I should not pay your bill until he tells me it appropriate to do so."

"I'm sorry, Mr. Dunston, I'm afraid I don't know what you are referring to." Michael could hear her fingers clicking on her keyboard.

"Your company has been denying me a wheelchair for the last year, forcing me at times to crawl from my bedroom to my bathroom and kitchen. You have all the documentation on the computer in front of you. All the letters I sent to you and all the letters you sent to me are right there on your computer. I have only been able to get ahold of Senator Kirk the one time, and he told me not to pay you for this quality health insurance until he told me it was appropriate. I can't go against my Senator. You're the Federal Government, so you should have an easier time contacting Senator Kirk then me. I'm just a citizen, and I was able to speak with him purely by luck. The matter is now in his hands, and once you can convince him to call me and tell me to pay you, I will be happy to do so."

"Well, Mr. Dunston, I'm sorry you've had an unpleasant experience, but I'm with the billing department, and I'm afraid we don't have access to the administrative matters."

"So, you have no knowledge of my case whatsoever?"

"No, sir. I'm sorry, but the only information I have is the account is way past due. But I will investigate this matter further, and you should be receiving a reply from us soon."

"That's great, Mallory; I look forward to that reply." The call disconnected, and the entire audience roared with laughter. The party broke up, and Michael and Catlin drove back to the hovel where together they prepared another delicious meal of Hamburger Helper.

CHAPTER 40

The following Thursday, Michael received a call which the caller ID said was originating from New York. Michael answered the call apprehensively, and the caller said, "Mr. Dunston? My name is Michelle Backes, and I am the Junior Grievance Coordinator for the National Care United's Department of Appeals & Grievances."

Michael glanced around for the digital recorder and discovered Catlin had taken it with her. He grabbed a notebook to document what he could. He had never talked to anyone in the company who provided their last name, so he needed to have proper documentation. He needed a name and a title.

"Hi Michelle, what was your last name and title again?"

"My name is Michelle Backes, and I am the Junior Grievance Coordinator for the Medicare & National Care United's Department of Appeals & Grievances."

Michael wrote the information as quickly as he could and felt a little insulted to learn he wasn't entitled to a Senior Grievance Coordinator. Michelle continued. "I've looked over your appeal, and all the documentation you sent us as well as everything Medicare & National Care United sent to you, and I wanted to let you know how sorry I am about everything that has transpired so far."

At that point, Michael was ready to attack, and he allowed himself to become snarky. "Yeah, well, the people in your company seem really willing to apologize for trying to kill me, but I'm still sitting here without a wheelchair."

"Yes, Mr. Dunston, I understand your frustration, and I am going to rectify the situation this weekend. You will be receiving a call from the Mobility Specialists Company on Monday. I am truly sorry you had this experience. It must have seemed as if we abandoned you."

"It certainly did, Michelle. I've been in this loaner wheelchair almost year now, and because of it, my spine is basically in fragments. I'm about to go to press."

Michelle was quick to intervene. "Oh no, there's no need to do that." I assure you I will get this resolved by Monday."

"Well Michelle, I don't want to have to play that card, but you have to understand, your company has declared war on me, and when I am at war, I have no problem resorting to nuclear weapons. I thought Senator Kirk was the biggest nuke I had, but he didn't seem to scare your company at all. Going to the press is the last weapon I have in my arsenal, and in wartime, you need to conserve your munitions. I'd prefer to keep that weapon in my ordnance in case I have to use it on a future occasion."

"Oh no, Michael, you don't ever need to bring in the press. I understand what you have endured over the last year, and I can assure you by Monday all the pieces will be in place for you and your doctor to select a chair appropriate for your condition."

"Okay, Michelle, so you understand that because of the diagnosis of your company's medical professional, which was reached without ever meeting me in person, I was denied a piece of medical equipment that I need to survive."

"Yes, Michael, I completely understand that, and frankly between you and me, I'm amazed you lasted as long as you did, and I sincerely apologize for what we put you through."

Michael wished he could record this conversation. This was someone who seemed to understand, but the company had deceived him before, and he had to solidify things.

"Well, I appreciate that, and I want to thank you for doing this. So I will definitely hear from Mobility Specialists on Monday, and what is the sequence of events after that?"

"Well, after hearing from them, you will meet once again with your physician and have David Gaiter from Mobility Specialists confirm his diagnosis is proper. After that, Medicare & National Care United will approve a wheelchair that is appropriate for your medical condition."

"Just so we are clear, Michelle, the companies you represent have agreed to stop trying to kill me and will now be providing me the wheelchair I need to survive."

"Yes, Michael." Michelle replied, clearly tiring of this man who seemed to want everything spelled out for him, "I will be sending you a letter detailing exactly what is required for you to receive your chair."

Michael enjoyed hearing the last two words of her sentence and decided to take another shot.

"So I should be receiving your letter in 10 to 14 business days then, right? I ask this because the last time your company said they were going to send me something in 10 to 14 days, 21 days later, the only thing I got was a bill."

"No, Michael, we'll be sending you a letter today and faxing your physician and the wheelchair company all the forms they need to get you the wheelchair as soon as possible."

"Michelle, I want to thank you so much for your help in guiding me through the maze and for being the only person in my health insurance company whose desire is not to kill me off."

"Yes, Michael, you can expect my letter early next week, and I will fax your physician and Mobility Specialists today, and the whole process should be resolved very soon. Thank you for your patience, and feel free to contact me if you have any more problems. I'm going to give you my direct number and all my contact information now. My direct phone number is 254-679-9580, and my Contact Information is Michelle Backes, Junior Grievance Coordinator, National Care United HealthCare Systems, P.O. Box 6106 Gatesville, Texas, 67528-9948."

CHAPTER 41

"The freezer is pretty full," Catlin said while handing Michael a glass of tea. She had been adjusting the packages of ground beef since she brought them in.

"Thanks," Michael responded. That White Widow strain made me really thirsty." He then addressed what was really on his mind. "Hey, do you have the digital recorder we've been using to tape our calls?"

"Oh yeah, sorry, I left it in my purse."

"Catlin. I've still got my insurance company dicking around with me. I need to record their calls."

"Yeah, I know I'll make sure you get it back in the morning." They spent the rest of the afternoon and evening talking and laughing, and both went to bed early.

Michael woke at 1:30 in the morning, with the insurance company phone conversation of the previous day rattling around in his brain. He decided he should document the discussion outlining the pertinent points and send it to Michelle. He gathered up all the documents he had received from Medicare & National Care United and wrote:

September 10, 2015

To: Michelle Backes
Junior Grievance Coordinator

Medicare & National Care United Department of Appeals & Grievances

P.O. Box 8052 Gatesville, CA 67528-9948 254-679-9580

From: Michael J. Dunston member number: 965881017

Dear Michelle,

Thank you for your phone call on September 10th, 2015. I am addressing this letter to you personally because you seem to be the only person within Medicare and National Care United, whose ultimate goal is not to kill me. I very much appreciated your apology for what has transpired so far and accept it wholeheartedly. As you are aware, in the eleven months this case has been in play, I have received thirteen items of correspondence from National Care United and Medicare. Those letters were the denial of medical benefits letter, ten bills for the medical benefits your two organizations provide me, and a letter from Debra Wilson stating that you had misplaced my address. This letter is dated August 3, 2015. You obviously have a copy of it. I am not faxing it or the ten bills because I don't have a fax machine and I don't want to bother the staff of my doctor's office by having them fax information that you already have.

Please tell the members of your billing department to quit calling me on Saturdays to demand payment for my health insurance. I'm often with people on Saturdays, and it is embarrassing when I get calls that have the appearance that I don't pay my health insurance bills. I explained in my letter dated August 23, 2015, that you will receive remuneration as soon as my attorney and Senator Mark Kirk tell me it is appropriate to provide it.

The most embarrassing collection call occurred on Saturday, September 5th, 2015. I was with a group of six people, not including myself, when an agent of your company called around noon demanding payment for the quality health insurance your company is providing me. I was forced to try to explain to the people I was with that my health insurance company was doing everything they could possibly do to kill me. This would have been difficult because all the documentation that proved this was at my doctor's office to be faxed on the following

Monday. Fortunately, two of the people I was with had already seen the documents and were able to explain that it was true; my insurance company was indeed attempting to destroy me.

Michelle, I truly appreciate that you seem to be the one individual within Medicare and National Care United who does not have this agenda, and I am delighted you called me on Thursday. I look forward to receiving your letter detailing that by merely meeting once again with my physician and having David Gaiter from Mobility Specialists to confirm that his diagnosis is proper, National Care United will approve a wheelchair that is appropriate for my medical condition.

It is now 2:52 in the morning, and I am so excited I am going to get a wheelchair appropriate for my condition that I can't sleep. The chair your organizations have forced me to sit in for the past eight months is hurting me so badly that I lack the vocabulary to describe it. I apologize that my vocabulary is limited. Still, I am confident that my physician who attended school for many more years than I will be able to explain the agony I am enduring.

Again Michelle, thank you for not trying to kill me.

Michael J. Dunston 230 Sycamore Drive, Willow Springs, IL 61278

cc:

The Honorable Senator Mark Kirk

Dr. Jonathan Stanton, M.D. (Primary Care Physician)

Pamela McMillan Attorney at Law

David Gaiter, Mobility Specialists Wheelchair Company

National Care United & Medicare Insurance

Michael mailed the letter early that morning and met with a 19-year-old epilepsy patient that afternoon. The patient was an enjoyable, intelligent, young black man named Devon with a good sense of humor. Michael explained to him how the CBD molecule would likely control his seizures and about the regimen his other epilepsy patients found to be successful. Michael told him about his patient, who was medicating with 200 mg of CBD spray and how she supplemented the spray with 0.3% THC to mitigate the depression that can be brought on by the CBD molecule alone.

"That amount of THC is well below the level of psychoactivity," he explained.

"Good because I pitch for my college baseball team, and I always need to be in control of where the ball is going."

"You're a pitcher?" Michael asked, an idea forming in his head.

"Yeah, I won 17 games last season."

"How hard do you throw?"

"My ball has been clocked at 85 miles per hour."

"So, you perform in front of large groups of people and never really get too nervous?"

"I never get nervous when I have a baseball in my hand."

"Would you be willing to throw in front of a group of people in Peoria on April 20th of next year?"

"Sure, if you can get me to a doctor who will give me access to medicine that controls the seizures without messing with my mind, I'll be happy to throw in front of any group you want."

"I appreciate it, Devon. You're going to be throwing indoors. Can you provide a catcher?"

"Sure. Will there be a scout there watching me throw?"

Michael hadn't thought that far ahead, but he had some contacts from his casino days. Baseball talent scouts were notorious gamblers. He'd make a call and try to get a scout to come to the event.

Michael said, "I'll try Devon, but you have to understand, this is just going to be a demonstration, and I don't need you to throw at top speed."

CHAPTER 42

The next few months were uneventful. Michael spent most of his time teaching medical cannabis patients how to medicate effectively while Catlin loaded safety deposit boxes in the various towns which housed their money.

April 20th arrived, and Michael and drove to Peoria for his trial. Catlin and the dogs stayed home. Michael was glad he didn't have to consider the ramifications if she chose to rip somebody's face off in open court. He once again medicated in the cemetery before the proceedings and drove to the courthouse. He submitted to the mandatory groping session required by security before making his way into the courtroom.

The moment he entered the courtroom, the Clerk called the Case.

"County of Peoria versus Michael J. Dunston." Michael rolled up to the table assigned to him. He would have preferred to have been closer to the Judge, but the seating arrangement was designated by the court to protect her for fear Michael might spring up and crawl across the courtroom and beat her senseless with his one good arm.

The clerk continued, "Mr. Dunston, you are charged with a violation of Section 11-605-1a of the Vehicle and Traffic Law of the State of Illinois, by driving Fifty-three miles per hour in a forty-five mile per hour zone on the Cedar Street Bridge between the City of Peoria and the City of East Peoria."

Once again, Michael chose to begin the proceedings by kissing up.

"It's a pleasure to see you again, Your Honor. I understand this is one of the last cases you have to adjudicate before you retire. Congratulations on a successful and stellar career."

The Judge smiled, likely envisioning her future of not having to associate with criminals like him.

"That's correct, Mr. Dunston. Today is my last day. How did you come across that bit of information?"

"I've spent the last four months researching all the players involved in this case." He looked directly at the prosecutor, who appeared extremely uncomfortable to learn this.

"Thank you, Mr. Dunston. You are the first person to congratulate me on my retirement." She looked directly at the Prosecutor, who once again appeared extremely uncomfortable.

"You're welcome, Your Honor, I'd like to begin with some last-minute motions."

"What last-minute motions?" The Prosecutor demanded.

"I have a list." Michael pulled a typewritten sheet of paper from his notebook and began reading.

"Oh, this is going to be a fun one." The Judge remarked, chuckling, clearly beginning to enjoy herself. Michael took it as a good sign, but Pam had warned him Judges sometimes seem to side with the defendant before slamming them with a guilty verdict.

"First, Your Honor, I have had a hell of a time determining who is actually labeling me a criminal. Is it the City of East Peoria, The City of Peoria, or the County of Peoria? I asked the people at the front desk of the Courthouse, and their response was 'Sir, we are not here to help you.'"

"That sounds like something they'd say." The Judge replied harshly.

"Objection Your Honor, the prosecutor grumbled. I don't think it's appropriate to impugn the integrity of the office staff of this Courthouse."

"Oh, pipe down. You know it's true. Have you ever tried to get anything accomplished in this building?"

"Does Your Honor really want me to answer that question?"

"No. Don't waste the Court's time. I want to hear the Defendant's motions.

"Well Your Honor," Michael responded, happy to be added back into the conversation, "I would like to know exactly who considers me a criminal. Is it the City of Peoria, the City of East Peoria, or the Entire County of Peoria? Whichever it is, I would like to challenge the claim on jurisdictional grounds. I was pulled over in the City of Peoria by an officer employed by the City of East Peoria, and I'm not certain he had the authority to do that."

"Nice try, Mr. Dunston." The Judge ruled, slapping him down. It is the County of Peoria who, to use your words, is calling you a criminal."

The prosecutor chimed in once more. "Excuse me, Judge. The County of Peoria has not called this man a criminal."

"Mr. Dunston, are you charged with a crime?"

"Yes, Your Honor, a crime which has the potential to cost me 1400 dollars in fines and untold increases in my insurance rates."

"Jurisdictional grounds don't work. Mr. Dunston." Michael hadn't expected they would and moved on to his next motion.

"Your Honor, I don't believe I've received a complete witness list from the People of Peoria County. I requested from the County a complete list of witnesses to the alleged crime in February and was only informed of one."

"It's the only one I need." The Prosecutor sneered.

"I also requested a list of all the workers in the construction zone at the day and time of the alleged violation."

"I don't need the construction workers as witnesses of your violation. The only thing I need is the expert testimony of the police officer who witnessed the crime."

"Alleged crime." Michael retorted. "You still haven't proven a criminal act occurred."

"Watch me."

"Okay." The judge interjected, "Let's get this trial started so we can move the docket along."

As much as Michael liked the judge, he wasn't interested in hastening her ability to get through her docket. He'd spent months researching tactics for beating this ticket, and he considered this as time the County had taken from him. During his near-death experience, he discovered how precious time was, and he was going to do everything he could to take it away from them. If he could delay long enough to get the trial continued until morning, he would consider it a victory even if he had to cough up the 14 hundred dollars. But it was still morning, and he envisioned no scenario in which he could make that happen. The clerk handed the Judge some papers, and Michael took the opportunity to speak.

"Your Honor, I would like to make the following motion. I move to dismiss this case based on the fact that the prosecution has completely ignored my written request to discover the officer's dashcam and body cam recordings. I have here a copy of that request, made on December 5th, 2016."

These recordings were the evidence Michael desired more than any other. He felt sure the dash-cam would prove no signs existed indicating the bridge was a construction zone. The officer's body cam would provide evidence the cop was both unprofessional and abusive. As a defendant, he felt certain as soon as these bits of evidence were presented in court, the judge would have no choice but to dismiss the charge. Somebody had to explain why Michael never got access to these recordings.

The prosecutor was forced to respond. "Your honor, according to State law, the defendant has four months from the date of incidence to request these recordings. As the defendant just stated, the request for these recordings was not even delivered to us until the middle of December; a full six months after the offense occurred."

"Alleged offense," Michael muttered, "You still haven't shown any violation of the law took place."

"That will happen later. The prosecutor sneered. "Your Honor, the fact remains after four months any recordings of incidents such as this are destroyed, and the county had no way of knowing the defense desired these recordings. In any event, whatever evidence might have been available by visual and auditory recordings is no longer available to either the prosecution or the defense. The prosecution had no way of knowing the defense desired this evidence until after the four-month window."

It was now Michael's turn to chime in, "Your Honor, I requested the recordings at my pretrial hearing as well as my preliminary trial. You were present on both occasions. The County had full knowledge I was requesting copies of the recordings of the officer's unprofessional conduct as well as the dashcam video, which would prove no signs were present indicating the area in question was a construction zone."

"Your Honor, the fact remains the defendant did not follow proper procedure for requesting these recordings, so the recordings were destroyed through a normal course of events. These recordings simply no longer exist because of lack of a timely request by the defense."

"As I said, Your Honor, I requested these items twice in open court and the fact the County chose to destroy them after my repeated requests indicate there was nothing on the recording to benefit it in its attempt to railroad me."

"Objection, the County is in no way attempting to railroad this defendant. "All it is interested in doing is imposing punishment for the commitment of a crime."

"No crime was committed. You are aware of this because you certainly viewed the recordings after I requested them the first time."

"Your Honor, the defendant, has no first-hand knowledge I viewed any such recordings, and I resent the implication I would destroy evidence which would exonerate a defendant. The fact is the recordings were destroyed in a timely manner through proper police procedures."

Michael had considered the recordings the strongest element of his defense and was disappointed to learn they no longer existed. Both he and the prosecutor looked to the Judge for a ruling.

"Well, Mr. Dunston, as a matter of law, even if the officer did act inappropriately, it has no bearing on whether or not you committed a crime within the confines of our County. The fact is you did not submit the written request within the four-month timeframe, and as a result, the recordings have been destroyed through proper police procedure. Whether or not the officer acted unprofessionally really makes no difference to whether or not you violated the law. Mr. Dunston, My role is the Judge. I am the umpire. I call the balls and strikes, and at this point, you haven't even thrown a pitch. Your motion is denied."

"Your Honor, this was, in reality, two motions. The first was the motion for the body cam recording, and the second the video from the dashboard of the patrol car. The only motion you addressed was that even though the officer called me a dick, the Court has no interest in it. I understand this, but we haven't yet addressed the fact the dash-cam would have provided visible evidence that there were no signs in the area indicating construction on the Cedar Street Bridge was taking place on the day and time listed on the ticket."

The Judge struck him down hard.

"Mr. Dunston, The fact remains. You did not submit your request for this evidence within the four-month timeframe, and the evidence you requested was subsequently destroyed. This was because of your failure to act in a timely manner, and the County destroyed that evidence at a legal time, and I presume lawfully. Is there anything else?"

"Your Honor, I'd like to reserve my right to appeal your decision on this matter." Michael wasn't sure if this was procedure, and it certainly seemed to frost the Judge, but if he lost the case, he figured an appeal would cause the County more headaches. Eventually, they were bound to get tired of him clogging their system and let him go.

"An appeal is certainly within your rights, Mr. Dunston, but let's see whether the County can prove its case against you. Mr. Prosecutor, please proceed with your Opening Statement."

"Your Honor, the People will show, through the testimony of Officer Richard Licker of the East Peoria Police Department, the defendant, Michael J. Dunston, was driving a white 2001 Aerostar Van on The Cedar Street Bridge between the City of Peoria and East Peoria. Officer Licker will also show that by relying on the use of a radar speed detection device, Mr. Dunston drove in excess of forty-five miles per hour, and he visually confirmed that for over half of one block distance Mr. Dunston was driving at that speed."

This opening statement by the prosecutor provided Michael with some much-needed information. First, Officer Licker was actually in the Courthouse; Michael had not yet seen him. Second, they would be relying on a combination of the officer's visual memory and a radar gun, which clocked his speed.

Michael had hoped the officer wouldn't show, and he didn't relish the idea of challenging an instrument of science. Still, he had taken a few physics classes and figured his understanding of the Doppler Effect was at least as strong as the officers. He hoped the trial wouldn't get this far, but if it did, he intended to test the cop's knowledge of the scientific principles on which his testimony was based.

The Prosecutor sat down, and it was suddenly Michael's turn to present his opening statement. Pam had told him not to make the mistake of revealing his strategy too soon and not to give his plan away by giving his opening statement at the beginning. By doing this, the prosecutor would have time to prepare, and he also wanted to tailor his statement until after he heard what Officer Licker had to say.

Michael spent a few seconds writing notes and then without looking up said: "Your Honor, I would like to reserve the right to make my very brief opening statement until just before I testify."

The Judge's anger at him had subsided, and she made her ruling. "Mr. Dunston, I like the fact you said you would make your opening statement brief. I see you have the ability to be passionate as well as long-winded, and if I get the sense you are trying to delay these Court proceedings, I promise I will step on you.

Michael was unhappy the Judge had ascertained his mission, and he responded with a meek "Yes, Your Honor."

"Mr. Prosecutor, please call your first witness."

"Your Honor, The State needs only one to prove our case. The State calls Officer Richard Licker of the East Peoria Police Department." The door to the courtroom opened, and a man dressed in a police uniform strode to the witness box. Michael didn't recognize the man, but the gun strapped to his side was familiar.

"Officer Licker, would you please describe the events which took place on the morning of June 11 of the year 2015?"

"On that particular morning at 10:05 during my routine patrol, I observed a white Ford Aerostar van traveling across the Cedar Street Bridge at a high rate of speed. This area was under construction, and I visually estimated the vehicle's speed at well over the forty-five miles per hour posted limit for the area. I used my radar gun to clock the exact speed of the vehicle at fifty-three miles per hour. I stopped the vehicle after it made a right-hand turn on Main Street in the City of Peoria. I later determined the driver of said vehicle was one Michael J. Dunston."

"Officer, is the driver of that vehicle present in this Courtroom today?"

"Yes."

"Would you please point out the driver of that vehicle?" The officer used his index finger of his right hand to point at Michael, and he had the feeling the officer would have preferred to have been pointing with his gun.

"Let the record show that Officer Licker has identified the defendant Michael J. Dunston. Were any words exchanged between you?"

"Nothing out of the ordinary. He didn't have his license handy, so I had him tell me his name, and I was able to obtain from dispatch all the information necessary to write the citation. I recognize the defendant as the driver who committed the infraction, and I cited him for the violation according to my authority as a public safety officer."

"So, Officer, you were able to determine Mr. Dunston was exceeding the speed limit both visually and through use of the radar gun as well?"

"Yes."

"And what was the speed of Mr. Dunston's vehicle?"

"I clocked Mr. Dunston's vehicle at fifty-three miles per hour."

"What is the speed limit on the bridge when the bridge is not under construction?"

"Forty-five miles per hour."

"So, Mr. Dunston was in a construction zone, traveling at a speed eight miles over the normal speed limit. That seems excessive, doesn't it, Officer Licker?"

"Objection," Michael said softly.

"Withdrawn. Officer Licker, was the area under construction and marked at the time of the violation?"

"Yes. The area was marked quite clearly with orange cones."

"Thank you, Officer. No further questions."

The Judge said, "Mr. Dunston, Would you care to cross-examine?" Michael chose to suck up again.

"Yes, Your Honor. Thank you for the opportunity. Officer Licker. Is it okay if I just refer to you as Dick?"

The Judge chimed in, "Watch it, Mr. Dunston."

"I apologize, Your Honor. I couldn't resist attempting to be friendly with the witness by addressing Officer Licker by his first name.

Officer Licker, you stated the area was clearly marked as a construction zone by orange cones. Where exactly were these cones located?"

The officer glanced at the back of the original ticket he held in his hand.

"I made a diagram on the back of the ticket indicating where cones were placed on the sidewalk on either side of the bridge."

"Your Honor, I'm going to object to the officer using notes to assist him in his testimony. The officer is referring to notes of which I was never made aware. I requested a copy of the officer's notes in my request for discovery. This request was submitted weeks ago and went virtually ignored. I ask that this evidence be excluded, and the officer's testimony be disallowed."

The Judge was obviously pissed, but there was no way of telling whether she was pissed at the officer, the prosecutor, or Michael. She reached out her hand.

"Let me see the note." Officer Licker handed the note directly to the Judge. "Let me see the Motion for Discovery."

The Court Clerk jumped into action and took the motion from Michael and transported it to the Judge. The Judge examined the documents and made her decision. "The objection is sustained. Mr. Prosecutor, the defendant followed proper procedure in requesting the officer's notes, and he should have had access to them before you wasted my time with this trial"

This was the first decision by the Judge that had gone Michael's way, and he enjoyed the victory silently. The Prosecutor was in a hole but dug himself out quickly.

"I apologize to the Court for this oversight and would like to propose that the Court grant a recess to allow the defendant the time necessary to study the officer's notes."

"Mr. Dunston," The Judge asked, "How much time do you believe you need?"

Michael considered. Here was a chance to get the case continued for weeks if need be. He could also compel the cop to come back in the morning. Michael liked the idea of inconveniencing Officer Licker immensely, and he realized the reason he had put so much effort into preparing for this trial was for the sole purpose of getting back at the cop that had insulted him, threatened him, and pulled a gun on him. However, the small victory he had achieved with the Judge clouded his judgment, and he spoke the words that would eventually lead to his demise. "Your Honor, there is no way of telling how long it will take for me to study the notes without seeing them. I propose you allow me an hour to look over the document to determine how long I will need. The note the officer is using may contain information which may require extensive research in order for me to prepare.

"Mr. Dunston, I will grant you one hour. It's time to break for lunch, and you can have the time to look over the officer's note. After the one-hour lunch break, if you feel you need time to conduct extensive research, you come back and explain to me the extensive research you need to do. You are not going to delay this trial. I retire the day after tomorrow, and I intend to leave my successor with a clean docket. We will adjourn for lunch until 1:15."

Everyone except Michael stood, and the Judge exited stage left. The Clerk of Court walked over to Michael holding the note the officer was using and said, "Mr. Dunston, I'll make a copy of both sides of this. The front side is the officer's copy of the ticket you were issued, and the back is the diagram he was using when he tried to testify. She left the room to make the copies, and the prosecutor oozed up.

"You know, this is just a traffic ticket. You're obviously guilty. Why are you making this more than it is?"

Michael was livid. " Four reasons, Mr. Prosecutor. First, I am not guilty. Second, if a construction zone violation appears on my record, my insurance rates will go through the roof. Third, if my wheelchair breaks down and I have to come to Peoria to get it fixed, and I so much as get pulled over for a burnt-out taillight, the County will call it a parole violation and pull my license. Finally, paying the County the fourteen hundred dollars you want would be rewarding that officer for calling me a dick."

"He didn't call you a dick; he merely said he didn't have time to watch you dick around all day."

"Ah-ha, Michael thought, *"so he had seen the video."* "OK, Mr. Prosecutor, you're right. He didn't call me a dick in much the same way I didn't call him a dick in open court."

The Prosecutor smirked. "Yeah, that was a good one. I've been trying to figure out a way of doing that for years, but it's harder as a Prosecutor. Allow me to address your concerns. I understand your anger at Officer Licker. The way he treated you lacked discretion and professionalism, but you exhibited the same lack of professionalism today in open court. Isn't that true, Mr. Dunston?"

Michael had no choice but to concede the point. The Prosecutor continued. "If your wheelchair needs to be repaired and you are pulled over for a broken taillight, I can assure you the County will not pull your license."

"Sure, like the Government employees in this County have been so helpful and trustworthy up to now." Michael could tell the remark stung the Prosecutor and was somewhat sorry he said it.

"Here is what I am authorized to do for you. I can drop the fine to 600 dollars, and when the probationary period is over, the violation will not appear on your record. This will not affect your insurance in any way."

"So, what you as an attorney are suggesting I do is plead guilty to a crime I did not commit. I'm sorry, Mr. Prosecutor, but I don't think it's in my best interest to take legal advice from you." That seemed to sting as well, but Michael didn't care.

"Mr. Dunston, I have to get approval for this, but I might be able to drop the fine to 200 dollars." Michael now felt as if he was talking to a used car salesman.

"Still the construction zone charge, though, right?"

"Yes, the State can't change the nature of the violation." The Clerk of Court came back and handed Michael the copy of Officer Licker's notes.

"Well, Mr. Prosecutor, let me look over the officer's notes and think about your offer of allowing me to pay you 200 dollars to plead guilty to a crime I did not commit."

"It will be cheaper for you in the long run. If you continue to waste our time fighting this, you will be found guilty, and it will cost you the fourteen hundred dollars."

"Well, Mr. Prosecutor, let me consider your offer and get back to you after lunch. I need to get outside and find some air that is not so oppressive."

CHAPTER 43

Michael gathered his notebook, shoved the officer's diagram inside, and left the room. The air outside the courthouse was pleasant. Spring had arrived early in 2016, and April 20th was a wonderfully sun-drenched day. It was a perfect day for planting seeds. The sun was shining, and although the day was not a national holiday, Michael always celebrated it.

He rolled down the sidewalk next to the Courthouse and spied Devon throwing pitches for the scout Michael had arranged to watch. The scout was a member of the Chicago Cubs Baseball Organization and a degenerate gambler. Michael was fully aware of how much money he owed the casinos in Las Vegas and was probably partially to blame for feeding the man's addiction.

Michael marveled at the power in Devon's arm. The ball striking the catcher's glove sounded like a rifle shot. He rolled across the grass and greeted the Scout. The scout was standing behind the catcher and holding up a radar gun to clock the speed of Devon's pitches.

"Hi Scott, thanks for checking this kid out for me."

Scott was astounded to see Michael in the wheelchair. "What the hell happened to you? The last time I saw you, you were leaning against a podium waiting to issue me another marker so I could give more of my money to the casino."

"Yeah, I'm not in the casino industry anymore. Prescription medicines caused me to have a stroke and lose the use of my left arm. That was also the last day I walked. I'm now teaching doctors and patients how to medicate with cannabis effectively. The kid is one of my patients."

"You mean this kid is throwing a ball at 87 miles an hour all potted up on reefer?"

Michael couldn't help but chuckle at the terminology.

"The kid has epilepsy and is medicating with a strain called ACDC. It doesn't get him high, and none of my patients use enough medicine to affect their ability to throw a ball accurately. How's Devon look anyway?"

"For as young as he is, he throws hard. He's got good control and a wicked curve. I can get him onto a lower level farm team. We have a club here in Peoria, and they can teach him some new pitches. There may be an issue if he ever makes it to the majors because I don't know what the League policy is on medical cannabis. The owners of the Cubs are pretty progressive, and if they can find someone who can help their team, I doubt they'll have a problem with it.

"Yeah, the Cubs need to try something new. What they've been doing hasn't worked."

"Well, anybody can have a bad millennium."

"Hey, teach me everything you know about the radar gun."

"What do you want to know?"

"I'm particularly interested in how they're calibrated," Scott called out to Devon, who, of course, was standing 90 feet away.

"Thanks, Devon, I've seen everything I need to. Just hang tight there. I'm going to want to talk with you in a few minutes."

Devon waved his gloved hand and sat in the grass with his legs crossed. The Scout proceeded to teach Michael the subtleties of the radar gun.

When he was finished, Michael rolled over to Devon and said, "Hey Devon, nice job man, Scott is going to talk with you in a second. Just remember, if you're allowed to throw in the Courtroom, you don't have to show your power. Just make sure you're there when I call you around 1:30."

"No worries, Michael; I'll be there. Thank you for introducing me to the scout."

"Devon, you and I are doing things for each other. This is what humanity is all about. I probably won't be able to talk with you much anymore today, but your certification visit with the doctor is next Friday. Stop by my house after that, and we'll talk, and I'll give you the form so that you can get the discount on your fingerprints."

Michael rolled to his van, retrieved his cell phone, and called Pam. He was able to reach her almost immediately. "Pam, the Prosecutor, offered a plea deal. If I plead guilty, they'll put me on probation for a few months, and he says it won't affect the price of my insurance, and if I get pulled over, they won't take my license away."

"Do you believe him?"

"Not really."

"Are you guilty?"

"No."

"Good, Michael. Don't plead. What you need to understand is the whole system is corrupt. Districts like the one you're caught in need money, and this is the easiest way to get it. Figure the Prosecutor is corrupt, the police are corrupt; even the Judge is probably corrupt. Here is my advice to you as a lawyer; go into the Courtroom this afternoon and have fun. Torture the cop as best you can and make him prove everything he says occurred. You know the law you were charged with. They have to prove every element of that law was violated. The Judge will give you some leeway because you're not a lawyer and don't know proper courtroom procedures. Try not to piss her off. If you can put her in a position where she has no choice but to find you not guilty, you've done your job. The law is your friend. Let it benefit you in the same way friends benefit you."

"I can get a continuance, Pam. Would you be willing to represent me for the rest of the trial?"

"No, Michael." I'm going to use your words against you now. When we met with my mother, you told us your near-death experience made you realize the reason we are in this life is to learn everything we can, so we are better prepared for the next one. This is a learning experience for you. If you lose the case, I'll handle the appeal."

As she always did, Pam ended the call abruptly. Michael put the phone down and cruised back into the courthouse with the mission of having fun.

He first decided to play with security. During the mandatory body search, when the guard's hand was in the appropriate area, Michael sighed deeply and said: "I've never been touched like this before." He considered kissing the guard on the forehead but decided that might land him in jail. He proceeded into the courtroom and tried to prepare himself for what would happen next. The prosecutor entered and crossed over to Michael.

"So, Mr. Dunston, I was able to get my superiors to agree to allow you to plead to the simple speeding charge with a fine of only 200 dollars."

"Still in a construction zone, though, right?"

"Yes, Mr. Dunston. It simply is not possible for me to change the nature of your crime."

"As I've told you on numerous occasions, Mr. Prosecutor, the only violation that occurred in your county that morning was the one committed by Officer Licker when he charged me erroneously for a crime I did not commit. I cannot, in good conscious plead guilty and pay the County money for abusing my rights. You are going to have to prove I committed the crime."

"Mr. Dunston, this is your only chance to get out of this. Pay the 200 dollars because if I have to spend the afternoon proving you were speeding in a construction zone, the State will not settle for 200 dollars. My advice is that you take this deal because you aren't going to get a better one."

"As I said before, Mr. Prosecutor, I don't think it is in my best interest to look to you for legal advice." Michael felt a sense of satisfaction when the prosecutor left in a huff.

Michael prepared his documents as the courtroom began to collect spectators. Word had gotten out that a simple speeding ticket trial had the potential to become interesting. It was rare one lasted through lunch, and Officer Licker had never been called a dick in open court before, and people were talking. The rumor among the spectators was a defendant in a wheelchair was going to talk himself into a contempt of court charge, and the Judge was going to have no choice but to throw his ass in jail. No one wanted to miss the entertainment an occurrence of this nature would provide.

The Clerk of Court announced, "All rise." Everyone except Michael stood up, and the Judge entered Stage left and sat down at her bench.

"Mr. Dunston, Do you need more time to research the information you obtained from Officer Licker's notes?"

"No, your Honor. I am ready to proceed with my cross-examination of Officer Richard Licker." A mummer of disappointed gasps went through the crowd of spectators when they realized he wasn't going to say what they hoped.

"Proceed Mr. Dunston."

"Officer Licker, would you describe the area which you claim was a construction zone?"

"The entire Cedar Street Bridge was under construction."

"Where were the signs indicating the area was construction zone located?"

"The area was indicated as a construction zone through the use of orange cones which were placed throughout the entire length of the bridge.

"Officer, how many lanes does this bridge consist of?"

"The Cedar Street Bridge is a four-lane road."

"Officer Licker, which lane was I in at the time you supposedly observed me breaking the law."

"You were in the left-hand lane, which is sometimes referred to as the 'fast lane.'"

"I see, were any vehicles in the lane next to me, in the right-hand lane, sometimes referred to as the 'slow lane'?"

"Yes, there was a truck next to you. I noticed you had to slow down to change lanes to get behind it to make a right-hand turn."

"So, Officer, did you have your radar gun trained on my vehicle, or did you have the gun trained on the truck in the right lane next to me?"

"I had my gun pointed at you. I always have my gun trained on the fast lane of that bridge."

"That's the radar gun you are referring to and not the gun strapped to your side. Am I correct?"

"Yes."

"And that was through the windshield of your patrol car. Am I correct in that assumption?"

"Yes."

"Officer Licker," let's get back to the matter of the orange cones placed throughout the entire length of the bridge. I've seen the orange cone you refer to in various parts of the lovely City of Peoria, and you have to agree, these cones come in the same shape and colors, but they have varying ranges in height. How tall were the cones lining the length of the bridge?"

"I think they were the six-inch cones."

"You think they were the six-inch cones, officer? If I were to tell you I went back and measured the cones after you ticketed me, and I found the cones to be a full foot tall, would that surprise you?"

"No, they could have been the one-foot cones."

"Officer, are you certain the cones even existed? Because I never actually measured any cones."

The officer looked uncomfortable, and the prosecutor jumped in to protect him. "Your Honor Mr. Dunston just told the officer he himself measured the cones, and now he is questioning the cones existence. I am not a philosopher, but if Mr. Dunston measured the height of the cones, this indicates to me the cones did indeed exist, and their existence proves they were placed on the bridge to indicate the area was a construction zone."

The Judge had caught on immediately. "You certainly are not a philosopher, Mr. Prosecutor. Court Reporter, would you please read back the last question posed by the Defendant?"

In a monotone voice, the Court reporter recited, "If I were to tell you I went back and measured the cones after you ticketed me, and I found the cones to be a full foot tall, would that surprise you?"

The Judge addressed the Prosecutor as if she were addressing a five-year-old, "You see Mr. Prosecutor; the Defendant phrased the question as a hypothetical. He didn't say he measured the cones; he asked if the officer would be surprised if his estimation of the height of the cones were different from their actual height. Isn't this right, Mr. Dunston?"

"To an extent, Your Honor. I'm really questioning the actual existence of the cones and whether they were present on the bridge that day or a day earlier or a day later than the day in question. I truly have no recollection of these imaginary cones and have seen no evidence they ever existed in the first place. The officer's recollection of the event is obviously cloudy, and it is apparent to me he is making up facts to obtain a conviction."

By this time, Officer Licker was irate. "The cones were right there on the sidewalk, lining down the entire bridge!"

"Okay, Officer," Michael replied, "for the time being, let's say your imaginary cones did indeed exist. For the purpose of our hypothetical, the question becomes, are these cones enough to indicate the area was a construction zone? Let's look at the law you accuse me of violating. The law is LLCS 5/11-605.1. This law details the speed limit when traveling through a construction zone. I refer you to the ticket you issued to me on June 11th of the year 2015. This is the law you are accusing me of violating. Is that a correct statement, Officer?"

"Yes, you were speeding in the construction zone on the Cedar Street Bridge on that date."

"As you remember it, I was traveling at a speed which constituted a hazard to the construction workers in the area. And as a Peace Officer, sworn to protect and serve, you can't allow some clown to go speeding through a construction zone and endangering the lives of the workers in the area. Am I correctly describing your reasoning for writing me this ticket?" Michael asked, waving his copy of the citation in front of him.

"Yes. My thoughts were strictly on protecting the workers in the area."

"Mr. Licker, how much of the morning of June 11th, 2015, do you remember?"

Once again, the Prosecutor chimed in. "Your Honor, I must object to that question. It is both argumentative and vague."

"I apologize, your Honor, I'll rephrase the question. I agree with the prosecutor. The question was argumentative, although I am not a lawyer, so I don't know whether the question meets the legal definition of vague. I will take the learned attorney's word for that aspect of the question. Here is a less argumentative, less vague question. Officer, do you remember what color shirt I was wearing on the morning you pulled me over?" The officer glanced down at his notes.

"Your Honor, I must once again object to the officer referring to his notes to refresh his memory of the event in question. He had the entire lunch break to study his notes so as to refresh his already shaky memory of the occurrences. He obviously has no independent recollection of what happened on the morning in question, and I move his testimony be thrown out entirely."

At this point, Officer Richard Licker became unhinged. "No! I remember the event very well. You were wearing green."

"Green, you are absolutely certain I was wearing green. Is this true officer? Because of the color of the clothes I wear is very important to me. I am currently wearing a green Hawaiian print because it's the nicest shirt I own. You are absolutely certain of the color of the shirt I was wearing that morning. Let me rephrase. Officer, with absolute clarity so you can convince me as well as this Court that you remember what took place on the morning of June 11th, 2015. This is a detail that will become very important to the court as well as me because I consider myself a bit of a fashion maverick. It is imperative to know that you remember the details of that morning clearly and express them, so we know for certain you remember. What color shirt was I wearing on June 11th, 2015?"

"You were wearing green."

"What kind of shirt was it?"

"I'm not sure what you mean."

"Was it a tee shirt or a dress shirt? Was it light or dark? Was it a mesh shirt? Was anything written on it? When I was wearing the shirt, did you find me attractive in any way?"

"Careful, Mr. Dunston," the Judge admonished.

"Forgive me, Your Honor; I am beginning to have too much fun and forgetting my sense of decorum. Just what kind of shirt was it, Officer Licker."

"I don't remember anything other than the color."

"So, it may have been a Tee shirt. Tee shirts usually have writing on them. Did my shirt have anything written on it?"

"Not that I recall."

"Thank you, Officer. That is probably plenty of questions to verify your memory about my clothes and my attractiveness in them. Let's see if we can establish who was actually driving the vehicle. Are you absolutely certain I was the driver of the vehicle you claim you observed violating the law on that morning?"

"Yes"

"What passengers were in the vehicle with me?"

"There were no other people in the car."

"And as a police officer, sworn to uphold the law, if you thought I might have been involved in any other crimes, you would have investigated, am I right? For example, if you suspected I was involved in a conspiracy to commit a murder or any crime for that matter, you would have investigated, am I correct in this assumption Officer Licker? In other words, if you had probable cause to believe a person might be engaged in criminal activity, you would investigate, and often-times detain that person. Is that a correct statement officer?"

"Yes."

"You had no reason to believe I was engaged in any criminal behavior other than speeding in a construction zone. Is this a true statement, Officer?"

"I had no reason to believe you were doing anything illegal."

"And if you had probable cause to believe I was engaged in something illegal, you would certainly have detained me. Is this a correct statement as well?"

"Yes."

"Officer, looking at past reports where your name is listed as the arresting officer, I see several arrests for a substance you refer to as marijuana. What probable cause did you have for these arrests?"

Once again, the Prosecutor interrupted. "Your Honor, I must strongly object to this line of questioning. The defendant is now bringing in other cases, some still in the investigation stage. The prosecution is willing to stipulate that if Officer Licker had evidence a crime might be occurring, he would have acted in his capacity as a Peace Officer to investigate and possibly detain the suspect."

The Judge was once again growing annoyed. "Mr. Dunston, would you mind if I ask a question to see if my phraseology provides you an example of how to better focus yours?"

"That would be most helpful to me, Your Honor. As a matter of fact, if you'd like, I'd allow you to take over the defense."

This response resulted in a few more titters from the gallery, which were completely ignored by the Judge. "Officer, if you had even an inkling that Mr. Dunston was engaged in some nefarious and illegal activity, would you have detained him so that you could have investigated him further?"

"I most certainly would have, Your Honor."

This was Michael's opening. "Your Honor, I am not familiar with the legal terminology, but at this point, I would like to call Mr. Dick Licker a liar."

"Objection!" The Prosecutor was now on his feet, and gasps rose from the gallery. Michael wondered if he had made a grievous error.

"Mr. Dunston, you had better be able to explain that statement, or I will hold you in contempt."

"Your Honor, I make this statement for a variety of reasons. I will start with the two most blatant. To begin, the officer stated the speed I was traveling presented a hazard to the construction workers present in the area. Written right here in the officer's notes on the back of the ticket as well as right here on the front of both his copy and mine are the words (and I quote now directly from the way it is written). 'construction zone/maintenance zone - Workers not present.' My second point is that the officer claims he does not remember any writing on the shirt. Given the officers stated predisposition for investigating possible criminal behavior, I would like to enter the shirt I was wearing on that day into evidence and ask if the officer remembers it."

"Mr. Dunston, why would the officer remember a shirt? Granted, you may think it makes you look attractive, but a shirt is a shirt, and any one is the same as any other."

"Your Honor, I'm certain you are aware of a very significant change in the law in the State of Illinois, which took place in September of last year. Up until that month, it was illegal for anyone to possess cannabis within the State of Illinois and punishable by a fine of 1500 dollars and six months in jail. Officer Licker was obviously aware of this law because he has arrested a significant number of people for this very violation. He stated under oath he had no reason to suspect me of committing a crime, and if he had, he would have detained me. Your Honor, this is the shirt I was wearing, and I submit at the time I was pulled over, simply wearing this shirt would have been enough evidence to suspect, detain, search and possibly arrest me. An officer as diligent as this one has proven to be could not possibly have missed a detail such as this. The Clerk of Court transferred the shirt to the Judge who examined the logo as well as the words *"Medical Cannabis Consultants"* emblazoned across the breast.

At this point, the judge began asking questions. "Do you remember this shirt Officer Licker?"

Patrolman Licker nodded. "Officer, the Court needs you to make a verbal response."

"Yes."

"Officer, on June 11th of the year 2015 was cannabis illegal in the State of Illinois?"

"Yes."

"Would not a shirt like this one have been considered probable cause to search the person wearing it as well as their vehicle?"

"Possibly."

"Yet you chose not to do so. Would you explain why you did not execute the duty you swore to perform and search Mr. Dunston? For all you know, he could have had an ounce or more of a schedule 1 narcotic in his car, and you totally ignored that possibility even though the evidence was sitting right there in front of you. If you had searched the car as you obviously should have, because you had probable cause, you likely would have found the defendant possessed a substance for which I could have imposed a 25 hundred dollar fine as well as a year in prison. Either you ignored State law or else your memory of the events of the day is faulty. Which is it, Officer Licker?"

"Your Honor, police districts in the State were instructed by the State Attorney General to stop arresting medical cannabis patients because she didn't want to prosecute any more. At the time, the law relating to possession of marijuana was being adjusted. I don't like it any more than you do. I believe as you do Your Honor; People who use a substance like pot should be punished, but I just did what I was told to do and let him go."

"Officer, I have never heard of the Attorney General issuing an order like the one you just described. I am forced to wonder if your memory is faulty here too. Due to a lack of evidence and your questionable memory, I am dismissing the charge of speeding in a construction zone against Mr. Dunston. Officer Licker, cannabis didn't become legal for Mr. Dunston until the plant could be legally grown in Illinois by people licensed by the State to do so. Mr. Dunston obviously does not have enough money to be one of those people, and cannabis was not produced by the people who do until five months after the day you let him go. On the day you stopped him, you had ample cause to search the defendant's car, but you disregarded Illinois law and sent Mr. Dunston on his merry way. I am forced to wonder how many other State laws you are choosing to ignore."

A wave of relief and satisfaction flooded over Michael. He had beaten the charge. The emotion was short-lived, however, and as he watched the beaten and beleaguered officer, the Prosecutor spoke up.

"Your Honor, there is a lesser included charge contained in this matter. Mr. Dunston was clocked by radar traveling at a speed of 53 miles per hour on a roadway where the speed limit is 45. The State intends to prosecute this violation of our law."

Michael was stunned. Who was this prosecutor, and why had he chosen to pursue this trumped-up charge?

"Your Honor, I'd like to request a short break to prepare my defense against this trumped-up charge."

The Judge looked annoyed. "5 minutes." Her gavel came down hard, and she stood up and strolled out of the courtroom.

Michael looked directly at the Prosecutor and carefully formulated his response. "Seriously?"

"Seriously, Mr. Dunston. As I told you, wasting my time is going to cost you. The maximum fine for speeding in this County is eight hundred thirty-nine dollars and eighty-five cents. Court costs are two hundred forty-three dollars. When you are found guilty, you will owe the County a total of one thousand eighty-two dollars and eighty-five cents."

"You are aware I did not commit the crime."

"It doesn't matter, Mr. Dunston. My firm has contracted with the County to bring in money, and so far, the only thing you've done is cost them. I'm tired of your antics and judging by the behavior of the judge; she is too."

Deep down, Michael knew he was right. He wondered if the Judge was even going to allow him to present his demonstration, but he had been backed into a corner. He had to try. If he lost, he would simply pay Pam to appeal the decision. He had already gotten half the case eliminated. It was now time for the battle to rage on.

"All rise." The Judge reentered the courtroom.

"Mr. Dunston, how do you propose we proceed?"

"Your Honor, I still would like to hold my very brief opening statement until right before I testify, and I'd like to cross-examine the officer as to the events of the morning in question. I promise I will keep my questions as brief and concise as possible."

"The Court appreciates that Mr. Dunston. I've never seen a simple speeding trial take this long."

Michael felt a sense of satisfaction in learning this. He didn't want to torture the beleaguered officer any further, but the Prosecutor had given him no choice. It was now time for him to do everything he could to win this trial even if he had to be deceptive to do so. The idea the charge against him was fictitious had never even been considered by the Prosecutor, and it was now imperative he prove the County had accused him falsely.

Michael knew the only law he had broken the morning of June 11th took place in Willow Springs when he inhaled some cannabinoid molecules before he departed for Peoria. He began his cross-examination.

"Officer Licker, you testified earlier that you visually estimated my speed. As a law enforcement officer, I'm certain you have some experience doing this and can do so with a good degree of accuracy because you have been trained in this throughout your many years on the force. Am I correct in saying you can estimate how fast something is traveling based on your experience as a Peace officer and comparing your estimate to what your radar gun says. Is this a correct statement, Officer?"

"Yes, the radar gun and I are generally very close." Officer Licker announced proudly.

"I see. So, through your years as a police officer, you have learned to estimate speed visually."

"Yes."

"And on the morning of June 11th, you visually estimated the speed I was traveling to be greater than the speed I was legally allowed to travel."

"Yes."

"And your visual estimation of my speed was later confirmed by using your radar gun."

"Yes, the radar gun confirmed my estimation that you were traveling at fifty-three miles per hour."

"Well, Officer, this certainly looks pretty bad for me. I now have two pieces of evidence against me; your visual estimation of the speed I was traveling as well as the confirmation of that speed through the use of your radar. Your Honor, at this time, I would like to provide a very quick demonstration. Because of my disability, I am not physically capable of doing the demonstration myself. I, therefore, would like to call Devon McDaniel and friend to assist in this very brief demonstration."

Devon and 'friend' were brought into the courtroom by the portly man in the red suit, and Michael said: "Devon, if you would please stand at that end of the courtroom and if your assistant would please take a position near the wall next to the witness box." The Judge was once again, beginning to grow annoyed.

"Mr. Dunston, how long is this 'very brief' demonstration going to take?"

"Honestly, Your Honor, the demonstration will take less time than it took to bring in the demonstrators. As I said, if I were physically capable of doing it, I would have done the demonstration myself. I ask that the court indulge me in this and allow me a tiny amount of leeway to compensate for my disability."

Granted, this was a cheap ploy, but Michael figured the cop had exploited the fact he was a medical cannabis patient to attack him, and the Prosecutor had escalated the war. Since he was now engaged in a war, Michael decided to resort to using nuclear weapons. "Devon, I'd like you now to throw this baseball across this courtroom to your friend who is now standing near the witness without blocking the officer's line of sight. You don't have to throw hard, but it is critically important you be accurate." Michael flipped a baseball to Devon, who did exactly as he was instructed. The ball sailed in and smacked against Devon's friend's gloved hand.

"Officer Licker, in your visual estimation, how many miles per hour was the object you just watched traveling?"

"I estimate the speed of vehicles, not baseballs."

"No, Mr. Licker, you estimate the speed of objects. One object is the same as another. This is physics, and it is simply impossible for the human eye to estimate the speed of any object accurately. If it were possible, the Policeman's eyes would be used to determine speed instead of a speed measuring device. I ask the Court to reject the visual estimation portion of your testimony."

"Granted." The Judge said.

To Michael, this was a minor victory, but it seemed to rattle the Prosecutor. "Your Honor, the State requests a recess to confer with our witness."

Michael figured if this was something the Prosecutor wanted, he should avoid it at all costs, and said, "Your Honor, you have already stated this trial is setting records in respect to how long it is taking to conduct. The Court would have to agree I have done everything I could possibly do to keep this trial as brief as possible while knowing nothing about proper courtroom procedure. The request for a recess is simply a delay tactic by the prosecution to try to salvage their rapidly disintegrating case. I am prepared to finish up my cross of this witness and to conclude my case. I ask the court to allow me to do so. If the Prosecutor insists on a recess, I request the trial be continued until tomorrow. I'm getting tired of the State's delay tactics."

Anger was visible in the Judge's eyes, and she came down hard. "No! Mr. Dunston, you were delaying this trial in the morning, and Mr. Prosecutor, you are delaying this trial in the afternoon. This is the last trial of my career, and I want it over and done with. No more delays by either side. I want this trial over. Finish up your cross Mr. Dunston."

"Yes, Your Honor. This won't take long. Officer Licker, my question is, where were you and your radar gun located?"

"I was at the end of the Cedar Street Bridge, and my radar gun was on the dashboard of my patrol car."

"Was the radar gun you used to check my speed calibrated the day you issued my ticket?

"Yes."

"Were you the officer who did the radar gun calibration that day?"

"Yes."

"Can you please show the court documentation that the radar tuning forks were tested and calibrated by a certified facility within the several months prior to the issuing of the ticket you issued to me?"

"Yes. I have all the documentation right here."

He produced some papers from a zippered notebook, exactly as Michael was hoping he wouldn't be able to do.

"Can you show by serial number that the tested tuning forks go with the radar gun on the dashboard of your car?"

The officer reached into his notebook and provided the documentation.

"How is the device typically calibrated?"

The officer was prepared for this question. He recited, "A vibrating tuning fork is placed in front of the radar unit, which produces a reflected signal to which the radar responds as though it were a moving vehicle."

"So, the calibration is all based on the Doppler effect. I am looking at the operating manual of the radar gun, which the State of Illinois uses, and I see the tuning forks used to calibrate a radar unit to read 50 miles per hour vibrate at a frequency of 1569.54 Hz. Is 1569.54 the vibration frequency of the tuning fork you use when you calibrate your speed monitoring device?"

"If that is what the manual says, that is what my tuning fork is set at."

"That is indeed what the manual says. I'm certain you are well versed in this manual, am I correct in that assumption?"

"Yes, I have studied it quite extensively."

"I'm sure you have Officer. You seem to be in your comfort zone with respect to the manual. The manual goes into quite extensive detail about the Doppler Effect because it is the scientific principle on which these radar units are based. I copied the Doppler Effect equation directly from the manual. Could you please explain this equation to the Court, so we can understand how it relates to the calibration of the radar unit?" Michael held up an eight by ten sheet of paper which the baseball scout had written the equation.

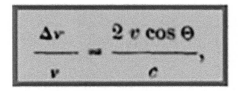

$$\frac{\Delta v}{v} = \frac{2\, v \cos \Theta}{c},$$

The Officer looked at the equation as if he were trying to read Klingon.

"That's okay, Officer. It explains this very simply in the manual. Let me read it to you directly. I'm sure you will remember this because you have studied the manual so extensively. Coefficient v is the microwave carrier transmitted by the gun, while delta-v is the radar signal received by the gun as reflected back from the moving vehicle minus v. C is the approach velocity of the vehicle relative to the ground. Θ is the angle between the pointing direction of the gun and the direction of travel of the vehicle, and c is the propagation velocity of the radar signal. Now could you explain how this equation relates to the frequency at which the tuning forks vibrate in layman's terms, please?"

Officer Licker sat in the witness box, stunned. By this time, Michael was certain he had everyone in the Courtroom completely baffled, and he chose not to torture the man in the witness box for very long.

"That's okay Officer, I'll explain it to you. Fortunately, Michael had the manual to read from. "To put it simply, what this equation means is, and I am quoting directly from the manual now: 'If the tuning fork is not vibrating at the required frequency of 1569.54 Hz., the accuracy of calibration of the unit could be affected dramatically.'

"Officer, are these tuning forks in your possession at all times, or does someone else have access to them?"

"Another officer uses them at times."

"So, Officer, you have no independent way of knowing whether the forks were ever dropped between the time the certified facility tested them and when you issued the ticket. I submit the forks were dropped, and the impact of them hitting the ground changed the frequency of their vibration. As I just read, according to the manual, enough change in the vibration from such an occurrence could result in a vehicle traveling at 45 miles per hour to cause a gun to read the speed as 115 miles per hour. Maybe the County feels differently, but to me, this is an unacceptable degree of inaccuracy.

"Your Honor, I submit this precisely what took place, and that the radar gun was not properly calibrated at the time I was pulled over by Officer Licker. I further submit the area was not a construction zone. If it had been, the State would have provided some evidence of this through the use of the dashcam video contained in the officer's car."

Officer Licker exclaimed, "The area was a construction zone! I gave the video proving that to the Prosecutor when he asked for it!"

The Judge stepped in. "And when was that Officer?"

Officer Licker looked through his zippered book. Michael marveled. This cop took meticulous notes. "August 27th, 2015."

"Your Honor, that is the day after my preliminary trial. It is the day after I requested these recordings in open court, and yet the prosecutor subsequently chose to destroy them. I don't know much about the law, but it seems to me a crime has been committed."

"It seems to me a crime has been committed as well. Bailiff, would you please remand the Prosecutor into custody and escort him to a jail cell." The Prosecutor was quickly handcuffed and escorted from the courtroom.

Michael couldn't help but reflect on the irony of the situation. He had wanted to get back at the cop more than anything but ended up destroying the Prosecutor instead.

Conversations in the gallery became intense, and the Judge brought down her gavel hard. Michael seized the moment.

"Your Honor, under the circumstances, at this time, I request the case against me be dismissed."

"Mr. Dunston, I was just about to suggest that. Case dismissed!" And the gavel came down hard again.

CHAPTER 44

Michael was in pain when he left the courthouse. He stopped at the cemetery and medicated with Gorilla Glue, a strain Catlin had obtained from one of Illinois's newly opened dispensaries. The medicine grown in Illinois was well controlled, and the State made sure it was free of molds, pesticides, herbicides, and all the other contaminates no wanted in their medication. He had brought the gram canister with him. Catlin had removed all the medicine except for a small amount she had provided for celebration or consolation after the trial. He called Catlin and let her know he won the case but didn't go into the details.

As usual, Catlin's mind was on other things. "Michael, every month, we get this statement from RSI Bancorp. It's for some credit card you took out last year."

"Yeah, that was the card we used when we went to the dispensary in Michigan. I threw a grand on it, and by the time we got home, it had around 6 dollars left on it. There isn't anything you can do with 6 dollars, so I threw the card away."

"Michael, every month since you threw that card away, the bank has been sending a one-page statement updating your account and charging you 2 dollars to do that. Your balance started at $6.42 on the day you threw the card away. A month later, it was $4.42; then, it went to $2.42, then 42 cents. Then it went to you owing the bank $1.58 then 3.58 then you owed 5.58, then 7.58. As far as I can tell, this will continue as long as RSI Bank is in existence. With a business plan as creative as this one, this bank is likely to be in business for a long, long time. They are essentially charging you 2 dollars to send you a sheet of paper."

Michael wasn't interested. He had a two-hour drive back to the hovel. Catlin would surely bring this up again, and he would fix this if she bitched enough. There was no uncertainty this would happen.

"I'll be home in a couple of hours. We'll talk about it then."

"Uh-uh. I'm heading to my parents until Sunday. I loaded up the freezer, so if you get hungry, you're on your own. I'll give you a call tomorrow night, okay? By the way, happy 4/20."

Michael wasn't sure how happy he was going to be celebrating 4/20 without Catlin and the dogs, but he would make the best of things, and he drove back to the hovel at a leisurely pace. By the time he got home, he was unbelievably thirsty.

Catlin has spent the day cleaning the house from top to bottom and had left a freshly brewed pitcher of tea on the kitchen counter. All it needed was ice, and Michael opened the freezer door to access the ice trays above his head. Catlin had loaded the freezer with ground beef, and when the freezer door opened, the provisions began to rain down upon him.

Epilogue

Catlin tried to call Michael on Friday and all-day Saturday. By the time Saturday evening rolled around, she was frantic. She needed to find out if Michael had gotten into some horrific car accident on his way home from Peoria. At 10 pm Saturday, she called the Willow Springs Police Department and asked them to do a welfare check on Michael to see if he was okay. At 11:30, an officer called her back.

"I think you better get back here, ma'am," was all he would say.

There was little activity around the hovel apart from a police officer and reporter conversing at the edge of the driveway as Catlin pulled in. She exited her vehicle and overheard the reporter asking the officer how the victim had died.

The officer responded sardonically, "As near as we can tell, he was pummeled to death by hamburger."

Catlin rushed into the hovel, and as she gazed at the chalk outline adorning the kitchen floor beneath the massive fridge, one thought dominated her mind.

"How am I going to launder all that clean money?"

CPSIA information can be obtained
at www.ICGtesting.com
Printed in the USA
LVHW041338310720
662069LV00001B/51